DEADLY FEARS

DEADLY FEARS

JESSIE MCCLURE

COPYRIGHT

Deadly fears

Copyright © 2020 by Jessie McClure

All rights reserved.

No part of this book may be reproduced in any form or by any electronic or mechanical means, including information storage and retrieval systems, without written permission from the author, except for the use of brief quotations in a book review. For permission requests, contact the author at Jessie@Jessie-McClure.com or through the author's website at Jessie-McClure.com. Include the subject line "Attention: Permission Requested."

First Edition

Edited by Line by Line Copyediting

ISBN: 978-1-7349351-0-3 (print)

ISBN: 978-1-7349351-1-0 (eBook)

Library of Congress Catalog Number: 2020907175

Printed in the United States of America

This novel is dedicated to my family members and friends who share my twisted humor and enjoy a good scare as much as I do.

CONTENTS

FATHER	1
PLOP INDUSTRIES	27
REVENGE	79
ORB C68	119
THE APOCALYPSE	141
DORIS AND ERVIN	169
THE REAPER	197
THE TRANSFORMATION	217
Acknowledgments	285
About the Author	287

FATHER

BLESSED BE THOSE HE HAS CHOSEN
TO HEAR

THE BEGINNING

"No," Yaeska said when the soft clank of bones broke her concentration. She squatted behind the dense bushes and breathed deeply, letting the berries in her hands fall to the ground. "Oh, Spirit Mother, do not let today be the day. Give us more time." Her gaze lingered on where her ebony hair touched the ground, at where her fingers clenched the warm soil, before she closed her eyes and prayed. Prayed as the beat of her heart increased and a wet line of sweat slid down her spine. Prayed as the pit of her stomach clenched with a knowing dread. The bones were never wrong.

Click-clack. Click-clack. The death rattles rose again from the ancient teeth and small skulls tied to the cord about her neck.

Fear spread up Yaeska's back. Only one thing made the necklace speak and left her legs weak with dread. She slowly stood and scanned the meadow, her hand clasped around the spelled bones to silence them, a part of her hoping they were wrong. Her breath caught in her throat when she found what she was dreading.

How could something so terrible begin as such a small thing?

The white speck twinkled from its place across the meadow, above the orange and purple wildflowers, heavily blooming bushes, and the meandering stream of the valley. In a cloudless sky, the birds flew and danced as if all was fine, not yet aware of the danger growing among them.

"Spirit Mother, help me," she said before twisting to look for her children. They picked berries further down the valley, their dark heads barely visible above the green cala'pa bushes surrounding them.

"Vanee! Easka! Come quick!" she shouted. Both raised their heads and peered at her over the shrubs, but neither moved. "Now!" Yaeska dropped her reed basket and lifted her skirt to run. In the back of her mind, she wondered how much time they had, even though she knew there was no point in speculating. No matter the answer, there was never enough.

They met in a small clearing in a cloud of dust. Dropping to her knees, she pulled them close and kissed them each on the forehead before staring into their wide, fearful eyes. *One last look, one final touch*, she thought before she uttered one irrefutable command.

"Run."

Scattered berries marked their path like shiny drops of blood as the kids escaped into the long grasses edging the tree line. *Not a sign*, she asserted, unable to look away, *just berries*. Not everything was meant to be interpreted, even if Haktu saw omens in raccoon dung. She held her breath until the twins had vanished in the trees, then she sighed in relief. In just a mile they'd be home. Safe and alive. She glanced at the pulsing blemish hovering a few hundred feet away, twenty feet in the air, and dropped her pack on the ground.

Six months she'd been learning the ritual, ever since Haktu dreamed of the hawk and weasel and their dance among the clouds. And now it was time to test his vision. Yaeska's hands trembled too much to untie the drawstrings, and she used her knife to slice the cords. The hawk's banded feathers were removed first and tied into her hair: one for courage, another for power. Next, she needed cleansing smoke. She grunted when her hands failed to do what she wanted, scattering the herbs and flints instead of laying them side by side.

"Calm yourself." She pressed her hands against her legs and looked to the sky. Her throat grew dry, and she shivered. She'd never witnessed the birth of the K'haylat, and what she saw was nothing less than magical.

White mist leaked from a bright hole in the sky and rotated like water spiraling in a ceremonial bowl. Minutes passed, and the fog grew larger and thicker with each revolution, expanding the circle's diameter until it touched the ground and appeared as opaque as a white stone. The swirling ceased, but dense fog continued pulsing from its interior, rolling out in tendrils of thick white mist that flowed in all directions, changing the circle into a throbbing cloud. It expanded east and west, up and down, and vaguely she wondered if it was pulsing from the other direction as well. Was there someone on the opposite side with fresh sweat beading along their upper lip like her? Were they running for their life as she'd like to do? Had the bitter cold reached them and begun to burn their skin and lungs, freezing their sweat into an icy sheath?

The skulls bounced against her neck and broke the mist's hypnotic hold on her. Yaeska shuddered and went to work mixing herbs with blood she drew from her hand, singing words of power before spitting globs of phlegm into the mix and spreading the concoction on the tight bundle of dry branches lying at her feet. It took four strikes of the flint before she got the bundle smoldering on all sides. She blew on the twigs with a soft breath, twisting the smudge stick to make sure every corner smoked but did not flame.

There is power in my blood. I can stop the mist. It will turn back at my magic. She reassured herself despite the doubt smothering her soul. The questions came again, unbidden, as she waved the branches in the air to see how much smoke they produced. Why was the spiritual leader, Haktu, the most mighty of their tribe, hiding in his wigwam like an old woman? Did he truly believe this twenty-winter girl capable of fighting an enemy as old as Mother Earth? That she could win when he could not?

He does because the blood of a warrior runs through my veins. Yaeska wobbled to a stand. *My grandfather was M'ayNactra, and I am the chosen one.*

She looked to the opaque wall that now stretched across the field and high above the trees, smothering everything in white as it extended to the sides and rolled closer. Her head snapped to the right to watch a great blue heron burst into the sky, surging away from the whiteness racing toward its legs. The K'haylat spread like fingers—thin white wisps stretching and clasping upward in an attempt to drag the bird down—before snapping together and bursting into nothing.

Her relief at seeing the harbinger of success and good luck escape was brief and short lived. The mist continued to grow, expanding up and out, moving closer with each second.

Yaeska turned to the side and began to dance. She moved her legs in the choreographed steps, moving faster and faster while waving the smudge stick in the air. Dusky smoke billowed, and a wolf howled in the distance. A rabbit dashed past her toward the forest.

"Aap hai thee'ka! Ta'han ko kai!" Dust from her dancing churned around her, dark compared to the brilliant opaqueness moving closer. It collected on her skin, accumulated in the sweat that fell into her mouth. Minutes passed, and the swish of her feet among the reeds and dirt was the only sound as the animals and insects now hid in fear. The scent of burning cedar, sage, and blood grew with the smoke, reassuring, but not strong enough to combat the fear growing inside her. Not enough to alter her belief that each second drew her closer to her impending doom. The air cooled, and her breath puffed out around her while the smoke swirled with the first coils of mist. Her sweat cooled into an icy cloak, and all at once she understood, no matter what Haktu said, that she would die.

No more children, no more tribe, no more life.

She raised her face to the heavens and sang louder, belting out her plea to the Spirit Mother to save her people while simultaneously screaming warnings to the mist of her power. Waving the smoking twigs in a figure eight, she pounded the dirt with her feet, dislodging dust to mix on her face with the tears flowing freely. She told herself she was larger than life and caused the earth to tremble, the air to fill with her strength. The beads sewn into the trim of her skirt jingled, adding to her display of power.

A woman's high-pitched scream broke through her concentration, and she stumbled to a halt. The song and steps forgotten, she turned, staring at the fog, which had drifted around her like two slowly encircling arms. Her head rolled up the thirty-foot wall to where she could see a small circle of blue sky. Behind her, the trees were still visible; the ring was not complete.

Yaeska swallowed and pulled the smudge stick to her chest. Just rabbits, she told herself as more death throes sounded. She'd heard the screams before and recognized their similarity to a human cry.

I can still run and make it home before the mist reaches the village.

Her hands tightened on the smudge stick. But that wouldn't save her. The village would know what she'd done, that she'd failed her destiny and fled. They'd burn her alive for not fighting for them—for being a coward. This was the only way.

"I am the one!" she screamed before returning to her ritual. Anger swelled as she danced and cried tears saturated with the misery consuming her soul. She sang the songs of her people as the circle closed and the sky vanished. Yaeska raised her sticks and dared the mist to battle.

Her heart soared when the gong atop the mountain clanged a warning. Her children had made it home. Her tribe had been warned. Another bell rang from a different village, and then another—each further away and quieter than the last. Earth and all its inhabitants were being warned one bell at a time.

Yaeska continued to sing and dance when the mist moved in. It surrounded her and drew closer, prodding her with icy tendrils as if testing this new thing. *This powerful thing*, she told herself even as the cool touch became sharper and an ominous scent of blood tinged the air. Her voice warbled as the pain grew, and when rivulets of red ran down her skin, her steps halted.

The mist surged inward, encapsulating her and ending the dance. Dark shapes shimmered into existence and moved silently over her still form. They pulled and cut, their dark eyes turning toward the world still not covered with mist.

Beyond her, the bells continued to ring, and the mist grew larger.

ONE HUNDRED YEARS LATER

Ten-year-old Avery pulled her head out from behind the curtain to glare at her sister. The pain in her belly was no longer little but a steady pulsing mass of anger and resentment throbbing with her heart, every thump an internal cry begging her to give it release. She clenched her teeth against the scream hovering on her tongue and shoved her head back under the protective folds of the curtain. *Shut up already, Jane.*

Her lips smirked as she placed her chin in her hand and fixed her eyes on the blackness outside. She could make Jane go to bed, without dinner even. That'd shut her up. Then she and Vail could sit with a book and listen to the popping of the fire while they tried to ignore the ringing of the warning bell. Her eyes flicked in the direction of his bed before the smile faded and her lips pressed tight in worry. Where were her parents? She hoped they were safe. A single cloud floated leisurely across the moon while her sister's voice dragged against her skin like chalk on rocks.

Avery jerked around. "Stop it, Jane," she hissed through clenched teeth.

"Stop what? Talking? We need to get Vail to the doctor! Look at him! He's sick!" Jane turned and thrust her hand toward the little bassinet next to the fireplace, as if Avery didn't know where he lay.

Avery moved away from her perch and limped to the window on the other side of the room. Timidly, she parted the curtain to peer at the blackness outside. The moon's rays gave a silver sheen to the path and trees in front of their home. No clouds obscured the stars above them. No fog blanketed the earth on this side of the house, either. She pulled the curtain aside and twisted her head to peer both ways down the lane. There was nothing but the steady thrum of the alarm, which had been going off for more than an hour now, warning them to stay inside—safe from the mist.

"Avery!" Jane shouted.

"I hear you, Jane," Avery snapped as she jerked away from the window. The curtain floated back into place, closing off her view of the outside. "Don't you think I'm worried also? You know I'd run him to the doctor myself, but the alarm sounded. What do you want me to do?" She turned and walked to the bench across from the fire. Her shoulders slumped as she sat and stared at the flames while Jane paced in front of her.

"The alarm only sounded an hour ago. Doc Howard is down the hill and over the rise. I run that path every day. It won't take more than fifteen, sixteen minutes . . . maybe twenty because we have Vail. If we leave now, we can be at his house before the fog gets here."

Avery considered her sister before standing and pacing opposite her. The sound of her right foot dragging across the floor filled the small space, overshadowing the popping of the fire and her brother's labored breathing. Her bad leg, normally not something she thought about, was the one thing making Jane's plan impossible. The trek would be much longer if she went, and they might not outrun the fog. Avery ran her hands through her hair.

I wish Mom was home, she thought as her chest tightened. More than likely their parents were holed up with a neighbor, safe and secure from the fog. As the mist never stayed longer than twelve hours, they'd be home tomorrow and could make the decision themselves. Her eyes flicked to the bassinet, and she sighed. Could he wait that long? She wished she knew if they had time to make the trip before the fog reached them. "The bell started ringing an hour ago, Jane. That's a long time. We'd never make it in time."

"How do you know? Is the fog outside? Did you see it?" Jane raised her arm and pointed in the direction of Doc's house.

Avery sighed. "No. I didn't. But—"

"Then we need to take a chance. Look at Vail. Look!" Jane hurried to Vail's bed and pulled the covers off him, exposing his small body to the open air. He whimpered but continued to sleep as Jane tugged his shirt up to display the puckered, red rash covering his back. She turned her head and stared at Avery with wide, fearful eyes. "He's got it. He needs the doctor."

Avery hurried forward intending to touch his red skin, but she drew back at the intense heat radiating off him in hot waves. She shook her head as a lump built in her throat. Tears welled, and she brushed them away. Vail had the pox and would die without Doc's care. She raised her head and met Jane's eyes. She didn't say anything, didn't need to. They couldn't let Vail die.

Jane reached over and pulled Vail's clothes tight before swaddling him in a receiving blanket. She turned her head to watch Avery grab a small travel pack and open the top.

Avery glanced at her as she spoke. "You can't take much. Just food for Vail and a little water for both of you. The fog should be gone by morning. I'm assuming Doc has enough food, but I don't know if he filled his water buckets before the alarm sounded. So you'll bring your own and extra just in case."

"Wait . . . aren't you coming?"

Avery refused to answer; instead, she limped to the storage cabinet in silence and opened the doors.

Jane removed her hand from Vail, placing her shaking fingers against her stomach in understanding. Her eyes slid down for a second, passing over her sister's leg before they rose to stare at her sister's downturned head.

Avery paused, staring at the now-filled pack. Her shoulders fell, and she closed the top before shuffling to the coat rack next to the door. With Jane's coat in one hand and her pack in the other, she turned and made her way to the bench. She sat and fidgeted with the ruffle on the coat without responding. Sickness welled in her stomach, threatening to move up her throat as she considered her words.

Jane stood and walked to her. She stared down at the top of her sister's head briefly before grabbing the sleeve Avery rubbed and giving the cloth a hard yank. Avery sighed and let the sleeve go.

"It's the only way, Jane." Avery wiped a hand along her eyes. "I'm two years older than you, so it should be me. But with my leg, I can't make that run in less than thirty minutes, even on a good day, and it's dark now." Her leg stretched out from under her skirt, exposing the shriveled calf, before retreating. A tear slid down her face as she grabbed the pack and motioned for Jane to turn around. Her hands shook as she tightened the straps on Jane's shoulders.

Jane stared at the fire. Going alone had never been the plan. For a split second she regretted saying anything, regretted hounding her sister for the last hour, but then her eyes slipped to Vail. Closing them, she took a deep breath to calm her racing heart. *I can do this.* "You need to be here when Mom and Dad get back to tell them where we are."

Tears slipped down Avery's face as she nodded. She reached forward and pulled Jane to her chest. The pain in her stomach had grown into something she knew was not anger, but fear. As sure as she was that they were making the right decision, she was equally sure they were making a mistake. She sobbed and closed her eyes.

"I need to go, Avery."

Avery pulled back and wiped her face before going down to her knees. "We should pray first."

She waited until Jane kneeled across from her before pulling her own cupped hands to her face. "Dear Father, who art in heaven, please protect my sister and brother on their journey. Please guide them to their end at the house of our doctor. Let their goal be reached. Keep them safe. Amen." Raising her head, she peered at her sister over her fingers.

Jane smiled tightly and whispered, "Amen," before standing. Neither said anything as Jane grabbed Vail and walked around the bench.

Avery opened the front door and moved aside. She stared out at the night, wishing for the cry of a coyote or the hoot of an owl. Even the droning of the alarm was preferable to the utter silence outside, but the alarm had stopped while they packed. Did it mean the mist had left and Jane would be safe, or did it mean the bell tower had been overrun and the bellringer hid inside? There was no way to know. They just had to wait. Her eyes slid to the grass and where the crickets cowered in deep holes. She closed her eyes when Jane moved next to her.

"I'll run," Jane whispered, "all the way to Doc's house.

It's not far, and the road is straight. Over the two hills and we'll be there. We can wait out the fog with him."

Avery nodded and peered west toward the hills. The rise at the end of the road blocked her vision, but she wanted to believe she'd see the unnatural glow of the fog if it was there. "Run fast. Just keep running . . . " Her voice faded for a second. "Don't stop for anything, Jane."

Jane crossed the door's threshold and walked into the yard. She breathed in the scent of dirt, grass, and the sweet fragrance of night before turning to see her sister raising her arm to wave goodbye. Jane started to raise hers in response then stopped—there was no reason to respond. Avery's hand had frozen in mid-rise, hovering below shoulder level, forgotten, as if she didn't realize she'd been raising it. Jane glanced at her sister's pale face and vacant eyes, and her spirits dropped even further. Avery stood before her, but she wasn't actually present. She was locked somewhere in her mind, away from here. Jane swallowed and backed away. "Goodbye Avery."

The road in front of their home was not really a road but a wide dirt track rubbed smooth by countless carts and feet. No matter how primitive, it was their lifeline to the surrounding areas. Head north to access the fields and farms, east or south to trade and reach the various waterways to fish, and west to find the ocean, and more importantly, the doctor. It was well known the roads were not the most direct route to anywhere. Cut across the fields, and you could take forty minutes off your trek to the lake. Go through the woods, instead of around, and you'd beat the road to the closest city by over an hour and a half. Continue through the valley, and a day's ride to Andenne was cut down to four hours. But there was one thing the roads had that none of the other routes did—safety. Over the years, small huts had been built every two miles to protect travelers from the mist.

But none, Jane realized as she hefted Vail into a more comfortable position, had been built on the westbound road between their home and Doc's. And it wasn't like this road wasn't used. People often passed this way with the sole purpose of visiting the doctor. She noticed them often—sick and injured, needing care—as she toiled in the garden or watched her baby brother. Seemed to her a nice warm spot to wait out storms would have been appreciated. It didn't have to be anything fancy. Just a room with a door so they could rest. Or where they could hide if they crossed those hills and ran into trouble between here and there since there was nothing—

Stop it, Jane admonished herself upon reaching the road. *Don't think—just run. Don't worry about what's out there.* It took only a minute to realize how futile that plan was. With her feet thundering on the hard dirt, impregnating the silent night, there was no way to ignore the abnormal silence, nor what it meant. It made her wonder what the animals knew that she didn't. What had they seen? Fear tickled the back of her neck, and she shivered. Vail cried weakly from her chest.

"Vail—" she huffed before stopping herself. Predators weren't on the hunt right now. They hid in their dens just like everyone else. She gave a small laugh that faded into a sob. One tear slid down her face as she wished for a wolf to howl or an owl to screech. Anything to cut the silence and tell her the danger had passed or at least let her know she wasn't alone. Knowing that wouldn't happen, she let Vail bawl, occasionally saying his name or patting his butt to calm him down, enjoying the sounds of him even if he wasn't happy. Eventually, his cries warbled their way to nothing and she was again alone with only her footsteps for company.

Her legs slowed on reaching the first hill. With screaming thighs and labored breath, she pushed onward, letting her mind ponder what might lie over the rise. Would the land

and ground remain clear, or would the fog cover the landscape like a blanket? What would she do if the mist waited below? Her steps slowed. Turn around? Could she outrun it? She almost stumbled to a stop when she crested the top, sure she needed to retreat, but there was nothing there to turn her back. She was safe, at least for now.

The town of Burlayn, in which she lived, spread for miles through the mountains. Her home sat in a deep valley, separated from her neighbors not just by distance but also by line of sight, and she often felt isolated from the rest of the world. Last to know of news, last to see the sunrise. As if in a fishbowl, the earth rose in steps around her home, leveling out at the top of the hills before rising again with the next mound of dirt. Thankfully, there were only two she needed to climb, with the last one descending on the other side for a good three-quarters of a mile. Then again it leveled, and Doc waited at the end.

Jane focused on the hill in the distance. The moon hovered high above the crest, the wind blowing the occasional cloud north across its face. The night was beautiful and peaceful, not matching her expectations. Maybe the bells were wrong this time, or the attack had ended.

The road began to rise. "Just over the hill," she said. "We are almost there, Vail." Hope bloomed in her chest, and she glanced at the fields beside her. Silver-tinged wheat sat motionless, waiting to be harvested with the next full moon. And when that time came, she pictured herself in the rows, with her woven hat and gloves, her twine and knife, prepared to work like always. *And*, she thought, *Vail will be healthy and gurgling in the grass with Grandmother, like he should be.*

Jane climbed with the earth and savored the anticipation coursing through her body. It grew with each labored inhalation, while her fear floated away with the warm breath of her exhalations. She was going to do it—get Vail to the doctor in time. She cleared the top of the hill and stumbled down the sharply descending road on the other side before sliding to a stop.

She'd never seen anything like the thick, luminescent fog coming from the north. It didn't drift as if driven by wind but moved south like a directed horde, smothering everything under a blanket that gleamed with an unworldly bright light from within. Maybe ten miles across, the mass had swallowed the landscape behind it as far as she could see, leaving nothing uncovered, not even the tops of the trees or the rolling hills of the skyline. It approached the road like a squad of soldiers marching in formation. Uniform. Controlled. Exacting. All except a wide swath far ahead, which moved much faster than the rest and had already crossed the road beyond the doctor's house. Jane's mind blanked, entranced by the otherworldliness, the beauty.

What are you doing, Jane? Her thought came to her in her sister's voice, echoing through her brain, forcing her from her stupor. Cold tickled her spine when she realized how long she'd been watching and how close she'd let the mist get. With a jerk, she stumbled down the hill, eliciting a cry from Vail that pierced the silence. He struggled within his swaddling, working one arm free from his cloth prison to pound the air in front of her face. And the edge of mist reacted, bulging in the area closest to her, swelling into a bubble.

Jane careened down the hill toward the lantern atop the doctor's house, toward the golden glow fighting against the darkness and the eerie illumination approaching them. With each step, the air grew colder, denser, settling in her lungs with an unusual heaviness, and she knew it was the edge of the mist reaching her before the rest. It muffled her footsteps until they no longer slapped the ground but sounded hollow as if they came from far away. Only Vail's wailing continued to rise, almost amplified, not hindered by whatever was happening. Her foot slid across a rock, and they tumbled down. Over the sounds of her heart pounding in her temple, her breathing loud and raspy in her ears, Vail screamed in fear.

"Hush, brother," she whispered, moving her bleeding hand off the ground to his head. "Everything's okay." A red slash appeared where she touched him, and she glanced away, her breath catching at the sense of dread it instilled in her. Pushing with her legs, she tried to stand, but she found the angle too steep and slid down another foot onto her back. After twisting to the side, she used her hand and struggled upright. Then she ran.

Her brother, who started off small and insignificant, had become lead to her tired arms. They burned and demanded she release their burden—it would be so much easier to run without him, they teased. But she wouldn't drop him. Couldn't. Not now. Not ever. Jane clutched Vail tighter and glanced to the side before facing forward. The mist was closer now, much too close.

Even with the doctor's house growing larger and the light growing brighter, she didn't seem to be progressing as she expected. Vaguely she wondered if there was some kind of magic holding her back. If something in the mist worked to make it happen. Jane swallowed and peeked at the fog again, then wished she hadn't.

The wall of mist was no longer a line but a rippling path with sections bulging outward from the original formation in delicate waves. The protrusions were small except the area nearest her, the one she'd noticed a moment before. It swelled into the darkness like a bulbous tumor, growing larger each second.

When she was halfway down the hill, she observed a small rip forming in the center of the bulge where it connected to the rest of the mist. At first a tiny black dot, the hole grew to a slit that opened and closed rhythmically like an eye. As the bulge grew, so did it—opening wider and staring at her for longer periods of time. Fear spread down her back in a cold line under its observation.

"It's not an eye!" she shouted suddenly, then sobbed. When the bulge surged toward her, the rest of the mist refused to let go and dragged the bubble back, extending and retracting like an animal staked to the ground by a stretchy tether. There was no eye watching her, just glimpses of the dark landscape through the hole in the fog.

But the tethers were ripping, the split lengthening, the eye gaping as the bulge got closer to her. Each surge made the connection to the large body of mist grow smaller until just thin ribbons at the edges held them together. With a sharp snap, one of the links broke, and an edge was free. The free section swung in her direction, narrowing the distance between them by half in one swoop before stretching like a snake toward her—the piece in the lead thinning until rocks and bushes were visible beneath the luminescent head.

As the snake-shaped mist accelerated across the ground, it stretched in an ever-narrowing line until it was nothing more than a reedy thread of white where it connected to the larger body. A soft puff of smoke and the end broke free. Now disconnected, it accelerated, and a vast space opened between it and the more significant mass.

Beyond the doctor's house, another section of fog struggled to break from the connecting wall of mist behind it, thinning and lengthening as the other had done. With an audible snap, it tore free and raced in her direction.

Jane stumbled and righted herself. Her breath exploded out of her in hot, dry, bitter-tasting air as the outermost extremities of the mist flowed over her. Cold and sharp, the cloud pricked her skin, burning as if hundreds of tiny knives pierced her through her clothes. Vail let out a shallow cry and beat against her chest. Jane's eyes bulged, and she screamed.

A less-translucent cloud moved in front of her face, almost obscuring the porch with its smoky essence. When she breathed in, a thin wisp slipped between her lips and down her throat, scraping against her flesh until she coughed the offender out. Slow licks of fire caressed her face and made their way down her neck to her chest as a delicate sheath of fog draped itself over her head.

Blood tainted her breaths now, and the cold made her ears hurt. A mere forty feet from the doctor's house, she called out, "Doctor! Doctor!"

Through the swirling fog, she watched his front door open and white light spill into the night. Jane sobbed as the doctor peered outside, worry creasing his brow under the flickering glow of the lantern. He turned his head toward her before something made him turn the other way.

A line of opaque mist pressed against her arm in a burning brand.

"No!" she shrieked through halting breaths as the doctor backed up and slammed his door. A vaporous mass followed, racing up the steps and over the wood, pressing against the doors and planks as it tried to get in. More rolled over the windows and up the walls until the house disappeared in a giant white cloud. Then it was moving toward her.

Moments later, the mist from the north and the west combined in an unsettling whoosh. Pinpricks moved down her body as the ground, trees, and the sky vanished in an impenetrable cloud. She was now surrounded by the luminescent vapor.

Jane jerked to a stop and screamed as hell-fire licked across her body. It felt like her skin had been peeled back, exposing her nerves to the cold air. Vail screeched and she glanced down, expecting to see something horrifying, skinless, but she found his smooth white flesh marred only by the slash of blood from her hand.

Then something brushed against her hip.

Jane twisted to the side and stared in that direction. There was nothing there. No creature. No shadowy shape in the white. "Leave me alone!" she yelled, clutching Vail tight. He fought against her, pushing at her chest while simultaneously trying to bat at his own skin. His screams filled her ears. "Just leave us alone!"

In answer, something touched the back of her leg, gently stroking downward in a soft caress. Another joined the first, and Jane froze. The fingers continued their exploration, marking her legs, her arms, and the curve of her shoulder with a cold brand. And no matter where she looked, she couldn't see what examined her. Then it pinched her, harsh and cruel, twisting and pulling the flesh on her waist. More followed suit, and their gentle touches became agony.

Jane spun in a circle, kicking at the air. "What do you want?" she yelled when she finally stopped. Her eyes bulged in her head, and sweat glistened on her skin, running into her eyes. She was shoved from behind and fell forward into something that scurried away. The contact slowed her enough to catch herself with one hand against the ground. Jane staggered upright, twisting to the side when something reached out and grabbed her wrists and tried to pull them apart.

"No!" she screamed and stumbled back.

But there was nowhere to go. More hands gripped her, stroking her face, tugging at her arms, pinching her flesh. She turned in a circle and screamed as if her voice would give her the power to scare them away. But the sound only seemed to inflame them, made them more aggressive and demanding.

Then one of them seized her cheek, pulling her forward with two thin fingers. She felt her skin tear and blood flood her mouth. Jane shoved her shoulder into the monster, and it released her. Suddenly alone, she glimpsed one of the beasts circling her.

She turned with it, staring into its eyes. Her blue ones to its lifeless black. Eyes much too large, too alien. Eyes that didn't blink. Halfway around they went until another creature grabbed her hair and pulled her toward the ground. Jane staggered back and tried to twist out of its grasp, but her legs crumpled. She contorted her body sideways and landed on her knee.

Ghostly impressions of a long, pale torso flashed before her eyes before vanishing into nothing. She dropped one hand from Vail and pushed herself upright. A gray form loomed closer, and she stared into a long, oval face. The creature grinned.

Jane screamed. They'd never known what existed in the mist. They'd never known who or what stole their people and animals. But now she did. She wrapped her arms around Vail and held on tight.

Long, silver fingers wrapped around her forearm and dug deep into her flesh, piercing her muscles. Jane howled and held Vail tighter. A loud rip and her sleeve tore apart at the seam. Blood poured from where they dug at her joints. Pieces of bloody cloth floated to the ground like confetti after a parade.

The scent of blood permeated the air, pushing the creatures into a frenzy. Gray shapes pressed toward her from all sides to grasp anything within reach. While one pulled left, another yanked right, tearing ligaments and tendons as they fought. Nails raked her body, peeling her skin from her flesh like the hide from a deer.

Jane's mind protected her, slowing things down until everything seemed to be happening to someone else. She didn't understand it was her arm being ripped from her body.

Nor did she recognize it when she saw it disappearing into the fog, clutched in long gray fingers. She slipped to the ground, fuzzy about where she was and what was going on as the fight over her flesh continued. From a distance she heard screaming, never realizing it was her own voice making the sounds. And underneath everything was the wail of a baby.

Vail, she thought, then everything went black.

MONSTERS

The scent of stew and pine trees filled the cozy cottage. A large fire crackled in the hearth as the pot hanging over its warmth bubbled. A silvery-gray hand stirred the stew with a spoon. It dug down to the bottom of the cauldron and pulled the meat and bones to the top where they were tested for doneness.

"The food's done," a female's soft voice announced.

"Children, come and eat!" a booming voice announced from behind her.

Laughter and the soft patter of feet came from upstairs. The tall, gray male listened to their descent as he made his way to his seat at the head of the table. A long runner of white linen decorated its top, adding a little elegance to the coarseness of the wooden bowls and bent spoons arranged on top of it. He dropped into his cushioned seat, exhausted, and looked up as he heard his children enter the room. Lights from the wall sconces shone a soft yellow on their smooth, bald, silver heads. They both looked at him with huge ebony eyes before starting toward their seats.

"Before we eat, I have a present for you both," he said,

reaching down and grabbing the basket next to him by its handle. It swayed as he pulled it up and placed it on a table beside him. "The hunt was good tonight. As always, God has provided and kept us alive." He pulled the blanket covering the basket back, revealing Vail.

He'd been bathed and lay semicovered by a small wool rag. Bright-yellow medicine accentuated the cuts on his face and arms, while a thicker, white cream coated the rash on his body. Vail's blue eyes opened to peer at them curiously. He gurgled and waved his arms in the air.

The girls' large, lidless, black eyes stared back at him without any emotion.

"It is sickly at the moment. I was thinking we should keep it and try to bring it to health. Let it grow before we decide what to do with it. It can stay in a pen in the backyard, and once it's grown, help us around the farm. I'll let it sleep down here until it gets better." He reached over and pulled the blanket up to cover Vail's torso more fully. "And if it ends up being more of a burden than an asset, we'll have us a nice feast. But let's see how this goes first."

Both girls stared down at the baby before making their way to their seats.

"It's so ugly," one said as she leaned forward from her chair to stare into the basket. "It's so pasty and round. How do you know eating it won't make us sick?"

Her dad snorted and ran a black claw across Vail's cheek. "They all look like this. Its illness will probably go away with a little medicine and care."

"What does it eat, Dad?" The other asked after sitting down and placing her napkin on her lap.

He shrugged and sat back to watch his wife move a steaming bowl of stew onto the table. Fresh bread sat next to it, waiting to be buttered. "I don't know. It came from beyond the fog. We'll give it what we eat and see if it survives." He watched as his wife ladled soup into the other bowls before moving to him. He smiled up at her lovingly as she filled his bowl. She may have gotten older in the hundred years they'd been married, gained a few purple veins in her silver skin, but her large, black eyes still gleamed and filled her face beautifully. She turned her giant head and smiled at him with a mouth full of dagger-thin teeth.

"Let's pray," he began as his wife sat down. Everyone brought their palms up and clasped their twelve fingers together above their heads. Their arms were much too long to clasp in front of their faces.

"Dear Father, who art in heaven, we thank you for the gift you have brought us. We thank you for the comforting mist you bring that shows us the way to our life-giving food. We thank you for always finding a way for us to survive and for keeping us safe on our journey. In your name, amen." He lowered his hands and let out a satisfied groan as he stared down into his bowl. His pointed white teeth dripped saliva in anticipation.

"Ahhh . . . the hands," he said as he picked up the small curled fist in his bowl. "They are always my favorite. All that delectable flesh nestled in-between the bones."

His family nodded in agreement as they each picked up a small piece of Jane and began to eat.

PLOP INDUSTRIES

POSSESSION LOGISTICS AND
OBTAINMENT PROFESSIONALS

ALL IN A DAYS WORK

The Minotaur slipped the last piece of wiggling flesh between his lips before wiping his hands on a soft white napkin. He chewed the morsel slowly as he ran the cloth over his fingers, enjoying the sensation on his hands almost as much as he enjoyed how the food wiggled in an attempt to escape his mouth. Once he had masticated the meat to a point where it no longer moved, he swallowed and gave a satisfied burp.

"That was good," Floyd muttered, crumpling the takeaway container between his large blocky hands. With a flick of his wrist, he sent the garbage into the air toward the wire trash receptacle next to his desk. It swirled around the edge for a second before dropping into the can with a plunk. He smacked his hand against his desk and grinned.

His wife, Satan bless her soul, made his lunch every night except Monday. That meant on Tuesdays he was free to eat out and pick from the menu at The Haunted Hound. Today's lunch had been exceptional, as they had his favorite: slivered ergen marinated with pickled onions.

His blunt black nails tapped gently on the top of his steel

desk while he considered the clock on the opposite wall. At four minutes to one, he should get back to his job matching humans to his demon clients, but he had an urge to call his son and hear what the doctor had said. Floyd wasn't one to believe in luck, but he couldn't ignore how wonderful his morning had been. The cantankerous owner of the company, Mr. Devour, hadn't been around to administer his customary verbal flogging this morning, saving Floyd an expense since his boss's caustic spittle burned holes in even his most expensive flame-retardant polo shirts. His restaurant had his favorite meal on the lunch menu. And he'd made a hole in one with his garbage. His black eyes glanced at the time again before he picked up the rotary phone handset and dialed his son's number. Maybe his good luck would transfer to his son and daughter-in-law.

"Hello?" grumbled a deep voice after the second ring.

"It's me. What did the fertility doctor say?"

During the long pause where his son said nothing, Floyd studied the picture on his desk. His son, so like him—tough, leathery black hide; large bull head topped by enormous horns; and muscular build—also displayed his mother's genes in the bright-blue spirals decorating his horns and chest. His lime-green eyes and tufts of spiky light-blue hair between his horns were also from her. That his son existed was a miracle in itself. His wife, Mavis, had warned him they'd probably never have kids if they mated. Damned if he cared. All he wanted was the beautiful blue demon with the curves and fetching laugh. Now, knowing the blending of their incompatible genes was wreaking havoc with his son's breeding ability, he wasn't so sure he should have been so selfish.

His son grunted. "We have options. On the other side. The human side."

Floyd grunted in return. Of course. His son would have to

leave Hell and seek treatment in the human realm. Their aptitude for technology more than made up for their fragile frames and worthless magical abilities. "We have a doctor under possession in Englewood, Colorado. I will come by tonight with the paperwork."

His son responded with another grunt and hung up the phone.

Floyd glanced at the clock and quickly depressed the push button to get a clear line. He twisted the dial to zero and stared at the institutional green walls while he waited for his secretary to answer.

"Lucinda," he said as he drew a manila folder from the top of a steel filing cabinet. "Send in the next client, please."

"Of course, *Floyd*," the sexy voice on the other end purred.

Damn Succubus, he thought as he grabbed a victim book from a lower shelf and placed it on his desk. "I've told you before, call me Mr. BoMaster, Lucinda."

The pitch of Lucinda's voice rose to her normal tone as she lost the seductive purr. "Yes, sorry, sir. I'll send in the next client posthaste."

Floyd hung up the phone and flipped the folder open to scan the first page. Dexter Bae—a Flurian. Interesting. He'd never heard of a Flurian visiting a travel agency before, at least not PLOP. His eyes ran down the page, stopping once before continuing on. They were a genderless species, and he wasn't surprised to find the space for gender had been left blank on the intake form. Still, it would have been nice if Lucinda had asked Dexter how it wanted to be addressed.

Floyd grunted and shook his head. Lucinda had rated Dexter a category two, which meant the Flurian had a pretty weak constitution and wouldn't get the highest-quality humans to select from, but there only needed to be one that piqued its interest. Floyd stood as the door opened, and then he stepped around his desk.

"Hello, Dexter," he said, extending his large hand. "I'm Floyd. Nice to meet you."

The tall, thin, opalescent-skinned fairy slipped a narrow hand into Floyd's and returned his shake with a slight squeeze. Although almost as tall as Floyd, who towered above most demons at seven foot seven, Dexter's lean frame didn't look strong enough to stand against a strong breeze. Everything about the Flurian appeared weak, from its handshake and shuffling feet to the tilt of its head when it glanced away. Even the piece of clothing it wore—a pair of white cotton pants layered in embroidered daisies—screamed *I am a victim*.

Floyd ignored his natural desire to dominate and flicked his tail along the ground. Fighting the Flurian would not only be frowned upon by his boss but would probably end with his death. The weak appearance and gentle demeanor of winged fairies were used to stimulate their victims into a desire to dominate, bringing them close enough to be poisoned and eventually devoured. Something Floyd had no interest in doing.

He sat back in his chair and waited for his client to get comfortable before they started their defensive posturing—an accepted ritual for all demon introductions. Minutes passed before the curious Flurian sat in the chair opposite Floyd's desk.

"I've never been here," Dexter said, running a hand against the leather chair.

"No, we don't get many Flurians here. To be honest," Floyd said as he leaned forward to cross his bulging arms over the desk, "you are my first."

"Ah, well then, do you have any questions you'd like answered before we begin? I'm quite okay with questions."

Floyd studied Dexter for a second while he thought. Demons of the magical kind often spelled their spoken words to guarantee outcomes they desired. As far as he knew, Flurians were not magically gifted. He needn't worry about promises and debts owed because of a misspoken phrase uttered. He could speak freely with this one. "To begin with, I'd like to know the pronoun I should use for you. I know your gender is neutral, but I've heard most of your kind have a preference when it comes to being described as a *he* or *she*."

"Hmph. Most of us do. I, personally, don't care but out of routine have become a *he*." Dexter twisted around in his seat and studied the walls. "You have runes spelled into these anemic-looking walls. I suppose those are for your protection, not mine?"

Floyd grunted before breaking into a smile. The large, block-shaped teeth filling his mouth gleamed as his nostrils flared. "Even without the runes, I am safe," he said. "I cannot be bewitched, charmed, nor enchanted." He reached his hand up and cracked it against the large expanse of bone crossing his skull. "My skull protects me from such. My thick hide protects me from physical threats. I am a powerful beast during a fight."

Dexter smiled, displaying the razor-sharp teeth filling his mouth. "And I," he said, "cannot be killed without you touching me, and if you do, I will inject you with enough venom to kill the devil himself. I would die, but not alone." As he spoke, his skin lost its milky, polychromatic tone, the colors coalescing into uniquely colored dots equally spaced over every inch of his body. The white of his skin remained flat, but the colored portions rose, becoming wickedly sharp points where venom formed tiny pearls. As quickly as they appeared, they vanished as his skin smoothed once again into a blemish-free hide.

Standard pleasantries and blustering completed, Floyd grunted and opened the drawer beside him. He flicked a pad of paper open on his desk and tapped a pencil against the lined yellow page. "So, Dexter, what can PLOP do for you?"

"PLOP—Possession Logistics and Obtainment Professionals. What an odd name." Dexter relaxed and tapped his fingers against his chair. "I want you to do for me what your name implies. I want to possess a human."

"Of course. But why? I need a better understanding of your needs so I can fulfill your desires satisfactorily. We here at PLOP have an exemplary record when it comes to placement. That only happens because of the time we put into matching every demon to a corresponding human. If I were to just pick any human, you might not get a full possession and instead become only a backseat voice in that person's head. Where's the fun in that? And there are dangers. Transferring your soul into a human who has a soul more powerful than yours could cause irreparable damage to yourself. So, take your time and explain why you are here so I can give you the best experience possible. I need to evaluate your demeanor, your thoughts, your desires . . ." Floyd's voice faded away, and he leaned over his desk with his fingers tented before him. "So, again, how can I help you, Dexter?"

Dexter pursed his lips for a second in thought. "I've always found humans fascinating. Even in elementary school when everyone else was in love with Hagen the Evil and Princess Eviscera, I was drawing humans. My classmates, and a few teachers, thought I was odd, or even disturbed, for liking such benign things. They assumed I'd grow out of my boring obsession eventually, but I'm twenty-six now and still find them endearing." He hooked one leg over the other and tapped his knee with a long finger. "I think it's time I fulfill a childhood dream and see the human world."

"Well, at PLOP you are among kindred spirits, Dexter, and you won't be judged. Most of our clients have a fascination with humans in some way." Floyd leaned back in his chair, glancing covertly at the clock. Already 1:43 p.m. If he didn't hurry, he wouldn't be getting to his son's house at a reasonable time. "But what do you want to do with the human? Don't be shy. I've heard it all."

"You have? What was the most interesting?"

"Oh, I couldn't pick if I wanted to," Floyd said with a low laugh that made the walls shake. "There are just too many options to consider. What I need to know is if you are looking at a single casualty or mass murder. Do you intend to extend your possession over months and delay the inevitable slaying, or will you kill your human immediately? Will you kill only the intended, or do you want to take out a crowd? Do you even intend to kill the possessed human? Or do you want your possessed physically or mentally maimed? How bloody do you want the experience? Do you want to bathe in the gore or give a clean death?

"We can charge you for a day possession, a week, a year, or an indeterminate amount of time. We can arrange for you to have access to someone with the skills necessary to cause mass casualties—a pilot or leader of a cult—or are you more interested in picking a target other than the one you possess? In that case, we'll set you up with someone who has access to your intended victim. Do you want a celebrity? We can possess his assistant or significant other. The president of a country? They always have hired guns to protect them. A child? How young do you want them? We can set up anything you desire, Dexter."

Floyd suddenly leaned forward and snapped his fingers. "I'd almost forgotten to tell you about our newest option! It's relatively unknown and the result of a suggestion submitted by an actual client, if you can believe it. Do you not want your vacation to end? You can now take possession of your human, do your deed, and then abandon them to live out the consequences of their action. We provide you with a hand-held scrying orb, spelled by our in-house witches, that enables you to watch their free fall for the next three months. Our team of demon-possessed private eyes will track and relay everything that happens, even if your human gets incarcerated. Last year we had a client who watched his human hang for his offenses a year after his possession was completed! That's a vacation that just keeps on giving, don't you think? Of course, I don't want to mislead you. The viewing wasn't free. The client had to pay a nominal fee to extend his continuing pleasure after the three-month period had ended.

"Now that I've talked your ear off, what does your heart desire?"

Floyd's smile fell as he noticed his client's discomfort. During his speech, the Flurian's skin had blushed to a pale pink until he appeared to be sunburned. Dexter had shifted in his seat and clutched the leather armrests so hard the material bulged and appeared about to crack. And his eyes—they sparkled unnaturally. Watching the Flurian swallow convulsively, Floyd could almost taste the vomit threatening to erupt.

"Are you okay?" Floyd asked as he eased back in his seat and extended his leg toward his garbage can. One large hoof pressed the container closer to Dexter before sliding back under the desk.

Dexter's eyes slid to the can before he straightened and dragged his hands to his knees. His voice was a high-pitched squeak when he spoke. "Yes, I'm okay. I'll just . . . I'll take the last option if you don't mind."

Floyd's eyes narrowed. Something didn't feel right. Dexter wasn't hitting the right cues nor stating the base desires he should be expressing. The Minotaur flicked the folder on his desk open and scanned the front page. "Are you sure? It's an expensive option. Our most expensive, as a matter of fact. Why don't you tell me the minimum requirement you have for this experience? Anything you'd like to see?"

An excited squeal from Dexter snapped Floyd's head up. His face blanked when he heard the word *snow* escape the Flurian's mouth. The guy might as well have asked to dance in a meadow naked. Under the full moon. With a priest.

"Of course," he lied while turning to the next page in the folder, "that's a common enough request. I'm sure we can find a human in the northern latitudes for you." Floyd stopped talking and pressed his jaws together. His assistant had missed a notation in Dexter's chart about his mental instability and unsuitability as a client. The Flurian was obsessed with happiness and beauty and got physically sick over thoughts of dismemberment and death. The demon should be committed, not sitting in his office. He was insane.

Damn it. Lucinda's main job was to cull the crazies from the client list, and what did she do? Not only had she accepted his application, but she'd sent him to Accounting where they took his money. Now PLOP would be out his payment and beholden for one wish if they didn't allow him to possess a human. Even worse, for Satan's sake, once that got out, it'd be all over the papers. They'd lose clients for sure. Who wants to sign a contract with a firm that doesn't follow through? He inwardly groaned. And then there was the favor. The last time the company owed a favor, he'd lost one of his horns. Damn thing took a year to grow back. And it hurt like hell.

"Excuse me," he said as he jumped to his feet. He smiled and nodded to the door. "I just remembered something I need my assistant to do for me. If you don't mind, I'll be right back."

Dexter continued to smile as he relaxed in his chair. The word *snow* seemed to have calmed him, and his skin was again smooth and pearlescent without a trace of the pink it had previously held.

Floyd closed the door behind him before letting his smile drop. He stomped to his assistant's desk, smacking Dexter's folder against his thigh as he walked.

"Lucinda, you messed up," he snapped. He threw the file on her desk and placed his hands on his hips. "Did you not check the Flurian's evaluation sheet?"

The fire-red Succubus raised her honey-colored eyes from the file cabinet in front of her to meet his gaze. She pursed her full lips for a second before whispering, "Did I miss something?" Dark lashes flashed as she blinked and turned her body completely toward him. The possibility of sex oozed from her, filling the room with an enticing aroma as she crossed her legs provocatively.

Floyd's brows lowered, and a trickle of smoke left his nostril. "Lucinda," he warned.

Lucinda rolled her eyes and stood. Her hips swayed seductively as she strolled to her desk, the delicate chains wrapped around her hips and breasts chiming with each step. She pulled the folder to her chest and examined the evaluation sheet.

"Hmmm, I guess I did," she murmured as she closed the folder. Her eyes slid up Floyd's hips and over his abs, paying close attention to the thick muscle over his breastbone, before meeting his eyes. "What happens now? Will I be . . . punished?"

Never again, Floyd thought as he ran a hand across his face. *I will never be talked into hiring a friend's cousin again.* He clenched his jaws tight and counted to ten. "No," he muttered, crossing his arms, "this is your first mistake. You won't be punished, not this time. But you need to refund Dexter his fee and write him an IOU for a debt owed. Do you understand what that means?"

"Noooooo," she drawled as she leaned forward against the desk. Long, dark tresses seemed to move on their own as they settled enticingly across her shoulders. One luxurious strand curled itself in the dark space of her cleavage.

Floyd stomped a heavy hoof against the floor. The desk shook, and Lucinda pulled herself upright.

"It means," he hissed, "you are beholden to the Flurian for one wish. This is your mistake, so it's your problem. Do you understand?"

The Succubus's face registered shock before she lowered her gaze to the floor. She gave a short nod as her hand moved to cover her mouth.

She's smiling? Floyd thought as his eyes narrowed and then widened. Wisps of sulfur-scented smoke escaped both nostrils now, gathering above his head like a small, dark cloud. Whether she had planned this, and he didn't think she had, rewarding her with owing someone a favor was probably a bad idea. The Succubus was getting off on the idea. Soon every client she approved would have an issue, and she would be beholden to each of them. PLOP would lose money, and she'd be the happiest employee he'd ever supervised.

Floyd yanked the folder from where it rested against her large, pendulous breasts. He caught his assistant's surprised look and snapped, "I'll handle this," before turning around.

Great, just great. He didn't want to owe this lunatic. Who knew what he'd request. Probably something illegal, like killing someone without a permit or on a Tuesday. No, he wasn't taking a chance.

He stopped before his office door and blew the last tendrils of smoke from his nostrils. Letting his shoulders relax, he walked inside with a plan.

"Thank you for waiting, Dexter. I appreciate you giving me your time." His eyes flicked to the victim book that lay open on his client's legs. "I, um, need to take this from you," he said as he tugged at the leather cover.

"But I've found humans I like."

Floyd noticed that as Dexter's grip tightened, the colors along his skin began to swirl. Alarmed, Floyd yanked the book away and stepped back with the book between himself and the Flurian. "Believe me, I'm sorry about the switch, but I don't think these humans are a good idea."

Floyd forced himself to smile. "Can I be honest with you, Dexter?" he asked, relieved to see the Flurian's skin returning to a relaxed state. At the Flurian's nod, he continued. "Your aura is a little softer than most of the clients we see. It's not a problem, as we get all levels of clients at PLOP, but it does mean this book isn't for you. For that reason," he continued as he moved behind his desk and scanned the victim books on his shelf. "I want to switch you to a book containing more compatible profiles. Just a second, and I'll have a whole new selection of victims for you to peruse."

His fingers brushed the leather-bound spines before stopping on a rough-looking binder. Not bound to impress their clients like the other books, the leather was thin, cheap, and cracked, the letters stamped in red, not gold. He drew it out and studied the cryptic codes along the spine and around the back. This was the one he wanted, a book of heavily medicated humans facing life commitments to mental hospitals. They were unacceptable candidates for possession—and any of them could solve his problem if selected.

If Dexter chose someone from this book, no one would hear about Lucinda's error, no profits would be lost, no favors would be owed, and Dexter would be locked away forever in the mind of an incapacitated human. Perfect.

Floyd turned and gave Dexter a large grin. "Here we go," he said as he placed the binder on the desk. "Pick anyone from this file, and you'll get the possession you deserve." He sat and waited, his hope fading as Dexter's eager smile wilted a little further with each page he turned.

Pressure increased under the horns atop Floyd's head. He resisted his urge to blow smoke and release his growing anxiety, having no desire to reveal his stress.

Today he hated his job.

Floyd tapped his fingers against the desk as the minutes passed, and Dexter's look grew grimmer. And what would he do if Dexter didn't find someone he liked? Tell him there were no other options? Force him to pick someone? Not possible. He could see the headlines now: PLOP —THE COMPANY YOU VISIT IF YOU DON'T WANT THE VACATION YOU PAID FOR. His jaws ground together as a slim, wispy tendril of smoke eased from his nose.

He had a pile of unprocessed victim packets stacked on the shelf behind him. He was tempted to search through them for other options but held back. The humans described within the packets hadn't been evaluated by one of PLOP's victim-acquisition specialists and couldn't legally be possessed. Damn bureaucracy—made things a thousand times more difficult than they needed to be. Fill out this form, that form, get it signed in triplicate. Bah. He'd been in this business for three hundred years and knew how to match demons to humans; he had a 99 percent survivability rate, for Satan's sake. If he thought a match would work, it'd work.

His attention returned to the Flurian when Dexter sighed deeply. An almost palpable sense of defeat filled the room, sending the pressure beneath Floyd's skullcap through the roof.

Floyd's jaws clenched as he pushed back from his desk and grabbed the box of forms off the bookshelf. Pulling it to his lap, he flicked through the pages quickly, not bothering to look at those without criminally insane stamped across the top. His fingers paused on a picture of a pretty girl.

Kelsey Freeman—committed to the insane asylum for killing two kids under the age of ten and attempting to murder another. One child died by drowning, the other by strangulation. Freeman was found by the local police department when the third victim went missing. Pentagrams, candles, altars . . . she was praying to Satan, said he spoke to her. Floyd snorted. Like the Almighty had time to waste on her.

Floyd let out a low grumble. The demon stationed in the intake center hadn't evaluated her yet. There was a chance he'd determine her too dangerous to possess, but that wasn't likely. Very few humans were capable of causing harm to demons. Normally only the religiously devout, and she definitely wasn't devout. She hadn't been drugged yet, but experience showed she would be soon. He casually ripped the admittance sheet off the packet and set it aside.

"Dexter, my man, I may have found the answer to your dreams." Once the papers describing Kelsey slid across the desk, he clutched his hands together and watched Dexter closely.

There was a moment of silence before Dexter nodded and grinned. "Is she somewhere snowy?"

Floyd stilled. "Yes," he lied, pulling the papers closer. His shoulders relaxed when he saw *AK* stamped on the form. "She's in Alaska, which is snowing more often than not. What we'll do is have you sign a long-term waiver to make sure you get the experience you desire. If the weather cooperates, you can come back tomorrow. If it doesn't, then you'll stay until you've been satisfied. How's that sound?"

"Perfect." Dexter leaned forward with his hands clasped in front of him. His long, narrow wings flew open and beat rapidly in the air before lowering back against his backside. He smiled wide, displaying his sharp needle-like teeth.

Floyd jerked his eyes away from the alarming vision and opened the drawer on his right. He saw every kind of demon in his job, but Flurians took the cake. So weak and nonthreatening until they smiled and raised those nasty little bumps on their skin. Freaks, even for demons.

Smirking, he removed the multiple forms Dexter needed to sign. Everything was coming together. There might even be time for another appointment before he left to see his son. His movements paused for the briefest second before they resumed. Or, he could leave as soon as Dexter was contained and miss rush hour completely. With renewed energy, he filled out a bank slip for the remaining funds Dexter needed to pay for the upgrade, then signed his name at the bottom.

"Here you go. I need you to sign these forms, after you read them, of course, and we'll be ready to go." He handed Dexter the papers along with a government-issued binding pen. The magical device glowed under the yellow light radiating from the bulb hanging above the desk. "Standard instructions," Floyd said. "Use the knife to open a vein, and fill the reservoir with your blood. The contract is binding once your blood touches the paper."

"No problem," Dexter said as he nicked his arm and drew blood into the glass end of the pen. He scrawled his signature in dark-blue blood across the forms with a flourish. As the pen inked the last letter of his signature, the blood darkened, and small puffs of acrid smoke rose from the pages.

Floyd grinned and stood. "All right," he said as he tapped the papers into a pile. He stapled them together and placed them in Dexter's folder.

"Follow me to the possession room, and we'll get your vacation started. Are you excited?"

"Oh yes," Dexter said as he slipped out the door and

waited while Floyd locked his office. "I've been wanting this experience since the first time I glimpsed the human world in the scrying ball at the fair. So magical. So beautiful. Seems dreams are possible topside."

Floyd turned his head away to roll his eyes. Beautiful? Magical? Snow? Where did this guy come from? He smiled at Dexter before stopping to allow another demon to pass. The narrow halls of the old building were barely big enough for him to walk in, much less him and another demon. As he sucked in his stomach and flattened himself against the wall, the passing shadow walker changed from solid to a shimmering cloud of darkness. The demon slid through the space between him and the wall with no trouble before transitioning back to his solid form. He raised a skinny gray arm and flashed the peace symbol before disappearing into an office.

"Well, dreams are also possible here at PLOP," Floyd said as they continued walking. "Here you are, on your way to the dream vacation you've always wanted. Life can't get much better than that."

There was a faint buzz behind them as Dexter's wings flared in excitement. "I know. I honestly didn't think I'd make it to adulthood. Life is hard when you have a delicate disposition like I have. No one understands or wants to listen. I might enjoy beauty once in a while, but that doesn't make me a bad guy."

Floyd struggled for a response for a second then shrugged. "You know, it takes all kinds to make the world go 'round." He jumped when Dexter squealed behind him.

"That's what I've been telling my mother forever. I can't wait to get home and tell her about my experience. Knowing there are others who want to see snow and a happy world might make her accept me." He stopped talking for a second before exclaiming, "I'll tell you something. I'm tired of her dropping me off at the therapist's when we're supposed to be going to the store. It's the same thing she does to Jasper, our hellhound, when he needs to see the vet! No offense to my hellhound, but I'm no dog."

Floyd glanced at him and laughed. He couldn't help it. "I'm sorry," he said, waving the smoke he'd emitted away from his face. "What a life, Dexter. Maybe you should write a book when you get back." He stopped walking when they reached a frosted glass door and pressed his palm against the steel plate embedded within the wall. His hand burned as the magic read his identity before allowing the door to slide open. He stepped to the side and waved Dexter inside.

"Well, maybe I will," Dexter said as he walked into the stark white room. He stared at a round mass of pale flesh sitting on a chair beside a door on the opposite wall. The transparent pink-tinged skin rolled as organs and liquid shifted beneath its surface. Eyes suddenly shimmered into existence on the side and slid along the outside membrane until they faced the front. Two sections of skin along the bottom stretched until legs touched the ground. A mouth, no more than fleshy bulges, formed under the eyes. "Hello, Mr. BoMaster. How are you today?"

"Fine, Bob. Thanks for asking. How are you? How's the wife and the pregnancy?"

"Good. The little ones are growing rapidly. We can see them moving under her skin now. So exciting watching the small blobs form and attempt to press to the surface. They should be popping out any month now."

"That is great, Bob. Someday I'll have grandkids, and we'll have to get them together. Should be fun." He glanced at Dexter. "You ready?"

"Huh? Oh, yeah." He continued staring at the blob as they went through the second door.

Bob stared back, his eyes sliding around his body to watch them as they passed.

"I've never seen one of those," Dexter whispered once the door shut behind them.

"Bob? Yeah, his kind don't tend to work in the public sector. Too conspicuous. But he's lived in this area his whole life and has a home a block away. Normally he works behind the scenes, but we have a few people on vacation and needed a guard. He's pretty easygoing and goes where we need him.

"Now," he said as he waved his arm around the room. "This is one of the rooms we use to home our long-term clients. You will be perfectly safe here. No one is allowed inside without approval, and you will be monitored every day to make sure your body is kept healthy until you return. Would you like to look around before we begin?"

He watched as Dexter moved down the aisle between the cots lining the white walls. Each bed had a small white table next to it, some displaying pictures of family and friends, others covered with candles and religious items. Nothing adorned the clients themselves except a thin blue blanket that covered their bodies. Dexter turned back, stopping for a second to stare at a square bed taking up one end of the long room. Twice the size of the other beds, the demon sleeping atop its surface barely fit inside the room.

"Whoops," Floyd said as he hurried toward them. He stopped beside the bed and picked up a glove lying on the bedside table. Using it like a towel, he grabbed the scaly arm hanging off the edge and placed it back under the cover. "His, uh, skin is corrosive. Can't touch it with your bare hands or you'll get a nasty burn. Makes bathing him quite a chore."

Dexter took a step back and stared at the creature nervously. "Am I sleeping next to him?"

Floyd glanced at the paperwork in his hands out of habit before shaking his head. "Nope. We weren't expecting you to need long-term care, so no bed was selected. Why don't we place you over here," he said as he led Dexter to a bed close to the door. "Go ahead and get comfortable. Put everything from your pockets in the drawer and remove your clothes. You'll find a nightshirt in the bottom cupboard. Just put your pants where you found your nightshirt. I'll get the doctor, and we'll start the procedure immediately. How's that sound?"

Dexter responded with a hesitant, "Sure." His eyes darted around before he leaned forward. "Do I change in here? With these guys?"

Floyd laughed. "No one in here knows you or I exist, much less cares if you change your clothes. You'll have privacy for a few minutes. I'll be back as soon as I get the doctor."

He hummed as he left the room, waved goodbye to Bob, and headed down the hall. When he reached the doctor's lounge, he stopped and looked around. Four large couches separated the room into comfortable sitting areas. At one end sat a demon reading a book. "Excuse me, Dr. TriDome," he said, "have you seen Dr. Lickster? He's on call." Three lizard-shaped heads, all located on one set of shoulders, turned to him. He stared at the center head, knowing LizBit was the most vocal of the three.

"I don't know. Go away," she said before turning to sip from her cup. The other two went back to reading the book held in the other hand without saying a word.

Floyd grunted and stomped to the other side of the room. He couldn't understand why diversiforms were always so difficult. Maybe more than one brain made them care nothing about others. The three other diversiform demons working at PLOP were inconsiderate and completely self-absorbed, just like Dr. TriDome.

"Overnight rooms or kitchen," he grumbled lowly as he

stomped as loudly as he could to the kitchen. "Would that have been too difficult to state?" Now he'd have to check both areas himself, and he hated checking the overnight rooms. The one time he'd walked in on Vane liquefying pieces of his dinner while it struggled on the floor had given him nightmares for weeks.

"Stan, are you in here?" he bellowed loudly as he swung the door open. He smirked when he heard one of Dr. TriDome's heads muttering behind him. Let the old biddies complain.

"Stan!" he continued yelling as he turned and walked across the lounge to the overnight door. His grin widened when the door opened and a human-looking head peeked around the corner.

"Floyd, what are you doing?" Stan asked. "Why are you yelling?"

Floyd grabbed the door and looked down at the diminutive male. Barely four feet tall, the top of his head just reached Floyd's hips. "I've been trying to find you!" he yelled again with a smirk. As Stan's eyebrows rose, Floyd nodded slightly toward the couch and Dr. TriDome.

There was a sigh before the doctor stepped out from behind the door. "I take it you have a patient?" He pushed a pair of wire glasses up his nose and studied Floyd. Shaggy brown hair with a hint of gray framed the doctor's inexplicably young-appearing face. A characteristic of his species, the Thermescian had a face as soft and flawless as the day he'd been born. Most of the time he didn't seem one hundred years old, much less six hundred; other times, like tonight, his exhaustion and age were almost palpable.

Even for a Thermescian he was old, and Floyd felt a little guilty bringing him a client in his current state. "Yeah, just one tonight, Doc. I'm leaving early, so you should be able to rest a little."

The smile Stan gave him was genuine. He nodded his head and walked to the hall. "Good. I'm feeling my age today. I'd like to rest and see if that helps."

"Is there anything I can do? Do you need me to stay late? Help?" His inquiry was real. As much as he loved his son and sympathized with his difficulties, Stan had no one but the people here. One of the last of his kind, he was completely alone in the city.

"No, no. Thank you, Floyd, but I'll be okay. Tell me about the patient while we walk."

"His name is Dexter, and he's a Flurian. Wants an extended stay with his victim."

"Sure. Extended stay. Must be nice being able to vacation as long as you want. Wish I'd chosen a different job when I was young. Should have been an actor or a politician. Worthless professions all the way around, but they have nice lives." He turned his head to peer up at Floyd. "What is it your son does? School teacher?"

"No, Darrius works at a gym training mixed martial art fighters. Loves the adrenaline, and the job keeps him in shape. Money's not the best, but he's happy."

"Kids. In my day, if we wanted to fight, we killed the kid down the street. How else do you learn? Now kids go to trainers and learn to fight safely. An oxymoron, if you ask me. Makes demons weak. Our kids are turning into pansies. You should see the politically correct crap the psychology student I mentor sends me. Praise Satan, how are we supposed to take over topside if our kids are scared of hurting each other's feelings?"

Floyd snorted and shook his head. "I heard about the rally at the embassy," he said as he touched the identity pad outside the long-term patient room. The door slid open, and he ushered Stan inside. "Was your student there?"

The doctor rolled his eyes and nodded. "Got herself

arrested. I picked her up at the police station an hour before her time ran out. Her parents refused to pick her up. Said they were ashamed of her. If she hadn't reached me, she would have been fed to the hellhounds. I hope she learned her lesson and will stop this nonsense."

Floyd slowed and shook his head. "I thank Satan I don't have to worry about Darrius getting arrested. When he's not fighting, he's watching human movies he's bought off the black market."

The doctor grunted. "Don't be surprised when you get a call from the police. They've been cracking down on that also. How undemon is that? Arresting people for stealing. What has this world come to?"

They stopped talking when they reached the second door and stepped inside. Stan immediately walked toward Dexter with his hand extended. "Hello there, I'm Dr. Lickster. I'll be guiding you through your possession today. It's an easy process, one I've done a million times before, so don't be worried. You'll pass with flying colors, I'm sure."

Dexter smiled from where he sat on the bed. He wore a well-worn, but soft, blue shirt. The same blue blanket the other occupants wore lay across his legs. "Okay, what do I need to do?"

"Just relax. I'm going to give you a sedative—nothing strong—just enough to make you comfortable." The doctor reached into his coat pocket and withdrew a long needle. His smile grew when he noticed Dexter draw away from him. He flicked the cylindrical portion of the apparatus with a long, slim finger, causing the golden liquid inside to slosh and drip down the sides in thick syrupy lines. When Dexter's eyes widened, the air around the doctor's body grew warm as dark energy oozed out of his skin. Shadows rose along his cheeks and eyes, rushing outward until the symbiotic demon inside him peered outside excitedly through his flesh. Stan's lips spread wider as he turned the needle upside down and removed the cap from the long, thin point. A drop of fluid beaded at the tip before dropping to the floor.

Floyd grunted and stepped forward, intentionally bumping the doctor's back with his knee in the process. "Doctor . . ."

Stan twitched before drawing himself upright and placing the cap back on the needle. The shadows vanished, sinking back into his body. It took a moment before the malevolent energy dissipated and a sense of calm returned to the air. "Pardon me," he said before turning to look at Dexter. "I'm sorry, what is your name?"

Dexter, whose two pale hands clutched the blanket beneath his chin, glanced up to the doctor's eyes and back to the needle before answering. "Dexter," he squeaked out as he sunk deeper in the bed and disappeared under the cover.

"Well, Dexter, as you well know, it's sometimes difficult for demons to ignore our base instincts. As a doctor, I'm trained to do better. I happen to be tired today and didn't do as well as I should have. I apologize from the bottom of my heart."

"Okay," Dexter whispered from under his blanket.

The doctor stared at the blue lump for a minute before turning to Floyd.

Floyd snorted, unable to determine if he was more amused or disgusted by Dexter's behavior. He shrugged before reaching over and pulling the blanket down. "Dexter, come out. It's okay."

"I really don't think so," the Flurian whispered as he sat up. "I don't think it's okay at all."

Floyd jerked back in alarm. Dexter's skin was angry and inflamed with venom flowing between the bright-pink bumps like a river through a valley. As if alive, the fluid moved over him but did not seem to be leaking onto the mattress or blanket.

"Don't," Floyd whispered, thrusting his hand down to stop the doctor from reaching forward. He stalled, an obvious solution to his problem within reach. "Dexter, would you like to cancel your contract with PLOP? If you are uncomfortable with this . . ."

"No! Of course not!" Dexter shrieked. He closed his eyes and took a deep breath before holding up his arm to display his perfectly smooth skin. "I'm sorry, I was alarmed. I'll control myself this time." He leaned back against the sheet and closed his eyes. "You may continue, Doctor. I just won't watch."

There was a moment of silence before Floyd dropped his arm and let his shoulders sag. He'd been so hopeful. He stepped back and blew a ring of smoke into the air.

The doctor glanced at the ring before moving to the bed. "Again, I'm sorry, Dexter. Let's get your vacation started." He stared down at the exposed arm for a second before sighing and pressing his hand to Dexter's flesh.

The injection completed, he stepped back and stared at the watch on his wrist.

"Okay," he murmured after a minute. "How do you feel now?"

There was a moment when Floyd didn't think the Flurian was going to answer, when he wondered if the Flurian had died, and his heart beat a little faster in excitement. It happened sometimes. But the moment passed when Dexter opened his eyes and gave a weak smile.

"I'm . . . much better," he said.

Stan nodded. "Good. Now, a little history before we begin. Every demon has the ability to move between the planes, to visit the human world through the act of possession, without visiting possession centers such as PLOP. Did you know that?"

"I . . . no . . . what?"

"Yep. It's true. Our souls have always been able to travel the divide without help, but our government feels it's unsafe for us to travel without being supervised. They say we are an endangerment to ourselves and need to be regulated. They are full of zonga shit if you ask me." He reached down and checked Dexter's pulse before giving another nod. "You are doing fabulous, Dexter. Just another minute and we'll be ready to begin.

"So, as I was saying, centuries ago the government felt the need to protect us from ourselves and enacted all these laws. Laws about when we could travel, who was allowed to travel, and how we could travel. Of course, whether the laws worked depended on demons doing what they were told, which, as we all know, meant the laws were doomed from inception." He shook his head. "It's against our nature to do as told. We require authoritarians, enforcers—someone to beat the snot out of us when we get out of line—if the goal is to make us conform. There's only one reason the government would pass a law allowing demons to self-regulate. Do you know what that reason is, Dexter?"

Dexter had opened his eyes during the doctor's speech and now shrugged. "I don't know."

"Money. They wanted it, and they came up with a way to attain it." The doctor walked to the cabinet against the wall and opened the doors. He brought out a large pendant hanging off a gaudy gold chain and studied the design carved into the front.

"After their regulations failed, the government passed a law securing the Nether between our worlds. A few witches, a little magic, and the space between the dimensions became as thick and impenetrable as tar—much too dangerous to travel through. Without proper support, even the most powerful of demons die within the sludge. When the law passed, not many demons cared. Most were happy terrorizing their neighbors.

"And the government noticed. They spent millions on advertising. Advertising that showed how magnanimous they were by keeping us safe from humans. Ads that were provocative and enticing. Ads that made the human more mainstream and tempting. Ads that gave demons ideas.

"Their plan worked. Not being able to travel the dimensions not only made demons want to travel, it made them demand a way to travel, no matter the cost. Remember, demons don't like being told what they can and can't do. Riots ensued, wars started. Demons who'd never cared about humans now killed for the chance to see one. And the government came up with a solution. Nice and tidy-like, if you ask me."

The doctor closed the cabinet door and shook his head.

"Taxes! That's what they wanted, and that's what they get when you pay PLOP for the privilege to possess a human. You pay us, we pay the government, and then your DNA gets marked so you can pass through the magically spelled Nether. And that is what the injection was for. The magic burns, which is why we mix it with a sedative and medicine to make the experience less painful. We wait five minutes to make sure the marker is coursing through your veins before we start the possession."

He moved back to Dexter's bed with a chair and the chain clutched in his hands. After setting the chair alongside the bed and sitting down, the doctor raised the pendant over the Flurian's face and whispered, "It's time to go, Dexter."

They were outside the sleeping room when the doctor spoke again. "So, are you going to explain why an obviously unstable demon is walking through the Nether, Floyd?"

Floyd said nothing until they'd passed Bob in the guardroom and stood outside in the hallway. "It's a damn mess," Floyd muttered once the door shut behind them. "He got through all our checks. I couldn't release him from his contract. I'm not taking on another debt when it's not my fault."

Stan looked at him for a minute before snorting. "You idiot. That weak demon is going to have the worst vacation ever. I hope you put him in an equally fragile human so he has a modicum of fun. Otherwise, his review is going to tank your end-of-year bonus."

"No, he's too weak for even that." Floyd glanced around before leaning as far down as he could, still a full head above Stan. "He's insane, Stan," he whispered. "He shouldn't be out in society much less possessing a human. I did what I had to. I sent him to a psychiatric hospital with a human who should be drugged to the nines for the rest of her life. He won't be returning."

The muscle in Floyd's jaw twitched while he waited for his friend to speak. Would he threaten to turn him in, or would he understand why he did what he did? He relaxed when Stan chuckled.

"Floyd," Stan said as he shook his head, "I think you've solved the societal problem of the ages. We should send all our crazies to the human world. Why keep them here? Let the humans deal with them. Once exorcized, their bodies will die, and we can feed them to the hellhounds and scavengers." He yawned and stretched his arms above his head. "I'd like to delve into your idea further, but I'm exhausted. I think I'll head to bed. Why don't we work on writing a proposal for the mayor tomorrow? You've got a good idea there, Floyd."

Floyd flushed. "Thank you. Sounds like a plan," he said as he clapped Stan gently on his shoulder. "Get some sleep."

The doctor waved a hand in the air and walked away.

Floyd glanced at his watch and smiled. If he left in the next thirty minutes, he'd miss rush hour and the inevitable mayhem that resulted when angry demons were stuck on the roadway. Yesterday had been a particularly bad day. One he didn't want to repeat. With that in mind, he hurried to his office.

He opened the top drawer of his desk and removed the forms his son and daughter-in-law would need for their possession: two physical authorization forms, two mental evaluation forms, two long-term waiver forms. Floyd sighed and ran a hand through the tufts of fur around his horns. He understood their desire for a baby, but going to such extremes verged on ridiculous. He closed his eyes for a second before returning to his task. No, they weren't acting ridiculous. He was the one acting foolish for forgetting he'd been willing to give up everything to marry his Mavis. This baby was his son's Mavis, and he needed to remember that.

A sound broke through Floyd's concentration, causing his eyes to rise to the doorway. It came again—an odd laugh . . . a yell . . . a scream? What was that? Floyd stood and moved around the desk with one hand trailing the metal. He tilted his head, allowing his ear to twist toward the sound as he moved to the door.

"Lucinda," he called, "do you hear that?"

His assistant came from her alcove down the hall. She sashayed toward him with her head cocked to the side as if listening but said nothing.

Electric screeches, a gurgle, and then thumping came from the other direction. They weren't screams, but somehow the unidentified noises unnerved him just the same. His tail flicked while his heart jerked violently in his chest. He swallowed and stared down the hall.

"I hear it," Lucinda said from next to his elbow, "but I can't place it." Her hand moved to rest against his spine as she shifted closer.

"Lucinda," he started, then stopped. Lucinda wasn't seducing him but appeared frightened as she stared around his shoulders in the direction of the noise. She chewed her lower lip, lost in thought and completely unaware of how seductive she appeared. A shiver crawled up his spine when he realized the Succubus had forgotten her biological need to seduce. He licked his black lips and turned away. "Go into my office, Lucinda, and lock the door. Don't come out until I come for you."

"Okay," she whispered as she slid behind him.

Floyd waited for the click of the lock before walking away. The floor was oddly silent. No sounds of talking, shuffling papers, or demons traversing the halls could be heard. Even the ventilation unit had cut off, removing the low hum he associated with the building. As he progressed, the glow of the yellow lights against the institutional green walls began to bother him, making him recall the human shows his son asked him to watch occasionally. Ghouls, ghosts, and monsters—usually they made him laugh. But now, feeling like he'd somehow become trapped in one of his son's movies, he wasn't laughing.

He hadn't gone far when he heard the smack of shoes striking the floor at a run. Already on edge, his body went rigid, and he squared his shoulders and lowered his head. Eighteen-inch ebony horns gleamed in the light. They were his weapons for the time being. Sharp and strong, nothing would get by them. Dark eyes stared into the distance as smoke slid from his nostrils. Tense seconds passed before a lizard-skinned demon appeared from around a corner. The demon raced toward him at a full gallop, mouth open, long tongue hanging from his mouth.

"Vander, what's going on?" He grumbled when the demon came close. Floyd's eyes dropped to the splatters of red on Vader's white smock. "Whose blood—"

They both turned as a scream rent the air.

"One of the patients woke. He's possessed," Vander hissed out. His unblinking black eyes widened as his tail swished anxiously behind him. "I'm going to call for a priestess and get him exorcized before he kills anyone else."

Warning bells went off in Floyd's head. "Wait," he said as he grabbed the fleeing demon's arm. "What demon?"

"A Flurian in the long-term patient room." He tried twisting his arm out of Floyd's grip before giving up. "I should go, Mr. BoMaster."

"Um—no." Floyd ran his free hand through his hair and blew out a puff of acrid smoke. Could this day get any worse? *Good Satan*, he thought, *if this gets out, I'll be here forever*. Talking to the police and insurance agents, filling out forms, and organizing a cleanse by the local priestess chapter would take all night. There were protocols he'd have to follow—bureaucracy at its finest. He looked down the hall and grunted. "Come with me, Vander. We need to handle this ourselves."

With Vander's arm locked in his fist, they made it to his office. He knocked and called out, "Lucinda, open up."

He pushed Vander inside as soon as the door opened. "Sit," he commanded as he grabbed the phone.

Floyd pressed the star button and hit seven. Overhead, the intercom clicked on with a beep. "Employees, this is Mr. BoMaster on the third floor. We have a Code Red. Again, Code Red. All employees follow procedures and meet in your designated areas." Next, he opened a drawer along the back wall and removed the long leather whip nestled inside. He clamped it to the hook on his belt.

"Both of you, collect your weapons and head to the cafeteria with everyone else. I'll be right behind you."

"Mr. BoMaster," Vander squeaked out, "I work in the pharmacy lab down the hall . . ." His voice trailed off as his skin turned a sickly pale green. "Toward the Flurian," he continued.

Floyd squeezed his arm. Vander couldn't run back and retrieve his weapon. "Okay. Just stay with me, Vander. I'll get you to the cafeteria safely." Floyd turned his attention to Lucinda. "We'll stop by your desk and get your weapon."

"I don't need a weapon," Lucinda said, running her hands down her breasts and over her taut stomach. "My aura will get me close enough to wrap my body around his. Once I do that, he's not going anywhere." She gave a sharp nod and pressed her lips tight.

Floyd understood she wasn't being suggestive but voicing her strengths. He shook his head. "Not this time, Lucinda. The patient is Mr. Bae. Touch his skin, and you'll die. Where's your weapon?"

She pouted, jutting her lower lip forward while leaning on one hip. "I don't like to use it, but the sword above the shelf in the alcove is mine."

Floyd nodded. "Let's get it before we head to the cafeteria. Everyone, stay alert and close together. If you see Dexter, let me know."

Floyd led the way out the door and into the hall. They reached the alcove, and he waved Lucinda inside. He stared behind him, an unfamiliar unease crawling up his back as the seconds passed.

"Got it," Lucinda whispered when she returned.

Floyd nodded. "Let's go. I'll guard the rear."

Lucinda held her sword in front of her as she crept forward. Vander followed close behind.

Floyd listened for an indication of where Dexter hunted, but he heard nothing but his own steps. His ears twisted to the back. A scream would be helpful—maybe three if he were lucky and Dexter had found Dr. TriDome. Then he'd know which way they should be going and the diversiform would be dead. He blew a puff of smoke and peered behind him. Nothing moved, but he got the feeling they were being watched. Tendrils of fear, not altogether unusual in Hell, spread from his spine to his hairline.

He grunted and unconsciously pawed his hoof before he stepped.

The lights flickered above them. On and off. Dark to bright.

All three froze.

"Keep going," Floyd grumbled. He glanced behind him and swallowed.

Lucinda stopped walking to peer around the next corner. She stared silently before her while Floyd stared behind. He didn't like the look of the shadows far down the hall where a few lights had remained off. Something moved within their depths, flickering and fluttering like wings catching the light. Relief flooded him when Vander stepped away, and he was able to follow.

Two minutes later they reached the cafeteria and slid into the room. Floyd looked over the demons standing around the tables. "Is this everyone?"

"We think those still alive are here," the garbled voice of the short demon from Accounting answered.

Floyd slid the lock closed before facing the crowd. He squared his shoulders and took a deep breath. Not many had made it. At least Stan, who gave him an exhausted half wave from a chair, was safe. "Okay," he said, "everyone's aware one of our appointments has gone terribly wrong. A client, Mr. Bae, has been possessed by his human victim. This doesn't happen often, but when it does, we've found the human involved to be much more powerful than the humans we are used to victimizing. They can be deadly as they take on the aspects of the demon they've possessed. But don't be alarmed. With our numbers, I believe we can handle this quickly and efficiently in house."

"I don't understand," a tall, birdlike demon with iridescent eyes interrupted. "Why are we not calling a priestess for an exorcism?" His head tilted to the side while he blinked rapidly behind thin round glasses. "This seems highly unsafe and irregular."

The agreeing grunt that escaped Floyd surprised him. He flushed and stepped forward to consider each of the demons in the room.

"I know it's unusual, but I think we should handle this ourselves. The possessor is nothing more than a young human girl. How she was able to possess Dexter is beyond me, but it happened—"

"She was a devotee," Stan interrupted.

Floyd shut his mouth and stared at his friend. His tail flicked, smacking him in the face before he responded. "What are you saying, Stan?"

Stan sighed, shook his head, and held up a sheet of paper he'd been clutching in his hand. "On her admittance form, it says she worships Satan. That's how she got in, Floyd."

Someone laughed in the background as a rumble of dissent filled the room. Floyd relaxed when he heard another demon voice the question he didn't want to ask.

"And why would that matter? Like Satan would waste his time on a human. We barely get to see His Exaltedness, and we live in his city."

Floyd heard the doctor mutter, "Idiots," below his breath before he stood to face the crowd.

"Devotees work both ways. If a human is devout to God, they have the possibility of fighting off the possession. If a devotee worships Satan, they have the possibility of returning along the astral plane the demon used to possess them." He stood for a second, glancing between shocked faces, before throwing his hands in the air. "Do none of you read your employee manuals? How do you think counterpossessions occur?"

Everyone went silent. No one moved or said anything as the minutes passed. When the room filled with smoke, heads turned to stare at Floyd. Floyd's tail whipped the air anxiously while he fought the pressure under his horns. He ground his teeth together and closed his eyes. He'd learned something today—that he was an idiot.

"Okay," he said, glancing around. "Thank you for the education, Doctor. But let's focus on solving our problem. We need to handle this without bringing in the authorities."

Grumbles filled the room, and he held up his hands. "Let me explain," he roared when no one quieted. He waited for silence before continuing.

"I don't want to be here all night. Hell-Land Security will have us filling out forms and answering questions on things that don't matter. What did you eat today? Who'd you eat today? Why'd you choose them?

"And what's the purpose? What are they hoping to ascertain? It's just a little possession gone wrong. It happens. Who wants to be here for the inquisition? Who remembers the last time this occurred? Terrance, do you remember what they did to you?"

A black and yellow centiloid demon leaned back in his chair and waved his feet in the air. Orange bulbous eyes widened as he screeched, "They made me remove my shoes

All in a days work 63

and scan my feet. Do you know how long it takes to remove and put on twelve pairs of sneakers? I only have two hands!"

"Exactly," Floyd grumbled. "What about the rest of you? How many of our friends were sent to the hellhounds after Hell-Land Security invaded their homes? Over a work-related possession! Why were they in our homes in the first place?"

This time he let the mumbles build until demons were exclaiming angrily about how they'd been treated. His lips curved into a smirk before he raised his hands again. Voices lowered immediately. "Let's take a vote. Raise your hand if you prefer we handle this ourselves."

With everyone in agreement, he continued. "We'll leave the weak, young, and old in the cafeteria." His eyes locked on the doctor until he got the dismissive wave he expected. Floyd nodded and went on. "The rest of us will search this floor. I doubt the Flurian's left this level with all the demons we seem to be missing. He's here somewhere, eating our friends, so we'll start searching rooms."

"Flurians are dangerous," the birdlike demon interjected. Five feet tall and covered in shiny white feathers, he held up two wings ending in clawed red hands before turning toward the group. "They are hematophagous demons and suck the blood of their victims. Their skin is filled with paralyzing neurotoxins that, if you are lucky, will kill you before they feed. If it doesn't, be prepared to die a horribly slow and painful death. Flurians like to play with their food, removing the blood while flooding the body with venom to create as much pain as possible. Believe me when I say you will wish you are dead way before you are."

"How do we kill them?" the shadow walker asked.

"Same as with most demons. Cut off the head, stab through the heart, or cut off the air supply. The problem is doing it without getting close. Those who weigh little need to be on extreme alert—one touch, and you'll die. Brutes like

Mr. BoMaster can handle more, but it will be painful." The bird demon finished his speech and turned to Floyd. "I will stay here. I am not a fighter and will be more of a hindrance."

Floyd nodded. "Everyone who can fight stand over here."

By the end of the shuffle, nine of the fifteen demons stood with Floyd. He looked them over, categorizing their skills and faults, before raising his hands to stop their chatter.

"There are nine of us. Those are good odds against one measly human. I know she has possessed a Flurian, which is . . . daunting, but the human doesn't know how to use the demon's innate abilities effectively. This gives us the advantage! Think—we know how things work in Hell, we know our strengths as demons, and she knows nothing. We just need to find her while she remains ineffectual.

"I believe it'll be easier to search the areas we know, so let's split into two groups. If you work in my hall, come to me. If you work in the hall with Mr. Falton, head over to him." His eyes flicked between the demons, stopping on a diminutive horned female named Yanna. Even eyeless, she somehow knew he watched and gave him a large smile. He smiled back before glancing down to her weaponless hands.

"Before we go, those of you without weapons head to the back cabinet and see what you can find to arm yourselves. I think you'll find swords and knives left by employees over the years." The demons hurried off, leaving Lucinda and Floyd alone on their side of the room.

"Weren't they supposed to do this before they got to the cafeteria?" Lucinda muttered beside him.

Yes, Floyd thought while giving a noncommittal grunt. They'd all signed the same emergency preparedness form when they'd been hired.

Lucinda shifted closer and whispered, "And what are we supposed to do with Mic? Why is he coming? The tiny butterball can't help us. You should tell him to stay here with the doctor."

"He wants to help," Floyd grumbled. "He's coming."

"Fine. But what is he going to do? He's a foot tall with no arms." She paused for a second before continuing. "Actually, I don't recall ever seeing his feet. Does he have feet? And what does he do at PLOP?"

Floyd pursed his lips and let a tendril of smoke slip out of his nostril. He realized he had no idea what the little pink Grumbling did. Spherical, with various-sized nodules covering his body, he had no arms or legs, and he slid along the ground as if on wheels—but, how was that possible? And what did he do at the office without arms? How could he possibly help, much less fight?

His pondering ended when Lucinda gave a seductive purr.

"Hello boys," she whispered, smiling brightly at the two demons walking their way.

Floyd glared at her before turning to the shadow walker and Mic. Of course, it was up to him to let Mic down gently. He would be blunt, he decided, but try to spare his feelings by being kind. Maybe lie and say they needed to leave him behind to protect the others. Floyd smiled, and the Grumbling swelled like a puffer fish, doubling his size before shrinking back to normal.

"I can't carry a weapon, Mr. BoMaster. But I have my own talents," Mic squeaked out before Floyd could say anything. Large baby-blue eyes surrounded by long, dark lashes fanned his pink skin. A light blush infused his cherub-like cheeks as he gave a timid smile. The tips of two white teeth peeked between his slightly parted lips. "I'm ready to fight."

Floyd gave a weak smile. All demons dreamed of their first fight. He remembered his and how proud he'd felt after beating the crap out of the weird kid who liked to run around naked. Bajul—he still remembered his name after all these years. "No problem, Mic. We need every fighter we can get. You are small, but don't be scared. I'll look after you."

"Oh, I'm not scared," Mic said while swiveling to stare at the rest of the group. "I've fought worse."

Floyd drew back in surprise. "You have?"

"Floyd," Dr. Lickster interrupted as he joined the group, "everyone's ready."

With a last glance down at Mic, Floyd turned to the demons standing before him. "Remember," he said, "we are doing this so we don't have to call Hell-Land Security. Work as a team, and let's take this demon down.

"Doc, barricade the door once we leave. Use the tables, chairs, and anything else not locked down. Even with the door secure, you should be prepared for a fight. If the Flurian gets around us, he may try to get inside. Everyone else, let's go."

Floyd strode to the exit and pulled the door open. Light spilled into the hall, creating a crescent-shaped area of brightness on the floor. Five feet on either side of the light, the hallway remained dark and shadowy. He studied the ceiling, noticing the two unlit bulbs over the doorway and a few more scattered through the hall. During the time they'd been inside, multiple bulbs had failed. Didn't seem right. He shivered and stepped outside.

The lights flickered, sending the hall into complete darkness for the briefest moment. Floyd slowed and glanced up again. His feeling of unease grew as the darkness returned. "What's up with the lights?" he muttered, rolling his head to squash the hair rising to attention along his neck. The light came back.

Mic raced forward along the ceiling to perch above Floyd's head. "Something about the possessed disrupts the flow of electricity," he said in a high-pitched voice. "We don't know why, but it's a common occurrence both here and in the human world."

Floyd grunted and continued on. So, being devout included worshipping His Excellence, and the possessed had the ability to screw with electricity. What else didn't he know? He heard a cough above him before Mic slid to the other side of the ceiling. "Sorry," Floyd grumbled. "I can't help the smoke. It's nerves—"

Floyd stopped talking. A red smear marked the space before him, flowing from the floor to the wall leading into a small storage room on the right. Red handprints decorated the doorframe and wall, sometimes punctuated by deep claw-shaped gouges. He called to the shadow walker. "Can you shadow and check the area ahead of us?"

"No problem," the shadow walker's deep voice rumbled before his body dissolved into a cloud of smoke. The particles spread until nothing could be seen of the demon at all.

Twenty seconds passed before a shape reappeared beside Floyd. Although the shadow walker didn't go fully corporeal, Floyd could tell by the slightly green tinge to his mistiness that it wasn't good.

"The silkworm is dead, and she's alone."

Cadence? Floyd's shoulders fell. She'd been a good demon. Reliable, responsible, respectful—the three *r's* so difficult to find in demons. She would be hard to replace. He grunted and walked to her body.

Dark blood pooled between chunks of the pale worm's body and splattered entrails. The five-foot-tall demon had been ripped apart, separated at her joints and tossed as if she were nothing. There were no teeth marks that Floyd could see nor dissolved areas to show she'd been feasted on. Just mangled pieces of flesh flung every which way. He stepped over the severed head that lay propped against the doorjamb and scanned the small room. He went back to the hall and peered to the right.

A loud clanging in the ceiling heralded the return of the ventilation system. Floyd looked up, receiving a face of stale air not scented by blood. An odd thumping noise made him pause, then he blinked and moved on.

Years ago, when he'd been a fresh-faced PLOP employee, he'd been witness to another possession that had taken twenty-two lives. The demon involved had been of the rare Vastendian line. Dark, deadly, and blessed with mind control, the demon infected the thoughts of everyone on the floor like a deadly virus. PLOP had become a war zone with demon against demon, brother against brother. They'd ripped each other apart, destroying one another in a bloody war that had raged for half an hour.

Thirty minutes. That's all it took for everyone to die. And the diminutive Vastendian had escaped through the air ducts, never to be seen again.

Floyd pulled his bullwhip from his side, wrapped the end around his wrist, and studied the ductwork above him. He'd never wanted to be small before—had always loved the size and strength he'd been gifted with. But, for the first time, he wished he wasn't such a large target. His size just might get him killed. Stamping his hoof, he pushed his worry aside as he neared the long-term patient room.

Most of the lights around the entrance were out. A lone bulb cast a yellow glow on the shattered glass covering the floor. The shards sparkled under the weak illumination, their glitter occasionally broken by the gelatinous gore splattered across their surface. Floyd swallowed and raised a hand to the identification plate. It flashed before he realized he hadn't needed to use it—the glass door had been shattered from the inside. The empty doorframe slid open with a soft crunch.

Charred lines marked where shots from Bob's laser

blaster had hit the wall, floor, and ceiling. The etchings were a road map of information, beginning at the opening of the sleeping chamber. Bob had obviously tried to keep the Flurian in the room, shooting at the doorway until the walls were burned a deep black. By following the charred lines, Floyd could tell the possessed had escaped to the right. The laser marks wrapped around the wall before moving across the floor where they ended at a large milky puddle by the door. What was left of Bob dripped from the ceiling and walls like mucus from a bad cold. One eye stared at him from where it dangled off a picture frame. Accusingly. Knowingly.

Floyd flinched and stepped toward the dark room beyond. The others followed as he advanced. He slowed at the sound of slurping coming from the blackness. Stepping to the side, he glanced at the others and nodded to the door. The others spread out along the walls.

Lucinda drew her sword.

The shadow walker pulled a shimmering knife from his belt.

Mic crawled to the center of the ceiling and flattened himself into a large pink disk.

Floyd held his whip loosely in his hand and called out, "Dexter, it's your old friend Floyd. Why don't you come out?"

The slurping stopped as something heavy fell to the floor. Feet slid across the tiles. "There's no Dexter here," a warbling voice crooned from the depths.

Smoke seeped from both Floyd's nostrils as his hoof pawed the floor. "Would you prefer to be called Kelsey?" His hand twitched, and he let the coiled whip slide off his wrist. The sexless Flurian was no longer a male, but a female, of that he was sure.

She didn't answer but slid forward until she stood just beyond the reach of the light.

Floyd made out Dexter's slim shape and found himself searching for the bright-red points weeping venom down her pasty skin.

"So, you know who I am," the voice that was not Dexter's stated.

"You need to return to where you came from, Kelsey." Floyd took an involuntary step back when Kelsey chuckled and moved into the doorway.

She posed, one hip cocked as she placed a delicate, pale hand against the door jab. The spaces between the small red points covering her flesh were shiny with wetness. "But why," she whispered as her fingers tapped the wood. "It's so much more fun here." Her lips spread, displaying sharp, needle-thin teeth.

Her eyes flicked to the left to where the shadow walker slunk closer to her by way of the wall. "Oh," she murmured, "what's this?" She dropped her hand and turned as her wings gave an excited beat behind her.

"Honey," Lucinda purred, stepping forward, "why don't you look this way?" Lucinda cast her eyes to Floyd and gave a slight nod in warning.

Floyd clenched his jaw as her aura magnified and magic filled the air. His body reacted as if she'd dosed him in an aphrodisiac, and thoughts of her beneath him filled his brain. He fought the urge to bellow his dominance and use the erection swelling heavily between his legs. Lust warred with honor, threatening to break his will. He slammed his hoof into the floor with enough force to crack the concrete, momentarily disrupting her spell on him. The bulbs blinked on and off above him. He blew out a rough breath and focused on the distracted Flurian.

Kelsey appeared to move in lurching, uncoordinated steps toward Lucinda in the flickering glow of the lights. Again, he was reminded of one of his son's human movies, her limbs popping and jerking in horrifying contortions. Her face grimaced while her neck stretched upward, every tendon and ligament displayed under her skin as she fought Lucinda's control.

Floyd stepped to the wall and slid sideways to try and get behind her.

Five steps from Lucinda, Kelsey flung her arms out and staggered back two steps. "No," she croaked as the skin along her face rippled with movement. A nose pressed outward from underneath her skin, jutting toward Floyd before sliding to the side to be replaced by the outline of a jaw. Fingers roved along the inside of her neck, etching lines downward before disappearing beneath her rib cage. Kelsey's soul squirmed inside the husk that had been Dexter's while she fought the draw of the Succubus.

"Please," Lucinda murmured as she ran a hand down her neck to gently stroke the space between her breasts. She licked her upper lip and whispered hoarsely, "Come to me." Sex oozed from her pores, filling the air with the hot scent of desire.

A groan came from the shadow walker. He stopped moving and stood rooted to the floor.

Kelsey's soul pressed outward again, pushing the skin along her stomach into the shape of a screaming human face. The image vanished, and Kelsey shrieked, "I am Satan's daughter! You can't seduce me," while arching her back and forcing her chest to the sky. She flung her arms out and her wings opened, beating the air like an iridescent fan before she flew toward Lucinda. The vivid red points on her body pulsed in the light, streaming toxins down her skin.

Lucinda screamed and lashed out with her sword. She twisted and tried to dash out of the way, but a finger, just one of Kelsey's long, slim fingers, touched her hand. Lucinda fell to the floor, twitching uncontrollably.

Floyd roared and snapped his bullwhip.

Kelsey turned to him, throwing her shoulders back as she flew higher. "Come and get me, Minotaur!" she screamed with a cackling laugh. She flew toward him with her arms extended.

A dark shadow burst from the corner to become a thousand dots of darkness before coalescing into the shadow walker. He jabbed his knife up into Kelsey's belly before vanishing into another cloud. Kelsey screamed and swung her arms down, trying to trap the shadow walker as he spread out and away. Blue blood spilled down her stomach.

Floyd flung his whip out, catching Kelsey on the arm where it wrapped in a tight grasp. His muscles bulged as he yanked back, ripping the arm off the demon. A deep bellow erupted out of him as smoke pooled in the air above his head.

Blood splattered across the ground under the severed limb. Kelsey screamed, "You will die, demon!" and flew at him, spewing blood with the beat of her wings.

Floyd flung himself out of the way and rolled across the floor. He turned as the demon careened past him into the wall. She hit with a thud and twisted around.

"No!" he bellowed as the shadow walker swooped in for another strike. "She'll kill you!" Kelsey was smart and would time her attack better this time—grabbing the shadow walker and killing him in the process. He couldn't let that happen. He dropped his bullwhip to the ground.

Floyd ran at the shadow. As the walker's form coalesced, Floyd wrapped his arms around his thin waist and shoved them both to the other side of the room. Sharp pain stabbed into his flesh, piercing his back as he passed Kelsey. He blew out a breath of air and slobber as he hit the wall with the shadow walker between them. Shaking his head, he stumbled to a stand—dropping the still shadow walker to the ground.

Floyd roared again, stomped his hooves, and charged with his head lowered.

Kelsey somersaulted over his head to land behind him before giving a thundering laugh. "You cannot win!" she shrieked as Floyd lurched to a stop against the wall.

He twisted around and pawed the floor again. As he prepared to throw himself onto Kelsey, hoping to impale her even if it killed them both, the ripping sound of hook-and-loop fasteners pulling apart came from above them. He looked up and watched Mic drop from the ceiling like a flat, round, five-foot-wide piece of pink rubber.

Mic landed on top of Kelsey like a blanket. His incredibly thin body stretched downward, inch by inch, over the Flurian's exposed legs. Kelsey screamed and struggled—her kicking leg the last thing Floyd saw of her before the edges of Mic's flesh connected and merged together.

Mic's skin bulged as Kelsey struggled inside her new prison. A face, distorted by fear with a mouth opened wide in a violent scream, pressed outward. As it twisted away, a foot slid down the pink flesh again and again. Outstretched fingers spread Mic into ever-thinning sheaths even as Mic's skin began to ripple like a lake suddenly hit with a gentle breeze. The small rippling bumps rolled faster until his skin surged in waves that grew larger as the seconds passed. With a sudden snap, the demon that was Mic, but nothing like the Mic Floyd remembered, grew smaller.

Floyd grimaced as the room filled with the sound of bones snapping and Kelsey screaming. Filled with the sound of grinding and sloshing as a drop of blue blood appeared on the ground beneath the shrinking ball. The spot grew larger as the ball shrank again, turning the spot into a puddle that spread across the white tile like a slowly growing pond. Bones continued to snap even as the screams dwindled to nothing and the sound of granular-sized pieces of bone mashing together like sand in a bowl was all that was left. Now the size of a highly inflated beach ball, Mic plopped to the ground. His eyes opened, and he let out a satisfied burp before giving Floyd a big grin.

Floyd stared at Mic's mouth. He couldn't get past the large white teeth dripping in Kelsey's dark-blue blood. He shuddered when Mic spoke.

"We got her," Mic squeaked out.

Floyd swallowed the bile in his throat and gave a slow nod. "Yes," he managed to say, "we did." He staggered back to lean against the wall. He didn't understand what had happened, why Mic was still alive. The Flurian's venom should have killed him.

Mic turned to stare into the long-term patient room before glancing down at the puddle beneath him. "Should I be cleaning up?" he asked, lapping up the flecks of blood along his lips with his tongue.

Floyd groaned and brought his hand to his face. He got it now. How he'd missed the obvious was beyond him. Mic, the pale-pink, innocent-looking Grumbling, was a scavenger demon, and eating was all his kind thought about.

Demons were not picky eaters and ate just about anything. Loins, ribs, brains—all was good, no matter where it came from, no matter what it came off of. But most demons couldn't afford the less plentiful wildlife of Hell and resorted to eating what was available: other demons. Even he had visited the local mortician to pick up a parchment-wrapped bag of meat when he'd desired something rustic. He had always worried, though, that he'd open the bag and find something familiar: a one-of-a-kind tattoo or a strange, nubby wart hanging off a bony elbow like a third nipple that he barely stopped himself from ripping off at every family reunion. Familiar was not good, not when it meant he knew who he was eating.

Mic rotated his body in a slow circle in Kelsey's blood until his lower half was a stark blue. He giggled and spun in a fast circle, sloshing blood everywhere.

Floyd's eyes were drawn to the blood like a magnet to metal. He couldn't look away.

Scavenger demons were immune to toxins and poisons, which is why PLOP hired them to remove deceased demons. It is also why scavenger demons were used to decide what went to the mortician for public consumption, while they ate the remainder. Floyd hadn't known any worked on his floor.

"Not yet, Mic," he finally said when the demon stopped playing in the blood to look at him. "We need to identify the dead before we clean anything up."

Floyd went to Lucinda and squatted beside her. Gently, he lifted her shoulders until she lay across his knees. He pressed a finger to her neck and found the steady beat of her heart.

"Thank Satan," he grumbled as Lucinda's head moved on his lap and her eyes blinked open.

"No, thank you, Floyd," she purred. She reached a hand around and gently stroked the side of his leg.

Floyd closed his eyes and shook his head. A thin stream of smoke leaked from his nose. "Lucinda. I'm still Mr. BoMaster."

She sighed and rolled to a crouch in front of him. She swayed slightly back and forth, setting the bells between her breasts to ringing. "One day, Mr. BoMaster, you'll want me," she said with a wink before she stood.

Floyd grunted. "Maybe. But I won't take you." He stood and walked to the shadow walker, whose hazy form leaned against the wall.

"Are you okay, uh, shadow walker?"

The demon laughed before answering. "My name's Roger." His body solidified completely as he stood. The vaporous gray cloud that had been his body came together to form a short, athletic demon with ashy-brown skin. His hair darkened to an inky black. His eyes, which Floyd would have guessed to be gray like his vaporous form, were a deep blue. "I've been better, but I'll live." He rubbed his back and shook his head. "I've never been hit by a train before."

Floyd grunted and flicked his tail. "Sorry about that. I didn't want her touching you."

"Oh, I understand. In hindsight, my plan was impetuous." He grinned and held out his hand. "Thank you for saving me, Floyd."

Floyd smiled and shook his hand. "Anytime, Roger."

Lucinda's voice came from behind him. "What happened here? Where's Dexter?"

Floyd faced her and waved a hand at the Grumbling. "Mic ate him."

Lucinda raised an eyebrow and peered beyond them to where Mic sat. Her face twisted into a look of distaste. "No kidding," she muttered. She made a retching noise and waved her hand in Mic's direction. "You might want to get involved in what he's doing."

Gagging noises came from Roger as his body shifted to a green mist.

Floyd clenched his fists and turned to the Grumbling. His stomach twisted, sending the acidic taste of bile up his throat again. He stamped his hoof. "Mic," he snapped. "I said not yet."

Mic rolled to an upright position and pursed his lips. His eyes slid away from Floyd to stare at a spot on the wall while a deep pink stain crawled across his cheeks. He'd been caught laying on his side with his tongue hanging out, gently lapping up Bob's gelatinous remains.

"He's a scavenger," Lucinda whispered.

"He's our janitor," Floyd mumbled back.

"Oh, dear Satan," muttered Roger.

As they stared, Mic slowly rotated his body until they couldn't see his face. The pink flush continued to burn its way over his flesh until the back of his head glowed like a florescent bulb.

Floyd shook his head. "I need to go." He glanced at the clock. "My son is expecting me."

"Then go," Lucinda said. "I'll handle the paperwork and cleaning everything up."

Floyd hesitated before nodding. "Thank you. I'll let everyone know Dexter is dead."

The crunch of glass followed him as he moved across the room and out the door where the lights no longer flickered but glowed a steady anemic yellow. He walked down the hall, his eyes skipping over the pools of congealing blood seeping out of rooms they hadn't checked. As he stepped gingerly over the blood spilling out of the storage room, he wondered how many dead they'd overlooked. *Too many*, he thought with a sigh, *but not as many as during the previous Code Red*.

His head snapped up as the breeze flowing from the ventilation unit stopped with an unusual rattle. The aluminum ductwork popped and cracked as something shifted within it. A slim, black, scaly finger slid out of the darkness to clutch the front of the grille. The Vastendian stared at him from between the metal slats, lips spread in a cruel smile. A voice wove its way through Floyd's mind.

"I smell blood," it said.

Floyd backed up and withdrew his whip. His son would have to wait.

This, he thought, stepping back, *is the worst day ever.*

REVENGE

SOMETIMES DEAD MEN DO TELL TALES

THE PLAN

Nora glanced up at her father before turning back to the fire. The popping of the wood did nothing to calm her racing heart. Instead, the sound agitated her, as if the fire had something to do with what was happening. As if the flames she saw reflected in the tears on her father's face were real and he was burning from the inside out. Burning like her mother. Nora shivered and hunched over, pulling her legs up against her chest with her arms.

Nora twitched as her mom belted out a short rambling sentence. She didn't turn, but from the corner of her eye she watched her mom pace. Sweat glistened on her mom's feverish face and dripped from the dirty-blond hair hanging off her head. Perspiration stained her shirt a dark brown where she cradled her arm against her chest. Nora's mother mumbled again, something about "almost there" and "decision was mine" before she giggled and glanced at Nora's father.

Nora rubbed a hand along her arm and looked down at her feet. She didn't stay turned away for long. Not when looking away meant her mother would die. Not when it was her ten-year-old focus keeping the fever from cooking her mother alive. She glanced up, then rubbed her toe in the soil and turned away again. She knew it wasn't true, but the small part of her that wanted to believe in miracles was scared of taking that chance.

Nora let out a pained sigh. Her mom was a walking corpse. Not a true one, like the undead who wandered the earth searching to appease a hunger they couldn't escape, but the other kind. The one people became when they were more dead than alive and unwilling to release that last breath and lie down.

Her father's voice broke into her thoughts like a jolt of electricity. She jumped and turned her head in his direction.

"Sit down, Nadine. Please sit down."

Nora laid her cheek against her knees and stared at the flames as her dad resumed pleading with her mom to rest. He'd been at it for an hour already, and it hadn't made a difference yet. Delusional pacing and muttering were things her mother could handle. Listening and following instructions were beyond her brain's capability when she was burning. Nora wasn't sure her mom knew where she was, or even who they were, much less remembered what dangers she invited by bringing attention to their group.

Nora felt a pang of remorse and closed her eyes. Her mother's voice rose in pitch as she giggled uncontrollably. Her father's voice lowered equally to whisper harshly for her to quiet down—as though the difference in tones would somehow cancel each other out and the fear of being found would disappear. But it didn't work that way. It never did. In a little while, her father would get off the log and wrestle her mom to the ground. Then she'd be bound and gagged for the rest of the night. And in the morning, she'd be lucid and back to the mom Nora knew. Unless she wasn't.

Unless this was the end and the black lines and sickly

green hue progressing up her forearm had finally poisoned her mind. Nora twisted her head to the side and wiped the tear that slid from her eye onto her pants. Sweet and slightly spoiled, that's how her mother smelled now; that's how Nora would remember her mother if she died today. Not clean like a summer breeze, nor spoiled like the zombies that reeked of decomposition and decay, but rotten like the fruit that had fallen off the trees and had been left to rot. Either way, the smell meant death, and death had grasped her family in its hot embrace. Again, in such a short time.

Nora jumped as her dad pushed against her back. She turned and looked at him.

"We need to leave early tomorrow," he said quietly, still gazing at his wife. "Go to sleep."

She nodded and pulled her blanket around her shoulders before she lay down. They'd been walking for over two weeks now, searching every town and city they'd encountered for medication to help her mom. Tomorrow they'd reach the last city on their tour—a city her father had chosen to be last because of the inherent danger within it. Nora closed her eyes and eventually fell to sleep while listening to the mutterings of her mom and the crackling of the fire.

DEATH AND REBIRTH

They left the next morning before the sun had risen above the mountains and only hazy red rays lit the lower edge of the sky in the east. Nora shifted the small pack on her back and copied her father as he scanned the forest. Since she usually smelled or heard the zombies before she saw them, she didn't look particularly hard for decomposing husks. What she looked for were the other dangers that were not so easily noticed until it was too late.

Cannibals roamed this land.

Nora and her parents crested a small hill and came across the flattened area of an abandoned campsite. Long blades of grass lay trampled to the ground from the base of the hill to the small crop of trees a quarter mile in the distance. Small fire pits still smoldered, sending thin wafts of white smoke into the air. Long, narrow wagon-wheel ruts rode off into the distance.

"Daddy," Nora whispered as she reflexively hunched down into the long grasses at her feet.

"It's okay, sweetling," he whispered back. He peered

around before stepping off the cusp of the hill. "They're gone."

Nora wasn't so sure as she followed her mom's steps down the incline. She scanned the trees in the distance and the hill they were leaving, sure they were being set up. Her mom's words broke through her anxiety like an icepick.

"Nora, come here. Don't look."

Nora danced backward, out of her mom's reach, and did the opposite of what her mother had warned. She searched the camp. Her stomach twisted into painful knots as the saliva coating her mouth evaporated, leaving her tongue dry and rough. Her curiosity tempered, she willingly accepted the pull of her mom's arms into the protection of her chest.

"I told you not to look." Her mom's words washed over her as she closed her eyes. The tang of fire and musky scent of old barbecue seemed more pronounced now that she'd seen what lay piled in the largest fire pit close to them. The blackened rib cage and butterfly-shaped pelvis stacked atop the mound of white bones did not sicken her as much as the head that had been carelessly tossed into the coals. Skin slack in death slid down the right side of the face as if it had melted like a wax candle. The left was not so encumbered, and a milky eye stared accusingly over a mouth that seemed confused. One edge flowed downward while the other raised in a grimace.

"Why?" Nora heard herself say. She quickly blinked her eyes and pulled away from her mother. She was not a baby, but she willingly returned when her mother's strong hand pulled her back.

"Evil heathens," her mom hissed. "They were starving and dealt a choice—same as the rest of us. Instead of living honorably and learning to live with struggle like we do, they took the easy way out and started eating their own kind. As if trying to stay out of the zombie's mouths wasn't enough of a challenge, now we have to be wary of our fellow man. There's no excuse for what they do. They deserve to die and be removed from the world in the same way they've damned so many others." Bitter anger tinged her words as spittle flew from her mouth to the ground.

Nora peeked at her mother's face before dropping her gaze to her feet. Her mother's eyes were bright and shiny, her cheeks pale except for the small pink circles at their tips. Healthy even. But her lips had twisted into a disgusted snarl while she stared at her husband's back. Nora swallowed and tried to pull away, only to meet resistance as her mother's hand clenched tighter about her arm.

"Sometimes," her mother whispered as she leaned down close to Nora's forehead, her voice so low Nora almost missed the words, "evil is closer than you think. Sometimes it isn't so obvious as a band of cannibals, and you only see hints of its existence until it reveals itself in all its glory when you least expect it. Sometimes that evil is worse than the evil you thought you knew—cloaked in the guise of a loving man." A small noise, almost a growl, came from her throat before she finished. "Sometimes, evil needs to pay."

Nora swallowed and pulled away from her mother. Away from the hands that attempted to grasp her with nails that had become long and sharp like daggers. She stumbled forward and didn't take her eyes from the green pack and large crowbar hanging off her father's back. Her mother was losing her mind, saying the most awful things because of the fever. It was the fever, nothing else. Her father was a good man.

The sun was hot overhead when they reached the edge of the city. From a distance, it looked like a fortress surrounded by a large concrete wall, with giant skyscrapers jutting into the sky at its the center. They walked the wall for miles, following the decades-old map residing in her father's brain, hoping time had not distorted his memories. As they climbed a small rise, Nora made out a road winding its way into the wall and heard her father let out a sigh heavy with relief.

"I'm so glad it's here," he whispered as he stopped to mop the sweat from his brow. He glanced at his wife and gave Nora a crooked smile before reaching down to his water bottle. "Drink your water. We may not be able to drink more until we find the pharmacy."

Nora sipped her water and watched her mom. Like a tide moving in and out, her fever had abated again this morning and would probably be back this evening . . . if she wasn't dead by then. Her mom's steps were slower today, probably half the speed they'd been two days ago, and every time they stopped, she asked to lay down and sleep. There didn't seem to be much life left in her. Not since she'd scared Nora with her spiel about evil.

Her mother cradled her arm against her chest, the fingers of her good arm mindful of the infected bite on her forearm. Nora clenched her teeth and shook her head. Her mother should never have searched that house alone. There were rules. Rules her mom had decided to ignore and was now paying the price for. She'd been lucky to escape the wild dog she'd encountered with only a small bite.

Nora glanced at her dad and put her water away. It was time to go. She nodded her head as her dad placed a finger against his lips. Her mom twisted to look at her from behind her father and gave a reassuring smile. Nora smiled weakly before glancing away.

Cars filled the abandoned street. They reminded Nora of an army of caterpillars marching from the trees toward new lands: front to back, separated by mere hairs, measuring in the hundreds, inching along as if pulled by a string that connected one to the next. This was the same, but instead of moving bugs, these were corroded cars with busted-out windshields, weathered frames, and deflated tires all pointing away from the city and down the road. They continued for miles—so far into the distance she couldn't tell if the chain of cars persisted or if the dark line she saw was nothing but the crumbling road.

A wave of trepidation worked its way up her back. All those people abandoned their cars, desperate to escape the city even if they had to go by foot, and she was heading inside. The spittle in her mouth dried as she followed her parents into the city.

She stepped carefully, mimicking her parents by walking where they walked, running when they hurried, bending low when they did. They stopped after a fearful ten minutes on the inside and crouched against the bottom of a car lying on its side. The air was dry and stale but corrupt with the slightly rancid scent of zombies.

Her father crept out, stepping quickly to the next car and squatting down. He peeked over the edge of the trunk before waving them over. Nora raced after her mom and sunk to the ground beside her. She cringed when her mom's voice shattered the unnatural silence of the city.

"Do you see something?" Her voice bounced between the buildings with as much power as a scream. Doves shot into the sky in a thunderclap of wings. Nora stared, transfixed, until she saw her dad reach around and cover her mom's mouth with his hand. Then she watched him nod to an alley across the way.

He removed his hand from her mother's mouth and returned to studying the street. Nora relaxed and slipped her arms around her legs. She closed her eyes and held on tight as her parents whispered next to her.

"Nora," her dad hissed, reaching over and shaking her leg. "Let's go." He crab-walked down the sidewalk before turning into a narrow alley between two buildings.

"Come on," her mom whispered, slipping her sweaty hand into Nora's and pulling.

Nora moved to a crouch and followed her. They were hurrying down the alley when she heard the moan behind them. It wavered in the breeze, forlorn and sad, sounding desperate in its misery. It happened again, this time ending with a warbled flapping noise. A ripple of fear crept up Nora's back, and she sucked in a quick breath.

Her dad ushered them into a crouch behind an old blue dumpster, and they waited. They were staring silently at the street when the zombie appeared.

What was once a woman was barely recognizable as human anymore. Her hair was mostly gone, and what remained hung in long, stringy red strands from a mottled gray skull. Her eyebrows were missing, but the ridge where they should have been protruded an inch above her sunken orbs. Cloudy white eyes rolled within their depths, not seeming to focus on anything in front of her, always searching. Her lower jaw had been ripped off, leaving an upper jawbone, ridged with broken teeth and a tongue that hung out grotesquely as she moaned. She walked slowly down the street, staring straight ahead with her arms hanging by her side.

Nora's chest tightened as if a vise was squeezing her ribs into her lungs. She tried to breathe deep but couldn't get much more than a small lungful. *Suck in*, she thought and tried again, but her lungs wouldn't expand. Her sight darkened around the edge, and she shifted around, suddenly feeling the need to run.

"Shhhhhh," her mom whispered as she slipped her arms around Nora's waist. She pulled her gently back against her chest and placed her mouth down close to Nora's ear. Her mom's hot breath tickled her sweat-coated skin.

"She doesn't see us," her mom whispered. "She won't find us." She placed her cheek against the side of Nora's head and held her tight. She squeezed gently until she felt Nora's shoulders relax and her breathing become normal.

Nora closed her eyes and breathed in her mom's scent. Whether the clean smell of sunshine and flowers was still there or existed only in her mind, it didn't matter. She smelled it, floating there beneath the stink of sickness. Her mother's skin burned against the side of her face, like a hot rock on a late summer day. Nora pressed into it, wondering if her cooler skin gave her mom any relief.

"Let's go," her dad whispered, glancing at them before he moved to the head of the alley. They crouched behind him while he watched the zombie disappear down a side street. He didn't speak until the moaning had vanished.

"When I was here before, my dad pointed out the pharmacy. I think I can find it again. It's not far, but we have to keep an eye out for zombies the whole time." He stopped talking and bent down until he was level with Nora. "We hide. We always hide unless we can't, right?"

Nora nodded and chewed her lips. She'd heard this talk before. Many times.

"Okay." He stood and stuck his head out of the alley. "Follow me."

The pharmacy sat three blocks from where they had entered the city, but it was much farther according to her father's failed memory. It took four hours to navigate the city and eventually find their way back to the right boulevard. Once there, they stood in the alley across the street watching the door for movement for what seemed like hours. It was impossible to see inside the store except through a small opening between the boards covering the glass door. And from where they stood, there wasn't much to see.

Nora jumped from her left foot to her right, hoping to lessen the pain in at least one of them.

"Stop it, Nora," her dad hissed as he twisted to the left.

She squatted, sighed, and leaned against the brick wall. The sun was hot, the city smelled like death, and her feet hurt. She wanted to sit down and rest, not stand in this alley for another half hour doing nothing. Her mom shifted into a crouch and made a little noise as if in agreement. Nora glanced worriedly at her mom's red face and glassy eyes. Either the fever was back and she was going to start muttering soon, or they were pushing her too hard and she was going to collapse. She touched her mother's arm, alarmed at the heat radiating up her fingers. They couldn't wait much longer.

Nora jumped as her dad suddenly raced across the street to the pharmacy. He twisted the knob and pulled at the door, but the bottom edge didn't budge. It held tight while the top shifted out and then slammed back into a closed position with a loud rattle that echoed through the street. Doves shot into the air. A ribbon of fear crept up Nora's back, and she scrambled to the head of the alley to peer around. She expected to see zombies crawling through the streets with their corruption preceding them in a repulsive cloud of flies or hear their disconcerting moans floating around the corner, but nothing had changed. All was silent but the hammering of her heart in her temple and the creaking, splintering of the door.

Her father muttered before bending down and shoving his crowbar into the slat between the door and frame. He pressed back and forth, widening the gap with every crack of the old, dry wood.

Hot sweat trickled down Nora's back and between her shoulder blades before soaking into the waist of her pants. Her mom pushed up against her backside and grasped her shoulders. Her hands squeezed, painfully, every time the door across the street creaked or banged.

"Please," Nora whispered as her mom breathed heavily above her. She didn't know if she begged for her dad to stop making so much noise, for a miracle to force the door open, or for her mother to back up, but she needed something to happen. Anything to make the fear and discomfort she felt disappear.

A loud snap split the air, and the door gave way, swinging open slowly. Her dad slipped inside, pulling the door closed behind him with a final thump. Nora held her breath and listened, hoping she wouldn't hear him scream.

The seconds passed, and there was nothing—no movements, no screams—nothing but a sense of weakness settling in her legs. She closed her eyes and prepared to run. Her mom gasped, and then Nora was dragged across the street to where her dad stood waving them over. He ushered them inside and shut the door firmly behind them.

"Daddy," Nora said and swung her arms around his waist. He bent down and hugged her back.

"It's okay, sweetie, we made it. There's medicine here."

His voice was excited, happier than she'd heard in a month, and she held onto him as long as she could. Once he let her go, she watched him walk to the back, then she turned to study the store.

They'd visited dozens of pharmacies over the last few weeks and all had been the same—dirty buildings with rows of dust-covered shelves and trash-covered floors and ceilings decorated with long spidery threads that looped around the defunct ceiling lights in wispy strings. Most still held relics of an old life that no one found necessary anymore: bright dog toys with squeakers that no longer squeaked, shriveled and crumbling makeup, and odd things like oscillating foot massagers and chin straps to help with snoring. But the important shelves, they were always barren.

This pharmacy was not the same. Instead of rows of organized products, the place looked like a tornado had come through and swept pill bottles and boxes onto the floor and shoved the metal shelves to the front of the room.

"What happened here, Daddy?" she asked, hopping over boxes to a clear space in the middle of the room.

Her dad glanced up from where he squatted, his finger marking the place he'd been reading in the *Pharmaceutical Drug Guide*. "Looks like someone tried to fortify the windows at some point. They tossed the medicine on the ground and stacked the shelves against the windows."

"But, where are the dog toys?"

"Sorry honey," he said, tossing a pill bottle back onto the floor and grabbing another. "This isn't like those other stores. It only carried medicine."

"Oh." Nora walked along the metal shelves curiously, trailing her hand along the dusty edges while she studied the containers on the floor. Without touching them, she could tell most were empty.

Nora turned to watch her mother limp her way to the back wall. Once there, she pressed her hand against the surface, paused, then lowered herself to the floor. Her hair hung from her scalp in wet strands, molding itself to her face and neck like a mask. Underneath, her face was red and dotted with tiny pearls of sweat. Nora watched a small circle roll down her mother's cheek, collecting sweat as it moved until it formed a large drop at her chin. It fell, splashing against her shirt in a vivid drop.

Why, Mom? Nora wondered as her shoulders fell. *Why did you go into that house?*

What could have led her to enter the dilapidated farmhouse they'd found outside the forest? Even though the building had seemed like the answer to their prayers, a place to hide from the cannibals chasing them, Nora had sensed something wrong as soon as she'd passed through the fence surrounding it. Evilness had leaked out the gaping entryway and glassless windows, stroking her skin with each step she took, silencing the birds and insects so incessantly active outside the perimeter. Fear had made her steps falter until she had lagged behind her parents by a few feet.

"Dad," she had whispered when her father had stopped walking to stare at the fathomless doorway before him.

His arm had shot up in a warning. Slowly, he had stepped backward, grabbing her mother's arm when he got close. "Not here," he had breathed to her as he retreated back the way they'd come. He'd barely glanced at Nora on his way to the fence.

But not her mom. She'd stared at Nora with her red-rimmed eyes up until the moment she'd passed her. Then she'd reached out and touched Nora's arm lightly while a soft sob escaped her.

Nora had followed without a word. She had understood her mother's pain and why she had cried. They'd all been in mourning. What she questioned was why her mom had gone back that night and crept into the house all alone. Why had she tempted fate with whatever hell existed inside? Couldn't she feel it?

Nora shivered and moved cautiously to the door to look through the boards covering the window. A weed rolled by but nothing else. Her eyes bore into the brightness, searching for anything to take her mind off her mother. She went down to her knees and rested her forehead against the door. Within minutes, she was asleep.

A medicine bottle rolled across the floor and woke Nora. She coughed and stretched before peering outside. Nothing moved; nothing had changed. She sighed and turned her head toward her parents' whispering voices. They sat in the back, sorting pills into small bags. Nora went to them and stared in surprise at the bottles piled around her parents.

"Why so many?" she asked.

"They won't be very strong, Nora. Mom will need to double the dosage to make them effective." He popped another bottle open and slipped the contents into a small leather pouch. As the pills clicked against one another, he grinned and winked. "There aren't many in each bottle," he continued, "but if we crack enough bottles, they'll add up to a nice little stash. Won't they, Mama?"

Her mother didn't answer but opened another bottle and poured the pills into the bag. Sweat glistened on her pink cheeks and across her forehead. Her lips were pressed together and curled at the corners in a secret smile; a sly and knowing pose that sent shivers up Nora's spine. Her mother's eyes slid to the side, glancing at her husband from beneath lowered brows, before returning to the bottles in her lap. There was a secret hiding behind those lips, one that wanted out.

Nora stepped back in alarm, stomping on a crumpled box.

Her mother twisted her head in her direction and smiled. Nora stiffened at the flat darkness that seemed to have invaded her mom's irises. Deep and endless, her eyes were no longer the bright blue of a summer day but dark and brooding, as if a storm brewed behind her lids.

Nora smiled, letting it fade as soon as her mother's eyes turned away. *It's the fever; it has to be*, she told herself, even though the words sounded false. *Eyes don't change color*. Nora brushed the thought away and turned.

Her steps were slow as she returned to the front of the store. There was nothing she could do about her mother, about the feeling that something was not right. Maybe the pills would fix her, and everything would get back to normal. She kicked a pill bottle across the floor and watched it clank against the door.

Somehow, she doubted it.

Peering through the gaps between the boards, she noticed a curtain fluttering against a window three floors up. Nora tilted her head to the side and froze. First a hand hooked around the faded cloth, and then a little boy stepped in front to peer outside. His small white face pressed against the windowpane while he watched the space between the buildings, unaware he was being watched.

Nora didn't breathe as her hand flew between the wood and glass of the door. Frantically, she waved it around, but the little boy didn't respond. She jerked it back and glanced behind her at her parents.

Her eyes went back to the boy, who watched the road outside. She'd had a brother until three weeks ago who was about that boy's age—five. When she remembered her brother's sweet little face, the way he laughed at everything, the way his blond hair flew behind him when he pumped his skinny little legs and ran, she wanted to roll into a ball and cry. Adam was gone. Lost. And probably dead.

She stared up at the little boy and yearned for the life her father told her existed before the zombie virus killed the world. What was she supposed to do once her mother died?

She'd be alone with her father: no more family, just him. A tear rolled down her cheek, and she brushed it off quickly.

Life hadn't been so bad before they ran into the cannibals. There'd been laughter and happiness even as they spent their days struggling to survive and their nights hiding. But the cannibals had destroyed everything. They'd forced them to run, forced them to stop searching for her brother when he wandered off during the night, forced their path to collide with the house that eventually made her mom ill. Maybe karma sent them to that horrid house after Adam disappeared. They should never have left him behind. They should have fought and found him. That was their job, wasn't it? To take care of those smaller than them?

With sudden clarity, Nora knew what she had to do and grasped the door handle. There was a boy outside, and he was still alive. Maybe he needed a family of his own. Her heart beat heavily in her chest, and the door opened with a loud creak. She twisted her head sideways, just enough to see her parents moving at the other end of the store, before she slipped outside.

"Hey," she hissed, waving her hands in the air. The boy's head whipped toward her as a little hand rose to press against the window. Nora smiled and motioned for him to come down. "We can take care of you," she mouthed with exaggerated slowness.

The boy's mouth fell open, and he shook his head back and forth. There was fear in the widening of his eyes, in the way he pounded lightly on the window then turned to peer down the street. Then he was gone, and only the fluttering cloth marked where he'd been.

She drew in a deep breath, and a ribbon of terror didn't crawl but raced up Nora's spine when she noticed what she'd been ignoring. The stink of the city had magnified; the stench of undead had grown stronger, thicker, and undeniable, as if the decomposing essence of millions of liquifying bodies had found their home up her nose. She swallowed the urge to vomit and let out a little whimper. "No," she whispered before turning her head. She stumbled back until the glass window of the pharmacy stopped her. Nora opened her mouth but found she couldn't scream. Couldn't get beyond the mass of zombies she'd somehow failed to notice. She'd never seen so many of the undead together. And they were so close—running, shambling toward her. All were in different stages of decomposition, leaking a stench she should have never missed. Nora pounded lightly on the glass behind her.

"Dad . . . " She tried to yell again, but only a weak whisper escaped her throat. "Dad . . ."

The door swung open with a loud bang and the sound of shattering glass. "Nora!" her dad screamed as he grabbed her arm and dragged her away from the window. He threw her over his shoulder and ran as her mother staggered after them with the bag of medicine clutched in her fist.

Nora stared at the zombies over her father's shoulder. They were old and slow and would have fallen far behind in a perfect world, but this world was anything but perfect. The horde grew as zombies came from alleys and side streets, from stores and the subway, streaming together in an unending line of hunger. The original group fell back as they were displaced by the new. Their moans intensified with their increased number, calling more zombies from across the city until the streets they passed were emptying the dead almost onto them instead of behind them.

"Run faster!" Nora screamed. "They are coming!"

Glass shattered above them, and zombies fell from the sky. Nora covered her head as they dropped to the earth, smashing cars and everything in their path, leaving a trail of plate glass and bodies.

Her dad turned down a shadowy alley. "Nadine," he called

over his shoulder, "hurry up! We can lose them here." He didn't stop or slow, but bolted through the shadows until they burst into a bright and empty street.

The zombies following them streamed into the narrow space in an uncoordinated line. At first they moved as one, slowing, but not falling behind as quickly as Nora had hoped. Then the lead zombie tripped, causing a cascading reaction of one zombie falling atop another. Skulls cracked and groans warbled to an end, replaced by the sounds of those still coming. Zombies were fighting to crawl over the fallen when Nora's dad turned and she couldn't see any more.

Her dad muttered, and Nora looked ahead of them. A large, empty intersection lay before them, but she knew something bad was waiting by the deafening moans floating from the connecting streets and her dad's tense shoulders. "Dad," she whispered, wanting to tell him to find another way to go. Too late, they entered the empty crossway. "Dad," she cried, expecting to be overwhelmed by the horde. Instead, she saw what her dad had noticed before her—long golden grass peeked through a crack in the brick wall at the end of the next street. Nora squeezed her father's shoulders and let out a blubbery cry.

She looked behind her and the half smile fell from her face. Her mom had staggered to a standstill.

She stared at Nora, her eyes large and bright with fever, her face glistening with sweat as she said, "I love you." With tears spilling down her face, she collapsed.

"Mom!" Nora screamed.

"Nadine!"

Nora's father shoved her off his shoulder and sprinted back to her mom. His arm slipped beneath her arm, and he attempted to pull her up. She pushed him away and crawled backward.

"No," she mumbled.

Nora ran to her parents. "Please, Mom!" she screamed, her heart pounding in her chest and the bitter taste of fear spreading through her mouth.

She glanced behind her mother. The horde flowed like a river out of the alley. They were still a block away, but the few in front were picking up speed, no longer hampered by the slower undead.

"Mom!" Nora yelled as she yanked on her shirt. The fabric ripped beneath her hands, sending Nora flying backward to the ground with the long swatch of cloth in her hand. She could feel the ground shaking as the hundreds of undead barreled down the asphalt toward them. Her mom looked at her and continued to cry, mouthing, "I love you," over and over.

Her dad stood and grabbed his crowbar. "Run, Nora, run!" he screamed as he moved in front of her mother and raised it to his shoulder. He reached over and yanked the strip of cloth Nora clutched in her hand. "Damn it, Nora. Get to the campsite," he snapped and turned away.

Nora stood and took a step back. Her mom raised her hand and cried while her dad looked at Nora one last time.

"We love you, Nora. We've always loved you," he said, his voice catching at the end. Turning away, he raised the crowbar in the air and screamed, "Run, Nora!" and began to swing.

She pictured them as she ran for the wall: her dad, standing tall, his crowbar raised over his shoulder as her mother sobbed against the ground below him. As the zombies closed in, she imagined his arms reaching out, slamming the crowbar against one brain after another, dropping the horde one zombie at a time until there was nothing left but him, her mom, and a mound of bodies. Yes, she could see it happening and tried to reconcile it with the noises she heard behind her. But no matter how hard she tried, no matter how she changed the story, it wouldn't fit. Because all she heard was screaming—horrible, agonizing screeching—until it suddenly ended. They went quiet, and there was nothing but moaning, shuffling, and the sound of eating.

And that was worse.

Tears rolled down her face as she jumped through the break in the wall and ran into the tall grass. She began crawling, not stopping until she heard the first zombie hit the bricks with a dull thud. At this point she lay down, curled into a ball, and cried silently with her face pressed into the dirt. One thing she'd learned well was to stay hidden. Out of sight meant out of mind to the undead.

She tried to silence her thoughts, but one kept returning like an annoying fly. If her mom had kept running, they'd have made it to the wall, and she wouldn't be alone.

Nora sat up, wiping the tears off her face as she peered over the grass. It had been an hour, and the sounds of the zombies groaning and shuffling in the street had diminished substantially. She rose a little higher, parting the yellow fronds. Shapes moved beyond the crack, but they seemed oblivious to the narrow divide that would release them from the city and, thankfully, oblivious to her as well. Moving into a crouch, she crab-walked to the tree line, then slid to the back of a tree and leaned against its hard bark. Light streamed between the leaves and branches above her, casting rays into the dark shadows of the forest. The small breeze flowing through the woods felt cool against her hot skin. She sucked in a lungful of the sweet air and considered her next step. The sky would be darkening in a few hours, bringing out the worst the world had to offer—things zombies even feared.

She needed to find safety while she had the chance.

Her feet were silent as they raced across the decaying foliage carpeting the ground. She breathed deeply, sniffing for zombies as she went. The highest concentrations were around the cities, but they still wandered the forests and outer regions in small groups of one or two and sometimes in bands. At least their smell would give them away.

If she could make it to a cave or a house, she could hide until she came up with a plan for the rest of her life. She swallowed her urge to cry over the thought of her father. What would he do? *Anything*, she reminded herself as her lip trembled, and she sped up. He would do anything to keep safe.

The sun had sunk low in the sky when she finally allowed herself to slow down. The city, which had etched itself into the dark recesses of her mind never to be forgotten, had faded from view as she walked deeper into the forest. She told herself it was far away, and she'd never see those towering walls again, but a part of her felt watched as if the crevice, and all the monsters it held, were just beyond the trees and waiting. What if she had walked in a circle and was now slowly making her way back? What if she popped through the trees ahead of her and emerged in a field of brown grass? Grass she knew only too well.

Nora stopped and peered around before veering off to the right where a smidgeon of pale light shined through the trees like a beacon. The vegetation grew less dense and spread out until the trees were behind her, and she walked through a dense meadow to a long berm of dirt rising into the sky.

Nora wiped sweaty hair from her forehead as she climbed her way to the top of the ridge in front of her. She hunched lower as the crest came closer, eventually easing herself across the threshold on her belly to peer through the grass at the road winding its way below. Her heart froze, then jerked angrily within her chest.

No, she thought as she let the vegetation fall back into place.

A tear slipped out of her eye and down her cheek. Somehow, she'd found them. They'd run for weeks from the cannibals, and on her first day alone she'd managed to make her way back to them—almost walking into their camp. She slid back down the hill with the image of headless bodies roasting on spits pushing her to move faster. There had been dozens upon dozens of cannibals sitting around the fire pits laughing as they watched the skin on the corpses blister and blacken over the flames. Worse had been the acrid smell of the burning flesh. Nora stared at the tree line with wide-eyed fear, desperate to get away.

There were innocent people down there, caged within iron wagons, like cattle waiting for the slaughter. Nora swallowed and tried to hold back a cry as another thought came to her. Was Adam a captive within one of those mobile prisons? She didn't know, but she couldn't go check. She wouldn't make it. The grass tickled her legs and shoulders as she ran hunched at the waist. Almost to the trees, the sense that she was being watched made her chance a look over her shoulder. No one stood on the berm or in the trees that she could see, but the feeling refused to leave. Swallowing, she ducked a little lower.

Something whizzed by her head in a flash of light and flowing air. Nora dropped to her stomach and looked behind her. There was the sound of another arrow zipping over her head and landing somewhere in the grass. Nora crawled toward the trees, pressing her knees into the dirt to propel herself forward. She wished the fronds above her were taller, thicker, and that the sky was darker, more concealing.

Harsh whispers floated through the descending darkness,

terrifying her in their ordinariness, paralyzing in how harmless they sounded. They were men's voices: one high, one low, both somewhere behind her. Nora screamed as an arrow pierced the ground beside her hand. She lurched to a stand and ran. Adam was gone. Her mother was gone. Her father was gone. She couldn't go like this.

"Don't run, little girl. We just want to play," a hunter called out, eliciting laughs from another.

Nora dived into the shadows and ran to the right. Branches whipped against her arms and face, and blood splattered her shirt. She struggled up a slope, using hanging tree branches to pull herself upward until she got a sure footing and could run again. Over the sounds of her escape, she heard them enter the forest behind her in a barrage of profanity.

Relief made her fly, made her feet barely skim the ground as she headed deeper under the canopy. *They aren't close*, she told herself even though she heard their occasional laughter and intermittent cussing over the snapping of twigs, the swish of branches, and the beat of her own heart. They were tracking her steps, she could tell that now, and until she found a stream or river, she had no recourse but to run and put distance between them.

An hour later, every breath was a stitch in her side and every step made her thighs throb. Nora could hear them behind her when she leaped a large root jutting from the earth like a crooked finger. Exhausted, she didn't leap high enough and caught her shoe in its curve. While tumbling to the ground, a twig ripped through the thin weave of her pants and pierced her flesh. She screamed and hunched over her injured leg, then glanced up into the sky. At some point, night had come, and the remaining light easing through the tree canopy was barely enough to illuminate the ground. She flinched as she stood, testing her foot cautiously.

"I see her!" someone yelled.

Nora shoved her way into the bushes, using her hands to guide herself through the thick vegetation. She realized she'd made a mistake when the snap of limbs and crunch of leaves seemed to be surrounding her. Briefly, she paused before pushing her way through the barrier and racing forward.

A bear of a man stood before her. He hunched his beefy shoulders forward as his lips spread in a wide grin, displaying decaying yellow teeth below a red bulbous nose. Wild, untamed hair hung off his face in dirty strands. Raising his hands, he beckoned her forward with a crook of his fingers. "Just give up," he whispered. "Don't fight."

Nora screamed and turned, only to find a face looming out of the bushes. The man sneered and stepped forward, letting his eyes rove over her body. "Yum," he whispered before licking his lips.

"Mama," Nora sobbed. She reached down and grabbed a large stick from the ground. It arced through the air as she twisted in a circle. The boy she'd heard earlier stepped toward her from the darkness, his too-large eyes matching the too-large teeth in his grinning mouth. Big ears stuck out from the greasy yellow hair on his head.

"Boy," he whispered, "she's a pretty one."

"What you talking about, Logan? She's just a child."

"She's not much younger than me. I think she's awfully fine."

Nora sobbed and whipped the stick forward when he stepped closer. The boy giggled and jumped backward.

"Let me have her, Roy. I don't have a girl of my own."

"We need food, Logan. She'll make a nice meal or two. You can't keep her."

"Please," he said as he brought a hand up to the sly smile on his face. "Let me have her. I'll need a girl eventually, and she's pretty." He giggled again as his eyes met hers.

"No, we need to bring her back to Bo. Strip her, then tie her up."

Nora's legs shook. She swallowed and widened her stance. *I'll kill them*, she thought as sobs wracked her body. Run, and if you can't run, fight. That's what her father always told her.

"Now," the calm voice whispered behind her.

Nora screamed and swung her stick as arms grabbed her body. They tightened on her limbs and clothes, ripping cloth and flesh as they dragged her to the ground. Pain slammed into her spine when she arched upward and was shoved back down. Her small pack jabbed into her back, and something sharp stabbed into her skin. The boy giggled and gave her a sloppy kiss before she could twist her head away. The fetid scent of dirty bodies wafted over her.

"Mom," she cried as her shirt ripped and young body was exposed to the air.

Adam, Mother, Father.

Adam, Mother, Father.

Their faces flashed behind her eyes as she struggled.

Nora sobbed as a hand dropped to the button on her pants.

I want to be with them, she thought as terror raced through her soul. *Just let me die*. She screamed as a hand cupped her chest.

The air suddenly churned above her. A cool breeze swept over her face, and the pressure on her pants disappeared. A shriek filled the sky, the high-pitched sound floating in the darkness around her: to her left, then to her right, then somehow high above her where she knew it couldn't be. The rough hands pressing her to the ground, previously stroking her skin with their sandpaper-like veneer, vanished as the foul-smelling bodies hovering over her head fell away. She lay sprawled against the ground.

Alone.

Nora barely breathed as she listened to the sounds of struggling. Feet thudded against the dirt, voices screamed in the night, and a cool breeze periodically blew across her skin. Something wet splattered her body and dripped down her face in hot lines. She lay perfectly still as the scent of iron engulfed her. *Breathe, and don't move*, she told herself. A loud thump and something fell to the ground close by. She turned her head and saw a dark object tumbling toward her like a lopsided melon, not quite rolling, but rocking back and forth until it settled inches from her nose. Logan's mouth gaped at her from his decapitated head. Nora screamed and rolled to her knees before standing. Her leg throbbed.

With her hands outstretched, she stumbled forward. The darkness made it impossible to see, but she could hear, and she focused on keeping the screams behind her. She continued through trees and bushes using her hands, even when the sounds of fighting dwindled to nothing. Bursting through a large bush, she found herself in an open space and on hard-packed dirt instead of spongy leaves. Bending down, she touched the ground and realized she'd found a deer trail.

She ran, scuffing her shoes against the dirt to make sure she stayed on the narrow path. After a quarter mile, brief glimpses of the night sky became visible through the thinning trees, allowing her to see the trail she ran. A rabbit darted across her path, escaping into the brush. Nora glanced behind her. No one seemed to be following. Whatever had attacked had saved her from those men. It could come for her, but for some reason, she knew it wouldn't.

Nora slowed to a walk and pulled her shirt around her chest, tying the pieces together until they covered as well as possible. She brushed the blood from her face with her arm. Then she walked, glancing into the sky where stars peeked through the leaves.

The moonlight had faded and soft golden rays lit up what had been dark minutes before. The light flowed over the trees and into the small clearing where Nora lay in the grass. She'd run through the night telling herself she needed to put as much distance between herself and the cannibals as possible, but that wasn't quite true. She had run from something much more sinister—from a constant feeling that someone was following her. She shivered and took another lingering look at the small cabin she'd stumbled onto an hour ago. She hadn't wanted to go inside in the dark, but now that it was light . . .

Don't let me die, Nora prayed, standing and creeping forward. The feeling of being watched had left before sunrise, and with its departure had come an overwhelming feeling of exhaustion. She needed rest, and she needed it now. She crossed the tall, untrampled grass to the cabin. Someone had taken the time to cover the windows with boards, which gave her hope. Nora swallowed and treaded the lowest step.

The wood creaked beneath her, bowing, but held her weight. She tightened her grip on the thin stick she held in her hands and moved to the door. After a quick bang against the door, she listened. She waited until she was sure nothing had moved on the inside before she reached down and twisted the knob. The door slid open without a sound.

She eased her head inside and took a deep breath. The air was stale and warm but not polluted with the smell of death. She edged inside and shut the door behind her. Thin ribbons of sun came in, bathing the small room with enough light to illuminate every corner. She picked up a two-by-four and placed it in the brackets on the door and wall, locking the door from the inside.

Nora sobbed and moved to an old mattress on the back

wall of the one-room shack. She dropped her pack and lay down, hoping exhaustion would take her away before she drowned in her tears.

Nora woke suddenly and stared at the wall in front of her. Chirping crickets and the high-pitched warbling of a songbird attempted to soothe her soul, but she couldn't get past the pain inside her. Only the ache of her stomach and the need to pee forced her to move. Rolling over, she stared at the windows where she could see the barest hint of light coming through the slats. It was too late to hunt for food but not to use the bathroom.

She moved to the windows and scanned what she could before opening the door. The porch gave a familiar groan, and she stopped to look around. A bird chirped and ran across the porch before taking off in flight while something small scuttled under the steps, but nothing lumbered from out of the surrounding forest. Nothing groaned and tried to bite her. Nora shuffled to a nearby tree and squatted.

An ache pierced her heart, and Nora looked up at the sky. She was alone now, with no one to tell her what to do or where to go. All she had were memories and the knowledge she'd learned from her father. That left her wondering what she should do now. She wouldn't go back to the city, but she wasn't sure she wanted to go home, either. Did she want to live in the cave she'd spent the last four years growing up in? With her father, she'd felt safe, but on her own, she wasn't sure she'd feel the same. She sighed, stood, and looked up into the darkening sky with worry. She'd wasted a day sleeping and didn't feel as rested as she should.

Rushing water caught her attention. Nora hesitated, thought about the time of day, then turned toward the sound.

She had a whole night to think about her predicament. A short walk to scout the area sounded nice as long as she made it back before full dark.

She found a small, overgrown path on the side of the house. It led away from the cabin and down a long incline in meandering switchbacks that gave her varying views of the surrounding countryside and the small river she sought. After a half hour of pushing her way through the overrun vegetation, she reached the actual river where it terminated at the edge of a lake. A bird hooted in the distance, and something splashed beyond where she could see. A low mist hung about the far end, and Nora found herself lost in the beauty for a moment before she remembered where she was. She bent down, took a long drink of the cold water, and headed back.

Maybe she should stay here. She had water and a house that seemed as secluded as anything she'd ever seen. Nothing indicated anyone had been here in ages, which worked for her. Sure, there might be an old road leading to the cabin, but she was betting it was so overgrown no one would notice it. Nora looked up when a rabbit burst onto the path and zigzagged across the trail before leaping under a bush.

Her minute of optimism faded, and she turned to walk back to the cabin. If her dad had been here, they'd have chased it. A tear slid out of her eye and she broke down in sobs. No matter where she went, she'd always be alone.

Night had fallen by the time Nora reached the cabin. She sniffed and ran her arm below her nose and took a step onto the porch. The screech of the wood pierced the deafening silence, and she peered around in sudden unease. Too wrapped up in her misery, she hadn't noticed when the birds and insects had gone mute.

Nora hurried the last few feet to the door and slid inside. She froze and brought a trembling hand to her mouth. Light from a small candle bounced off the walls and board-covered windows, flickering into the corners and along the ceiling. Slowly, she bent down and looked under the bed, then turned and locked the door. Her legs collapsed, and she slid down to rest against the wood. Where had the candle come from? Nora noticed a small basket sitting beneath the table and felt the hairs along her arms rise in alarm. She swallowed and peered at the windows.

There were large gaps between the boards that had not bothered her before. Now she studied them, acutely aware how vivid she'd appear with the candle burning beside her. She glanced at it as a shiver slipped up her back, then returned her gaze to the windows. The light would stay. Sitting in darkness didn't appeal to her either. Minutes passed, and her stomach grumbled loudly.

Nora shifted closer to the table. Someone had helped her last night and could have followed her here, possibly leaving the basket. But why? And what was wanted in return?

She pulled the cloth from the top of the basket and held it tight. Her stomach growled, and she studied the darkness through the wood slats. Her hands worked the soft cloth while she tried to ignore the scent of cooked meat and fresh bread wafting from the floor. Saliva coated her mouth, and her stomach rumbled again. She swallowed, tasting the warm bread on her tongue, and turned back to the food. She stroked a piece of hard crust and looked up.

A shadow moved on the porch.

Nora screamed and scrambled back to the wall. She raised a stick in the air and ignored the way it shook as her eyes flicked between the two windows. A tear streaked its way down her flushed face.

The door shook within its frame, and then something sharp scraped down the boards.

Claws were what she pictured and what sent her heart

reeling. "What do you want?" she shrieked as sweat poured down her back to pool at her waistband.

The porch creaked.

"Shhhhhh," a voice carried through the broken window. "Don't cry, my sweetling. Don't cry."

No, it couldn't be. Nora dropped her stick, and she stood. "Mama?"

Soft humming came to her, the familiar notes caressing her skin in a familiar pattern, enveloping her in their fold. Nora closed her eyes. "It can't be," she whispered. But the song continued; the words now sung were the same she'd heard every night since she'd been a baby. As the last line warbled to an end, she stepped forward.

"Mama?"

"I'm here, Nora." There was a soft scratching at the door and then an urgent whisper, "Let me in."

Nora's hands touched the wooden beam barring the door. She swallowed and leaned her forehead against the wood. How could she be here? A tear slipped down her face while she fought the urge to lift the lock. This couldn't be happening. Her mom was dead. Along with her dad. Along with Adam.

She was alone.

The humming began again. Nora cried as the words of love and togetherness cascaded over her like a waterfall of cleansing water. It had to be her. No one else knew about the song. No one alive, anyway. She stepped back and opened the door.

The light from her candle flowed a few feet onto the porch but didn't pierce the ebony nothingness further out. Even the stars hung back tonight, hidden from sight by low-hanging clouds. Nothing accounted for the singing, and Nora leaned further out so she could scan the clearing. Something darker than the night shifted within the vegetation. A shadow among shadows that sent unease skittering across Nora's shoulders like small fingers walking over her skin. She shuffled backward into the room while clutching her shirt to her chest.

"Mama?" she whispered through lips that trembled. Her limbs felt suddenly weak as she realized she'd made a mistake. She should never have opened the door. Nora jumped forward.

The sickly sweet scent of spoil and fresh sunshine flowed into the room as something thin and bright moved across the yard to the deck. The body didn't waver as it rose up the risers and made its way across the floor. Instead, it floated, smoothly gliding toward her, a tall, thin, glowing version of her mother. Skin as pale as death, pupils no longer blue but the darkest black, their edges tinged in deep red. Crimson lips pulled back in a smile, exposing long, sharp incisors that hadn't existed before.

Nora screamed and fell to the floor as the vampire entered the room and the door shut behind her.

"Shhhhhh," the creature said as she floated toward Nora. Crouching down, she raised a hand, no longer tainted with black lines and green flesh, to stroke Nora's cheek. "I've not come to kill you, child. You are my only one."

Nora whimpered and scooted away from the cold hand until her back pressed against the wall. She stared at the thing that was once her mother, at the smooth way she twisted her head to stare with eyes more alien than human.

The creature reached out and grabbed the basket of food. "You are hungry," she said as the food slid across the floor. "Eat, Nora. I can feel your hunger."

Nora ignored the basket and stared at her mother. Her hair, so slack and greasy yesterday, floated along her shoulders like golden thread. The imperfections across her skin, the small cuts, abrasions, and normal discolorations from a life spent in the sun were now gone. This wasn't her mother as she remembered her, but there was no denying who sat before her. "How, Mama?"

The smile Nadine gave her sent terror down her spine. Her skin grew cold where the ebony eyes touched her, and her throat grew tight as her mother's gaze lingered on the pulse beating along her neck. When her mother's eyes rose, and her blood-red lips spread into a grin, a whimper escaped Nora.

"Oh, the how is not too long, sweetling. I'll tell you the story," she whispered as she leaned forward and lowered the cadence of her voice. "Eat."

The scent of roasted meat grew intense, drawing Nora's gaze even though she fought the attraction. Her lips parted, and the smell coated her tongue. Saliva flowed freely, and she swallowed as everything dimmed in comparison. The basket slid closer until it touched her knees. Her mother's arm drew back to lay against her lap.

"Eat," she whispered again, this time with a weight to her words that surrounded Nora and invaded her thoughts. Intense hunger, like nothing she'd ever experienced before, forced her to lean down and sink her teeth into the charred flesh. She savored the nourishment even as her mind questioned what she did.

The flesh slid off the bones, filling her mouth and stomach with the smoke-flavored mass, filling her mind with nothing but a compulsion to eat. The more she ate, the stronger the order became, the more she gnawed on the edge of a bone hoping for more.

"Good girl," Nadine purred from across from her. "You are my perfect daughter. So sweet, so beautiful. So trusting." She leaned forward from where she'd sat on the floor across from Nora. "Are you ready to hear my story now?"

Nora froze and raised her eyes. She swallowed the food in

her mouth and sat numbly staring at her mother. Why couldn't she think? Stay focused? All she wanted to do was eat. Her eyes slid down to the roast before they rose again.

"Eat," her mom whispered.

And Nora ate.

"I didn't want to die, not at the end," Nadine said as her eyes tracked the food Nora lifted to her mouth. "But in the beginning I did, after your father killed Adam."

The fog within Nora's head thinned. Adam? Her dad killed Adam? Her hands slid down to her lap. He couldn't have. Adam wandered off. She looked into her mother's eyes and felt the fog returning. No. She shook her head and looked away, trying to focus.

Her dad killed Adam?

That didn't happen. Tears pricked her eyes, and her head shook slowly back and forth. "You lie," she said, fully comprehending what her mother said. "Daddy wouldn't do that."

Her mother's lips curled back in a snarl, and her teeth clenched together.

A blast of cold air assaulted Nora, coating her skin in a frosty sheet. Nora shuddered, immediately regretting her words as she watched her mom's hands stretch and her fingers curl like talons in front of her body. "I'm sorry," Nora whispered, cowering as her mother disappeared beneath the thing that now lived within her.

Black sludge seeped from her pupils into the whites of her eyes before spreading out the corners like spidery webbing down her cheeks. That darkness continued to course through her veins, raising ridges across her skin in lines of black—changing her flesh into something alien. Something unnatural. Her mother lunged forward. "That bastard did!" Sharp fangs flashed as she leaned back and bellowed into the sky.

Nora screamed, dropping her food onto the floor. She

pressed back into the wall, wishing she could disappear as her mother's anger crested.

A cold wind charged through the cabin, filling the room with the sound of rushing air that was not quite loud enough to cover the words coming from her mother's mouth.

"He used Adam to get away from the cannibals. Left them a gift so they'd give *him* some time to escape. He didn't know I watched him walk off with my boy. Didn't know I saw what he did. Didn't know I knew why he returned without him."

She screeched again as her hands slammed into the floor and sent a loud crack through the cabin. The floor dented in two distinct depressions where she'd punched.

"At that moment, I wanted him dead," she hissed, "but I wasn't strong enough to do it myself. I couldn't do it, and I knew you were next. The cannibals were still chasing us and wouldn't stop. It was only a matter of time until he gave them you, and I wouldn't be able to do anything. I was trapped, and I didn't want to see you die. Nor did I want to let that monster live! So, I waited until he slept. Then I crept away and went to the small house."

Her mother rocked back on her heels and closed her eyes. She whispered to herself, and the veins began receding back into her skin. The wind slowed and then vanished, and her eyes opened. They were again white around their ebony irises.

Nora swallowed and remained still.

"I was weak," her mom whispered. "I went to the vampire to die. I crawled through the broken window, stepped into his den, and found the tunnel below the ground. I cried the whole way, thinking of you, Nora, knowing that I'd abandoned you to a certain death. By the time I'd changed my mind, it was too late. The vampire had woken, and he'd found me."

Her face went slack as her gaze grew distant. She'd gone

silent, and Nora took the time to absorb what her mother said about what her father had done. He'd murdered her brother to keep them alive. Fed him to monsters. Tears slid down her face, and she lowered her head. She looked up when her mom spoke.

"I had hoped to change and make your father pay. I wanted to rip him limb from limb, to feed from him the same way he let those monsters feed off my boy. I wanted him to pay for his sins, but I was too late. The zombies got him."

She leaned back as her eyes again focused on Nora.

"I want them dead," her mother whispered. "All of them. I want them ingested as they did my son. They will pay now, where your father could not." She grimaced and leaned forward, her long fangs shining in the candlelight.

Nora shivered, unable to look away.

"Was that you last night?" Nora asked as she wiped a tear from her cheek.

"Yes." Her mother cocked her head to the side. "Eat, sweetling."

Her stomach rumbled, and her eyes drifted to the basket. The scent of meat and bread smothered the smell of decay coming from her mother and the smell of mold and rot in the cabin. Thoughts of her mother, father, and even her brother vanished as she gave in and pulled the bread to her mouth. She ate and ate, not stopping until the bread was gone and she saw her mother floating before the door. She swallowed the food in her mouth before whispering, "Why are you alive? Why didn't the vampire eat you?"

Her mother's look became sly. "The vampire liked me," she whispered. "He offered me another option. Become like him, share his home, live forever. I would not have done it, but my thoughts kept returning to you. Maybe, with the power of a vampire, I could save you and damn that man who killed my son. I agreed to his proposal and let the vampire bite me." She drew the sleeve of her long shirt back, showing Nora the two small depressions in her skin where the infected animal bite had been.

Her fingers gave the small dimples a loving caress. "The zombies took that man's death from me, but they left me alone. They could smell what I was becoming and let me make my way to the dark safety of the buildings. I woke that night, completely reborn, and immediately searched for you. No one was more pleased than me to find you so easily." She leaned forward to grab the remaining meat from the floor.

"I am alive because of you," she said with a lowered voice. Her smile spread, revealing teeth long and sharp. Something slick and thick dripped from her fangs onto the floor. "Without you, I would have given up. Without you, I couldn't seek my vengeance. Now I'm going to keep you safe, sweetling. I will not let you die. You will never be alone again."

She leaned closer and whispered, "As long as you eat, Nora."

Nora shuddered as fear slid up her back. "Mama—"

"Eat," she ordered.

Inexplicable calm flowed from Nora's center and out her limbs. Her shoulders relaxed, and a warm haze filled her mind. She took the meat from her mother's hands. Hunger again consumed her, and she looked down at the meat covered in dirt and leaves. "Thank you, Mama," she said as she took a bite. She chewed thoughtfully for a minute before asking, "What kind of meat is this, Mom?"

Her mom smiled. "Just eat . . ."

ORB C68

AND THE MIST

THE HISS

Tim Rectorm did a quick calculation as he dropped his toolbox to the ground. Ninety-eight days he'd been sequestered in these mountains. Days that ran together like water in a stream: hours merging into days, days into months, months into years. Nights that took an eternity to pass. He should be home running with his dog along the waterfront, sipping margaritas in his favorite restaurant, and enjoying a nightlife that included more than wishing for a shot of whiskey.

But he wasn't.

Not for the first time he wondered if he'd died, and this was his hell—stuck forever in an alien mist studying alien objects waiting for something alien to happen. How Earth's first alien invasions turned into the most boring project known to man was beyond him. He wondered if his counterparts in China or Africa were experiencing the same disappointing realizations in their outposts.

He tapped C68 lightly with his hand. The alien artifact was a perfect sphere. No dents or imperfections marred the exterior nor were there seams indicating how the orb had been pieced together. It was a solid, inexplicably warm, mirror-like material that reflected everything on its surface. Spoiling the alien beauty were the numerous black rubber tubes secured to its side. Two centimeters wide, they extended from the transmitter at Tim's feet to various points along the orb's surface, protecting the wires inside the tubes from the elements.

With a seventy-two-inch diameter, this particular orb was the biggest of the twenty Tim's group monitored twenty-four hours a day, seven days a week. Only Tim had the arm length necessary to check for detached sensors along the top, giving him the task of driving here at the crack of dawn every few days. Often, like today, while marinating in his own sweat in his biohazard suit, he wondered if being tall was more a punishment than privilege. There were no rewards for working on C68 other than being able to brag to his coworkers that only he could do it.

Tim bent down and began laying out his gear while he listened to the silence of the mist. He'd heard nothing while hiking through the tall evergreen trees to get here—no birds cawing, animals crawling in the brush, or trill of insects as they searched for mates. His steps and the clanking of his tools had been muffled and hollow, oddly one note and unnerving. He could blame the layers of pine needles covering the ground, but mostly, he blamed the fog. It was even worse down in the crater with the orb. It felt like another world in the thick white, with the alien artifact, and the abnormal stillness. Somehow the mist absorbed sound waves, leaving everything in a perpetual vacuum. Tim stiffened when a voice suddenly blasted into the quiet of his biohazard suit.

"How's it going out there, rectum?"

Tim shook his head at the juvenile name play while he smacked the speaker in his helmet with his hand. The voice reverberated in his ear long after his coworker stopped talking—finally warbling its way to a wheezy hiss before disappearing. Tim made a mental note to get his own biohazard suit repaired when he finished this run. If he'd done it a week ago, he wouldn't be wearing a borrowed one from the visitor's closet. One that was not only almost a decade old but besieged with its own problems.

"Children, children," he replied. "I have access to copious bottles of hair remover. Who knows what kind of trouble I'll get into with five bottles of that shit at my disposal." Shrieks and howls came through the speaker. "You laugh, but keep it up, and you'll feel my wrath. We'll be known as the Outpost of the Follicly Challenged when I'm done." He grinned as they continued to chortle from their location within the outpost forty-eight miles from him. He'd thought the mayonnaise-filled donuts would have stopped the mocking but obviously not. It didn't really bother him; thinking up pranks kept him amused. At the continued laughter, he realized it might be time to put plan Hairless Apes into action. A poker game, sizzling wings, and a sleep-aid beer chaser would set the stage. After they were knocked out, a little hair remover would complete it. "Call me rectum one more time and you'll rue the day, I swear."

"Old man, you try another stunt like the may—" Jake's voice cut off abruptly with a feminine squeak.

Inwardly cringing, Tim leaned against the orb as Dr. Linda Leakhert's voice came over the microphone.

"What the hell is going on here?" she snapped at his coworkers.

"We were just—"

"Oh, don't even start making excuses. You're harassing Tim again, aren't you?"

Tim snickered and went back to work with his crew's arguing filling his suit like a sweet serenade. He'd have something to goad the jackholes with when he went home tonight. As words like "degenerates and irresponsible" and "immature baboons" drowned out their excuses, Tim laughed but found himself sympathizing with his coworkers at the same time. He'd come under Linda's punishing umbrella and biting tongue more than once and knew how they felt. Not that it influenced his feelings about her in any way. She was tough but fair.

Standing, Tim studied his reflection on the orb's silver surface. He looked like a boy playing scientist in an ill-fitting biohazard suit that bulged around him like a yellow balloon, two sizes too large. Belts cinched around his upper thighs and waist kept the extra material from hanging heavily around his hips and feet but resulted in cumbersome blobs around the belts. He sighed as he moved back into position. He looked like an idiot.

Tim ran his hand along one of the rubber tubes until he found a loose section. He slid a screwdriver underneath and tugged until the piece detached from the orb in a long line. He examined the impotent glue, not surprised to see holes pocking the surface as if corrosive material had been misted all over it. He scraped at the crumbling gunk with a finger and watched pieces fall to the ground. The fog had caused this. The same fog unsuspecting people breathed on a daily basis, unaware it was composed of an unclassified molecule that dissolved adhesives, corroded metals, and ate away at cement. At least the air at the government's research outposts was canned and clean—too bad the same technology wasn't available to the average Joe. Tim's lips pressed together in concentration as he used a knife to cut the remaining adhesive off the tubing without piercing the rubber.

"Damn fog," he muttered as he shut his knife and picked up his grinder. The wheel whirled while he roughed up the area where the tube would lay once glued down. He pressed hard, not worried about gouging the surface. In fact, he wasn't so sure his grinding scratched the material at all, but if there was a chance his effort helped the glue adhere even minimally, he'd do the work.

Linda's deep voice came through his speakers loud and clear, so he knew she was speaking only to him. "I can't believe I'm locked in the outpost with the children. Again."

Tim shook his head at the exhaustion coloring her voice. She'd been quiet and withdrawn lately, her lack of sleep evident in the dark shadows under her eyes and the lethargy in her movements. He'd hoped by talking to her before she'd retired last night that she'd sleep a little better. And if a romantic interlude had occurred, it would have been icing on the proverbial cake. However, nothing had worked as he'd wanted. Instead of finding answers to how she felt about him, he'd been sucked into her anxiety-riddled conspiracy like an insect to a bug zapper. And like that bug, now that he'd seen the light, he couldn't see anything else. He'd lain awake long after he'd left her room, unable to forget all they'd discussed and quiet the fear in his mind. For now, he didn't let her know how much her worries had influenced him. "Oh, the children are just blowing off steam, Linda. All harmless fun. We've been cooped up in the middle of nowhere for almost four months. Everyone's a little stir crazy."

"They are scientists, Tim. They should be acting like professionals, not children. I've been here the same length of time, and you don't see me running around like an idiot."

Tim smirked at the vision of Linda letting loose, then flushed when it morphed into her leaning against the wall in sexy lingerie and giving him the come-hither look he desired more than anything else. He pushed the image away, aware they weren't that close. God, he wasn't even sure she knew he was interested. "Of course not, we're fossils next to those young bucks, Linda. They need to expend their energy in some way. If not, they'll explode, and we'll be dealing with fighting and drinking and who the hell knows what. You need to remember how young they are."

He heard Linda slap her hands against the desk before she spoke. "Fossils? You think you're a fossil? You used plastic wrap on Lane's bed and wrapped it like a fucking Christmas present two months ago. I should be yelling at you for your shit, but I know you are just responding to their antics."

He couldn't help the snort that escaped him as he thought about the fifteen minutes Lane spent cutting the filmy material from his mattress. "Lane deserved that. You know he was the one who placed those silver cow balls on my truck."

"Tim, you like those—never mind. It doesn't matter. My point is they are too old and too intelligent to be acting like out-of-control children. I need them to grow up. They are goddamn scientists, and they spend more time joking around than they spend analyzing the orbs."

Analyzing the orbs? Analyzing data that never changed? The thoughts passed through Tim's brain before he shook his head and dismissed the questions. "They are young, Linda. Alan is barely out of his teens."

"Oh, please. He's twenty-three and definitely old enough to act responsibly. Jesus, he has two PhDs! I shouldn't be wasting my time parenting him."

"Alan has an IQ rivaling Einstein's, but he's still young. Don't hate me for reminding you, but we were thirty when he was born." Tim waited for a second before stating the shocking fact again. "Thirty, Linda."

Tim thought about breaking the silence that followed his statement with a joke but decided against it. For all he knew, the speaker had finally wheezed its way to its final death, but if not, he didn't want to interrupt if Linda was seriously considering his words. He relaxed as a sigh slid through the speaker.

"Fine," her breathless voice said. "How's everything going out there?"

"Everything's as normal as expected. I've found two areas where the adhesive detached. I'm repairing the last one now." The gentle whirl of the grinder comforted him in the unnatural silence permeating the fog.

"Two? Already? Jesus Christ. You are using the urethane acrylate?"

Tim smiled. "Of course, Linda. Why are you surprised the glue has degraded? I haven't been here in three days."

"I know. You are right. I'm just a little edgy today."

Tim grunted and opened a tube of adhesive. He squirted a thin strand along the same path the old rubber tube had followed and closed the container. Moving fast, he pressed the rubber straw into the gummy paste and held it tight.

"I still don't like it," Linda muttered. She paused for a second before asking, "Have you seen the newest data? The orbs are heating up. There's been a fifteen-degree increase in the last ten hours. And this morning, one of the sensors caught movement from inside an orb in zone seven. Stephen thinks it was seismic activity his sensor picked up, and he's working on a recalibration, but I'm not so sure. What do you think it means?"

Tim snorted. "What does any of it mean? The aliens? The fog? These orbs? None of it makes sense. We sit here day after day, learning nothing new, and we act surprised when something new happens." He flinched as soon as the words left his mouth. "I'm sorry, I didn't mean—"

"That's bullshit, Tim. You said exactly what you meant because they are the same words you used last night! How can you still believe that after what we discussed? It does make sense—all of it. The spaceships that arrived nine months ago released something into the air that is modifying our atmosphere. They—"

Tim looked up and caught the reflection of his own pale face in the orb. He didn't want a repeat of the conversation they'd had the previous night. He wanted to go back to when things were calm and familiar. To a day ago when he hadn't known her theories on the aliens, and his biggest concern was whether he should tone his humor down or ramp it up. "Linda—"

"No, don't Linda me—not again. Those alien assholes are terraforming. You know it. I know it. It's so fucking obvious it's ridiculous! The lights they shot into the atmosphere weren't visual messages scientists were supposed to interpret and respond to like some goddamn *Close Encounters of the Third Kind* movie. Those colors created this damn fog and changed the composition of our air! The only thing I want to know is what's the fucking point of these damn spheres? Why were they released? What are they supposed to do? Are they going to fucking hatch—which is my fear—and if they do, what the fuck is going to crawl out of them?" Her sentence ended with her last words squealing in his ear like a balloon slowly letting out air.

Tim smacked his speaker in irritation. "Linda—" he stopped and hit his helmet again. The speaker gave a last squeak before going silent. "Linda, can you hear me?"

Her harsh breath came through the microphone before she issued a soft, "Yes."

"I'm almost done. Let me get back to camp, and we can talk this out. We're all scared, but the worst thing we can do is buckle under that fear. We'll figure this out. Together." He waited, his breath held, no longer seeing himself in the reflective surface of the orb but her face as it had been the night before—tear streaked with eyes so bright they appeared feverish. She'd been close to the edge, ready to walk out of the unit and strike out on her own. His heart jerked at the thought, and he whispered, "Linda?"

She answered as if he hadn't spoken. "I have a bad feeling about this, Tim. The atmosphere's still changing, almost on a daily basis, and electrical systems are frying because of the fog. People are dying, animals are dying, crops are dying . . . What's next? These orbs? They were dropped off three months ago and have been completely nonreactive. But not anymore, Tim. Stephen says earth movement; I say they are coming to life. And I guarantee they aren't filled with some gift from God to save us."

Tim blinked rapidly a few times before he reached up to rub the sweat from his brow. His gloved hand smacked the plastic partition over his face with a loud thunk before lowering. Linda wasn't wrong. The orbs had always been a little warmer than the air temperature, but like a man waking from a dream, he suddenly realized heat rolled off C68 in waves. Pulsing, scorching. At least fifteen degrees higher than when he'd arrived. The surface was no longer just warm; it was hot.

Honestly, more than a tiny part of himself agreed with Linda and thought they should run while they had the opportunity. "Together," he whispered, "I know we can get through this. I don't know what that entails since I don't know what's coming, but we'll live. Just wait for me. We'll come up with a plan. Something that will cover the most likely scenarios—"

Linda interrupted him, her voice hitching as if she were crying. "And if the best plan is to leave? To get as far away from these things as we can? What will you say then?"

Tim opened his mouth, intending to persuade her to stay, when an unpleasant sense of doom washed over him. His breath eased out of him as he looked around. Turning back, he placed his gloved-covered fingertips against the orb before dropping them to his side. He wasn't psychic—didn't believe in anything supernatural—but until nine months ago, he hadn't believed in aliens, either. His intuition told him to think before he made any rash decisions.

His role with the government was theoretically important, but without data to interpret, he mattered little to anyone. In the last three months, he figured he'd become the highest-paid maintenance man in the United States, one with more experience on a grinder than any other scientist in the area. He'd love to have new data to interpret, but did personal curiosity make staying the smart choice? Did he need to be the guy who interpreted the data? No, he did not.

Tim chewed his lip. As of last night, unanswered questions were invading his sleep, disrupting his normal even-keel outlook, and sending him into instances of panic. The aliens were terraforming, but why? Were they displaced and looking to cohabit Earth peacefully? Or was there a sinister purpose to their manipulation of Earth's atmosphere? Would the changes continue until the air became incompatible to Earth's existing life? Would life above ground become something humanity left to the past as people moved underground to live in the tunnels and caves that still contained unpolluted air? Scientists around the globe were already investigating the possibility. Should he and Linda join them?

Or should they stay where they were and continue blindly collecting data until the alien's plan reached its inevitable conclusion? Did he want to take that chance? The lights shot into the atmosphere were just colors: streaming yellows, blues, greens, and an occasional red. No physical objects that scientists could find. No chemical signatures known or unknown to man. Just colors exploding over every continent in the world.

Nothing explained the temperature changes that had begun immediately around the world, changing the topography forever. Both the Greenland and Antarctic ice sheets were melting at an alarming rate, while the sea ice of the

Arctic had become a shadow of what it had been. In the Pacific Northwest, where Tim lived, whole cities had fallen to the ravages of the sea. Seaside, Long Beach, Ocean Shores, Bellingham—all were gone or only a sliver of what they used to be. Even inland cities were not safe. The Columbia River had swelled way beyond its boundaries and flooded his hometown of Portland, Oregon, destroying one of the bridges that crossed from the city to Washington State.

The thick and unyielding mist made the remaining landscape something new and alarming. Enough that standing in the middle of a forest in the middle of his state's backyard felt alien. Tim turned his head and looked into what was now considered the distance. Twenty feet at most.

And what about the orbs? Three months ago, the aliens returned in mass, dropping into the atmosphere with shocking silence and precision. From their small aircrafts came thousands of orbs, each shot to the earth with unbelievable exactitude. No orbs landed within fifteen miles of one another. No orbs wrecked during landing. And no one knew what existed inside them or what their purpose was. They had proven to be impenetrable to everything known to man. And the ships had disappeared as quickly as they'd arrived.

Tim shook his head as his shoulders fell. Did he really believe the aliens wouldn't come back once the atmospheric changes were complete? No. Did he think they'd be pleasant —arriving to shake hands in air they could now breathe? Probably not. He sighed and dropped his hand to his side.

"Tim? Are you there?" Linda's voice sounded worried.

Maybe getting out of here and preparing for a doomsday scenario would settle the disquiet brewing inside both of them. Those plans might be the only things that saved them. Tim's shoulders relaxed.

"I'm here," he whispered. "Look, let's talk when I get

back. If what makes sense is for us to leave, then I'm willing to go. We can head to the hills, maybe join the other scientists already investigating caves as an option for the future. I honestly don't know what we'll do, but I do know we need to have a plan, not take off at the spur of the moment—"

Tim was cut off by unknown voices screaming on Linda's end of the speaker. His shoulders tensed as he strained to listen, but their words remained muffled, unidentifiable, as if Linda had pressed a hand over the microphone. Linda's voice joined the discussion, but she didn't allow him to hear. He let out a heavy breath to ward off the dread building inside him. This wasn't good.

"Run!" Linda's voice suddenly screamed over the speaker. "The orbs, they are opening. Run, Tim!"

Tim stumbled back, then turned and ran to the edge of the crater. His breath was harsh in his ears but not as loud as the screaming coming through his headset. He focused on Linda's voice as flashes of their relationship went through his mind. *I waited too long*, he thought as the dread gave way to fear.

Even with his heart pounding angrily in his chest, each palpitation like a hammer trying to crush its way through his ribs, he still felt the faint vibration that rolled through the ground beneath his feet as he ran. The urge to turn was intense, but he focused on the lantern sitting on the steps leading out of the crater.

Tim let out a labored breath and grasped the guide rope leading up the stairs. He moved recklessly, disregarding the rocks and sticks jutting through the dirt, and hustled up the steps as quickly as he could. He jerked to a stop when his pant leg caught on something sharp.

"Damn it," he muttered and gave his leg a hard yank. The rubber gave way with a loud rip, and his foot went flying into the next step. He stumbled forward with his hands splayed out in front of him. Through the thick confines of his gloves, he registered the repeated sequence of vibrations flowing through the ground before he pulled himself up.

"Tim, are you okay? Tim?" Linda sobbed quietly as she spoke.

"I'm . . . I'm okay." He stopped for a second to catch his breath. His suit was weighing him down. Almost fifty-five pounds in rubber and insulation. Fifty-five pounds that might be hindering him more than helping him at this point.

"Tim," a voice intoned, one that took him a moment to recognize as Jake Lasting, the man who'd called him rectum earlier. "We are getting reports from all over the US about the orbs. They are opening, and creatures are emerging. Things . . . things you can't comprehend. You need to get out of there. Get in the truck and get back to camp."

"I'm trying. This damn suit is weighing me down." Tim took one step, and then another, continuing on until he was almost to the top.

"Then drop it," Jake said. "We've never proven the chemicals the orbs are emitting is dangerous."

Tim snorted. Taking the final step, he pulled himself out of the crater. This was a common argument between him and Jake. Tim, who followed protocol for everything versus Jake, who didn't give a shit. The cowboy versus the sheriff. He gave his standard response in-between labored breaths. "We've never proven otherwise, either."

After a moment of silence, Jake's strangled voice came over the mic. "I'm not joking this time, old man. What's coming out of the orb will kill you. Hurry your ass up, Rectorm."

A shiver crawled up Tim's back like fingers going for a walk over his spine. He breathed out as he whispered, "Then I should take it off?" Everything slowed as he waited for Jake to answer, his brain frozen and unresponsive.

"Yes."

Tim gathered his resolve and turned toward the crater as he ripped open the fasteners on his glove. The noise from the underlying zipper unzipping made him peer up. He shivered under the layers he wore as if a cold breeze blew through his suit, but moist heat met the exposed skin of his hand.

"The, uh, orb looks the same as normal. Nothing has opened. But I can feel vibrations in the ground. They were faint when I began to run, but already their pace and intensity have increased."

"What are you doing, Tim? Get out of there. We don't care what you see, just get home." Linda's sentence ended in another sob, and Tim felt a pang dig deep into his heart. He threw his unzipped glove on the ground, then removed the remaining one.

"Linda, I'm explaining what I see as I remove my suit." He swallowed the lump that came from nowhere and filled his throat like a lead ball. "I need to talk, Linda." He almost choked on the sour taste of fear that filled his mouth.

"Okay," Linda whispered, "please hurry."

Tim ran his hands along his legs and unstrapped the belts holding his suit to his thighs and waist. The too-large suit billowed around him as if he'd instantaneously gained forty pounds. He pulled the large, protective shell off his head and dropped it to the ground, but he left the inner rubber headpiece surrounding his neck and skull alone because they contained his mic and speaker.

He breathed deeply and placed his hands under the snaps on his chest and worked them open. The metallic, wet scent of the air filled his lungs as mist stroked his face in a soft caress. He drew in another deep breath as he pulled his arm out of his suit and wondered how many more breaths he'd be taking.

A hiss, soft and continuous, rose from the direction of the

orb. Tim froze at the sound, his breath catching in his chest as a memory flitted up, unbidden and insignificant, but somehow fitting. He could feel the air whipping through his hair as he raced around his yard, shooting a nail gun at the fence and trees. Bam! Bam! Bam! Cops and robbers. Joy and excitement. They'd gone hand in hand until he'd shot the tire of his father's truck with a two-inch nail. That joy had shriveled, morphing into an all-consuming fear that had caused his bladder to sink low and grow heavy. The thought of his father's belt had sent him racing to the shed with one thought on his mind—if there was no evidence, there was no crime. With all the strength an eight-year-old could muster, he'd attacked the nail, yanking back on the hammer with a muscle-bulging pull that had thrown him to the ground. The sound of air hissing its way out of the rubber hull had flushed his momentary relief away. He'd known instantly he'd made a mistake.

This hiss was the same.

Tim shivered and went back to removing the buckles and zippers along his suit. As he shrugged his second arm out of the orange material, he looked up at the orb. The suit slid down and puddled around his ankles.

His movements ceased. "Oh, dear God," he whispered as his breath caught in his throat. He took a step backward, forgetting about the mountain of rubber attached to his feet, and fell onto his backside. His breath whooshed out as his head snapped back and hit the ground.

"Tim, what's going on? Tim?" Linda's frantic voice broke into his consciousness.

"The," he answered, pausing to pull himself onto his hands, "the orb is opening." He stared at the white billowing out the top like steam from a teapot. A wild, alien scent washed over him, setting his nerves on fire and filling him with an inexplicable urge to flee. He scrambled upright and kicked his legs out in an attempt to throw off his suit. The heavy weight refused to budge. Tim leaned forward and gripped the orange material with his hands as he looked up.

"Linda, it's splitting open, venting gasses into the air. The smell is horrific. There are slits moving down the sides—like the lines on a beach ball." Tim managed to get one foot out of the boot and began working on the other. Large drops of sweat rolled down his face, where they caught on the edge of rubber against his chin.

"Tim—"

"The, the sides of the orb are now curling downward, like a, uh, banana peeling. Yes, it's a banana, and the sides have rolled down enough that I can see into the orb and—" Tim's voice stuttered to a stop. His hand slid from the foot he'd pulled from his boot, and he stumbled to his feet. "Heaven help me," he whispered.

Then he ran.

The dark shape he saw crawling out of the thick mist seeping from the orb haunted his mind. The way the figure rolled its torso upward to stand on four long, spindly back legs until the creature stood around five feet tall. The way its hard black exoskeleton shined with the filtered light reflected off the four segments making up its body. The way its many arms waved randomly in the air, the three sharp-pointed fingers on each opening and closing reflexively. He couldn't remember the shape of the head because his eyes had focused on the teeth. The many, many sharp teeth that sparkled as the creature opened its maw and seemed to yawn.

"I'm running," he whispered, his bare feet thudding against the dirt. Linda and the others continued speaking into their mic, giving instructions and yelling encouragement. He ignored them and focused on the shapes in the fog: trees that were large, nondescript columns that didn't lose their smooth texture until he was almost running into them, bushes that resembled gray blobs. He scanned the trail anxiously, looking for the one shape that might save his life, but the red truck was nowhere to be seen.

Tim's head snapped back as an odd clicking came from behind him. It was close, way closer than he thought it would be. Tim stumbled to a stop and turned in a slow circle until he faced the direction he had come from. He let out a raspy breath and edged backward in the silence.

"Tim, can you hear me?" Linda's voice whispered.

"Shhhhhh," he hissed, running a shaking hand across his sweaty forehead. Some of the clicks were low and drawn out, while others were high pitched. They tickled his subconscious, and he knew he was missing something. *Come on, Tim*, he thought when they went quiet. *Think. You are a scientist. You can do this.*

The clicks returned, and bats immediately came to mind. They used echolocation to visualize their environment. What if the sounds he heard were from the creature trying to get through the woods? Maybe it couldn't actually see, and if he stood still, it might mistake him for one of the trees. He pondered this silently, then moved to the edge of the trail where a tree would be directly behind him. Swallowing, he tried to become one with the vegetation.

A second later, a dark shape materialized out of the mist, sliding into existence like a dark apparition. It froze, a nondescript blob no different than the trees and bushes surrounding them. As shapeless as he hoped he appeared. He kept his breath shallow and slow, unnerved by the creature's sudden silence.

A click broke the noiselessness, sending fear down his spine when he realized it didn't come from the creature in front of him but somewhere to his right. *There were two. Twins? Or had they been designed to hatch together to reproduce?* Tim clenched his hands to stop them from trembling. From his peripheral vision, he saw another blob shift within the shadows. It clicked softly, moving closer. Tim let his breath out slowly and pressed his hands flat against his thighs.

Should I run or wait them out? The thought had barely formed in his mind when Linda's voice exploded in his ear. He fought the urge to clamp his hands over his ears; instead, he dug his fingers into his thighs.

"Tim, what's going on?" she said, her voice warbling at the end into a piercing squeal.

The creature in front turned at the sound, and he swallowed the bitter taste of fear that coated his tongue. Multiple arms stretched forward, fingers clenching and unclenching until the one on top motioned with a pointed finger in his direction.

Tim's legs weakened, and he pressed one hand against the tree behind him. The alien clicked loudly in response, and he froze, waiting for it to make a move.

It didn't, and the forest remained terrifyingly silent.

Tim peered through the side of his eye to study the other alien. His heart squeezed tight. He scanned the trees, the shadows, an area closer to the first creature, but it wasn't there. He couldn't find its darker shadow hiding where it had been before. He couldn't help the low whimper that escaped him as he turned his head slightly. The creature was gone. Then he heard a twig snap somewhere to his left, and he knew. It was hunting.

Tim screamed and ran. His heart thundered in his chest as nausea gripped his stomach in its strong grasp. "Please," he cried, eyes scanning the path. Where was the truck?

"Tim? Are you there, Tim?"

A whispered sob against his ear.

The trees thinned as he reached the end of the path, allowing more light to stream through the canopy above him.

He hurtled under the trees they called the twin witches for the large humpbacks on each and the long overhanging branches that seemed to be reaching toward each other. Their long limbs resembling arms with fingers that arched across the trail, marking the end of the trailhead.

Leaves rustled on the ground behind him. "Tik. Tik," they called. One to another, louder, more aggressive than before.

His name flowed across his ear. "Tim? Where are you, Tim?"

His foot left the moist path, slapping painfully down on the rock-covered parking lot toward the dark shadowed shape in the far corner. The slight gleam of red in the fog made his hope soar.

Click tik. Click tak. The sound of feet sliding on gravel.

He stumbled across the biting rocks to his car. "I'm here," he cried, "I made it."

Linda sobbed on the other end while Jake gave instructions. "Get in, Rectorm. Get home now!"

Tim's hands slid along the smooth front panel toward the door.

He yanked on the handle, but he knew he was too late. Knew by the clicking that seemed to be getting louder and more animated. Knew as the wild, meaty scent of their flesh became more pronounced. The hairs along his neck rose as a click thundered behind his ear.

"Let me in, let me in!" he shrieked as his fingers pulled again. The door remained closed, and his hand jerked painfully off the chrome rod. Something cold and sharp pierced his side as claws dug deep into his upper arms. He screamed and heard Linda's returning cry as something bit deep into his neck. In seconds, all went black, and he passed away with "I love you, Tim," echoing in his ear.

THE APOCALYPSE

THE FRYING PAN, AN UMBRELLA, AND
ONE LAST MEAL

THE LAST MEAL

Todd shuffled into the kitchen, blinking rapidly to combat the brightness of the room. The kitchen's yellow paint glowed in the sunlight in stark contrast to the darkness of the bedroom he'd just left. It was a color he'd chosen ages ago to imbue himself with a sense of warmth and contentment when nothing seemed to be going right. And nothing had been going right for a while now. Even so, he was surprised when the stir of something stronger than apathy began to grow in his chest.

Then he looked at the dead body rotting in the yard outside.

He scratched his protruding belly and pushed a strand of greasy hair off his face. Turning away from the window, he briefly considered taking a shower before dropping his hand to his side in disgust.

What's the fucking point? It must be noon at least. He glanced at the dead clock hanging lopsided on the wall like a prophetic depiction of his life—already dead but not quite willing to fall down. Todd scowled and turned away. No one cared what he looked like, whether he smelled, or what time it was. He had nowhere to go. Nothing to do. No one to visit. Everyone was dead, save those too stupid to give up, and even they'd die eventually.

People like me.

He bent down and opened the propane valve, then lit the stove's burner. He glanced at the ingredients he'd laid on the counter and sighed. Chorizo and rice. In a past life, he would have been drooling at the thought of such a delectable breakfast, but he couldn't find it in himself to get excited anymore. Maybe he should have picked something else from the cases of meat stacked in his bedroom. Something exotic like canned sturgeon or deer. Or even those delectable turd-shaped Vienna sausages or salty meatloaves of Spam.

He dropped the red-tinged meat into the warm pan and stirred it slowly. There was another option he hadn't considered. He could have chosen something sweet for breakfast, like peaches in sweet syrup over oats. Why hadn't he thought of that?

"Maybe," he muttered, his voice rising in pitch as he exaggerated his whining, "because peaches were not on *the plan*. They don't fit my goddamn *schedule* because they aren't for breakfast but *only* for special occasions." Todd yanked a cupboard open and grabbed a tin of dehydrated onions off the shelf. He opened it, sprinkled some on the meat, and added an eighth-cup of water to the mix. Stirring it all together, he suddenly grumbled. "What the fuck is that supposed to mean, anyway? *Special occasions?* They don't exist anymore." *Not when we're probably the only two people left alive in this godforsaken place.*

Or when no one knows what day it is, he suddenly thought, turning to stare at the calendar hanging, neglected, next to the window. *American Prepper* blazed across the top, over a group picture of three women and two men standing high atop a mountain. They were all smiling, holding guns and gas masks while wearing their go bags, looking attractive and happy. He wondered vaguely how their apocalypse was going before sighing and returning to his breakfast.

Yeah, he should have picked something else. He had dehydrated eggs and milk for pancakes. He could have whipped up a crepe . . . His spatula froze over the pan as his eyes rose to stare out the window. Then he smiled. He'd almost forgotten about the lone can of dehydrated guacamole he'd found hidden behind the garbanzo beans last night.

"It's Christmas," Todd whispered, hurrying across the kitchen and open hallway to the closed door of his bedroom. He went inside and grabbed the large 109-ounce #10 canister from where he'd placed it on top of his dresser and hugged the aluminum to his chest. Guacamole. Maybe not fresh, but after months with only canned food, he wouldn't care.

He danced as he moved around the kitchen. He could barely stand the wait, knowing the flaky green powder he spooned into the water-filled bowl would soon be guacamole. He held the bowl tight to his chest and whisked away, breathing in the spicy avocado scent that grew with the thickening mix. The sound of his utensil clanking against the metal filled the small kitchen. Finally, with a bob of his head and a flourish of his arm, he dropped the bowl and whisk onto the counter.

"Ka-bam! Guac-a-molé!" he said, emphasizing each syllable and ending with a wild laugh. He placed his hands on his hips and did a little dance before regaining his composure. With unsettling quickness, reality settled in, and his face shifted to its familiar morose mask.

The guacamole is nice, but it won't fix anything. He turned to the calendar with its empty page of activities. Life wasn't going to get exciting just because he made guacamole. Nor would it bring back his neighbors, family, or friends. It hadn't changed anything. His eyes slid in the direction of his roommate's room. It definitely wasn't some magic sauce that would make his roommate disappear, that's for sure.

He pulled a plate forward and methodically layered a tortilla with the refried beans, rice, chorizo, and guacamole. He knew it was cruel to want Gordon gone. If it weren't for him, he'd never have gotten his crap together and been prepared for the end of the world. His pre-Gordon stash of beans, rice, and pasta wouldn't have lasted him more than a couple months. Gordon was a paranoid lunatic, but his capacity to organize and plan everything down to bathroom schedules was amazing. They'd worked well together preparing. It was when they weren't working that Gordon became a pain in the ass.

Todd moved to a small table that separated the kitchen from the family area and sat down. He glanced around the open-concept living area before letting his gaze scan the neighborhood again. Nothing new to see. The one-way shades allowed him to look outside while stopping anyone from observing him from the street. That was important in this post-apocalyptic world—$1,000 well spent, if he thought so himself. Too bad he hadn't been able to afford shades for the other rooms. Todd cringed when the vinyl chair across from him squeaked as it was drawn away from the table. He hadn't heard the bugger leave his room.

"Well howdy-do, Todd," Gordon said as he waved his hands at the window. "Look at that sun! What a glorious day!"

Todd jerked his seat to the side so he no longer faced the table and his roommate, but to the left and out the window instead.

He took a bite of his breakfast and gazed at the wasteland they lived in. Although not an affluent area, his street had been clean and well cared for before the apocalypse. His neighbors had always been busy washing windows he hadn't thought were dirty, mowing lawns that hadn't grown from the previous week, trimming leaves from bushes one delicate leaf at a time. With the maintained community park across the street, he'd spent many a morning happily viewing the outdoors from the bank of windows covering the walls of their living room.

But no more. A jungle had sprouted between the swings and slides, spreading through the crumbling bark chips and across the once-elegant running trails like some type of infection. Small trees poked their delicate tips above a lawn that had grown to over a foot tall. The only barrier he could see to nature's takeover were the cars abandoned where they'd ceased moving many, many months ago, and they weren't exactly safe from nature's invasion. Things were finding ways to grow on the dirt, in the windshields, and through the tire walls. As a great actor had once said on Todd's favorite dinosaur movie, nature finds a way.

On the street, in the grass, and even half inside Mrs. Miller's townhouse down the road, the cars lay like decrepit reminders of what used to be possible. Rusted and broken, they'd never run again. They'd never take someone from one frivolous event to another. Maybe somewhere in the world cars still moved, but here, in Birkenridge, the only things moving were the plants—growing up and out in their attempt to take back what was once theirs—and the birds that feasted on the bodies left to rot in the sun.

Todd's eyes flicked in his roommate's direction before turning away. And Gordon wanted to talk about how glorious the day was. What an ass. Todd flinched as Gordon's high-pitched voice broke into his thoughts.

"Is that Spam? You shouldn't eat that," he admonished.

Todd didn't bother correcting Gordon, but he took a bite of his burrito and savored the spicy taste before turning his head to stare at his roommate. Their eyes met across the cold plastic of their dining room table in a silent exchange of words.

Don't go there, Todd warned with a narrowing of his brown eyes.

Gordon's baby blues, shiny and wide with anticipation, blinked rapidly, innocently, as if they hadn't comprehended Todd's warning.

Todd stopped chewing and blew an angry breath out his nose.

Gordon gave an encouraging nod and scooted forward in his seat. Bony elbows attached to stick-thin arms plopped down on the tabletop as his cadaverous face loomed closer. *I am serious,* his eyes said with a slow blink. *Would you like to talk about it?*

With a sigh, Todd lowered his burrito and swallowed. He stared at his oblivious roommate for a minute before giving in.

"It's chorizo. Why shouldn't I eat it?" he asked, knowing their silent exchange wouldn't end until Gordon had his say. *Don't bring up poisons,* he thought, even though he knew he was asking for a miracle. Their fights always began the same: eating meat was inhumane, Todd's vegetables weren't organic—

"Because it's filled with awful hormones, terrible GMOs, and all kind of additives you shouldn't be eating. How many times have I told you this? Do I have to go through this every day with you? Where are the organics? The lettuce? The kale? The tomatoes? Any vegetables at all, even canned like I have? You could have at least stocked up on some organic superfood shakes like I did. Just add a little water, and you've got your nutrition for the day even if they aren't the most appetizing. Of course, there are powders you can add to make them taste better. Powdered fruits for sweetness, a little broccoli to add bitterness. Seriously, you're killing yourself with the way you eat," Gordon paused and took a small sip of his shake before adding, "one disgusting bite at a time." His shaggy blond brows wiggled over his eyes as he waited expectantly.

Todd rolled his eyes and studied the burrito clasped in his hand. Gordon had skipped his whole spiel about killing animals and gone right to genetically modified vegetables. Great. They'd only have to go through half their allotted time of fighting today. There wasn't much he could say about the lack of tomatoes and lettuce, but he did have the guacamole. He smiled and took another bite. "Guacamole is a vegetable." He chewed for a second before adding an afterthought. "And I used masa for the tortilla, which is corn." His eyes tracked a piece of half-masticated tortilla as it flew from his mouth and landed on the table.

"Ugh," Gordon muttered. His face twisted in disgust, his forehead wrinkling beneath the long hairs that had fallen from their normal place covering his receding hairline.

Todd liked to call Gordon—with his bulging eyes and tall, cadaverous frame—a praying mantis dork behind his back. Now he was a praying mantis dork with a comb-over. Todd grinned.

Gordon noticed Todd's look and smoothed his hair back over his head. "First, close your mouth when you eat. That's disgusting. Second, avocado is a fruit, not a vegetable, and that concoction you call *guacamole* is filled with so many additives and preservatives it ceased being a fruit or vegetable long ago. And don't bring up masa. Masa is a highly genetically modified crop. Poison, all poison."

And there it is, Todd thought in irritation, *back to poisons*. He shook his head and watched Gordon use a straw to drink the green shake in his cup. The goo flowed up the tube in a slow, thick line toward Gordon's waiting lips, his face turning a delicate shade of pink while his eyes bulged from the exertion.

Todd took a bite of his burrito and dropped his gaze to Gordon's sports cup. The thick mixture foamed at the top like pea-soup-colored pond scum. He wrinkled his nose, making the same face Gordon had previously held. "And what are you drinking now?"

"Something of my own creation! Protein powder, wheat germ, dehydrated vegetables including kelp, kale, zucchini, broccoli, and parsley, xanthan gum to thicken it, and one lemon. Frozen lemon, of course. With the apocalypse, I can't be choosy." Gordon sat back and held out his glass. He shook it in offer and again waggled his shaggy brows. "Would you like me to make you one? You'll *love* it."

"No," Todd muttered around a mouthful of tortilla.

"Oh, come on, Todd. I'm telling you, you start drinking my shakes, and you'll become a new man. Your skin will clear up, your waist will shrink, and you'll no longer have to worry about the cruel side of humanity."

"What the hell are you talking about?"

Gordon gave a small laugh and waved his bony hand in the air. "Oh, Todd. Don't you remember me saying you reminded me of something, but I couldn't remember what? I figured it out last night, when you were busy sucking down that disgusting slop you made with the Spam. Now, excuse me for stating something I'm sure you've heard many times, but you resemble a toad: short, squat, pimply. Todd the toad, or toady Todd—I'm sure the variations you've encountered were much more creative, but my version should get the point across." Gordon swung his arms out to encompass the room. "With a *huge* dietary change, I'm sure we can have most of your problems solved within a month!"

Todd's burrito-filled hand smacked the table.

"And don't worry," Gordon continued as he reached over

and swatted Todd's hand, "I'll be behind you the whole way. Once we get your obvious problems taken care of, we'll work on those things your diet can't help." Gordon's grin spread across his face. "Like your lazy eye. I'm no doctor, but I'm sure with a little tape and focusing exercises we can fix you right up!"

Todd's eyes narrowed as he felt the vein in his neck throb. Gordon had just called him a frog. With a lazy eye. A pain raced up his jaw, and he forced himself to unclench his teeth.

He blew out a slow breath and stared at his burrito. When would Gordon's fixation on his diet end? Since he'd run out of fresh food and started drinking his smoothies, he'd become unbearable. Todd raised his head. "Why don't you sit somewhere else, Gordon? Like in the living room?"

Gordon turned to peer over his shoulder at the couches behind him. "Where? On the couch?" He turned back around and shook his head. "Todd, be serious. You know as well as I do that I don't *eat* in the living room." He leaned back and crossed his legs. "You should know this.

Sometimes I feel like you don't pay attention to me at all, Todd."

Heat flooded Todd's ears. He turned sideways to stare across the room at the entrance to their apartment. Wasn't much to look at besides a small half bath on the left of the barricaded front door. Continuing to the right, he could see the door to a small hall closet, the closed door of his bedroom, then a dark hall that led to the remaining two bedrooms. He took a bite of his burrito, chewed a moment, then suddenly swiveled his head to stare at the half bath again. His eyes narrowed slightly before he smiled. "You know, I've noticed you use the bathroom quite often. Six, seven times a day. Maybe you shouldn't drink so many smoothies. They seem to fill you with shit."

Gordon's face appeared to slide downward like wax under

a hot lightbulb. His eyebrows fell to hover over his narrowed eyes in a long line. Lips, once raised in excitement, turned down at the ends in definite displeasure. His cup hit the tabletop with a thump. "My drink has fiber in it, making me regular. There's nothing wrong with my bathroom habits." He started to take another sip, and then stopped. "And bathroom habits are not appropriate topics of conversation nor observation. I'd appreciate you dropping the subject."

Todd took a bite of his burrito and chewed for a minute. His face broke out in a grin. "I don't know if you've noticed, but the paint is peeling off the bathroom walls. I think the adhesive is dissolving because of your poop vapors. I may have to charge you for the repairs."

Gordon's pale skin flushed and his eyes narrowed.

Todd leaned back in his seat and grinned. Sparks were practically flying out of those baby blues now.

"You should talk," Gordon hissed. "Your once-a-week habit not only burns the nostrils and eyes, but it fills the house with a god-awful stench that makes me think the hounds of hell have rotted in your intestinal tract and exploded out your bum! It's not I, but you, who is causing damage with your foul, poisoned defecations!" Gordon's mouth snapped shut in a thin, almost nonexistent line.

Todd leaned forward. "Twice a week," he whispered with a conspiratorial wink, "but thanks for observing."

Gordon jumped up, knocking his chair back in his haste. He turned and walked, seemingly toward the half bath in the corner, before making an abrupt right as if he knew what Todd was thinking.

Todd laughed and turned back to his suddenly-exciting meal. He groaned. "Vegetarians don't know what they are missing," he mumbled as he chewed. His eyes rose and met the hot glare of the sun through the window. Squinting, he turned away to stare at what remained of civilization. Then he sighed. Almost four months had passed since he and Gordon last stepped outside their door. That this was to be his life, stuck in a flat with Mr. Personality until he died, was almost more than he could bear.

"Hoot, my ass," he muttered, resuming his chewing. His eyes flicked to a faded picture of him as a little boy and his mother. He studied her pale blue suit and perfectly manicured nails for a second before his brows lowered into a scowl.

Renting to Gordon had been her idea to help him pay the rent he owed her. He'd felt hopeful when she'd told him she'd found the perfect roommate for him. Then he'd met Gordon and assumed she'd made an honest mistake until he noticed her eyes sliding in his direction when Gordon had clapped his hands and exclaimed over the molding. Next had been the smile she'd hidden behind her tightly controlled lips when Gordon commented on the idiot box in the living room. He'd known then. The sly, manipulative dog.

"Todd, you need a roommate," she'd explained when he'd confronted her, "and he's the best I could find on such short notice."

Yeah, right.

She'd stood with her arms crossed before her. "Now, don't look so despondent. He'll grow on you. He's a hoot. You are six months late with rent already. I'm only doing this to help you."

Yeah, right.

Then she'd given his arm a quick squeeze. "And if you really don't like him, you can always move!"

Todd took another bite of his burrito. And there it was— the real reason she'd signed Gordon to a five-year lease. Sly mother-fucking dog. He glanced at her picture with grudging respect before flashing her a peace sign. She'd been smart, he had to admit it. A woman to be proud of.

"I'm going to show you someday, Gordon," Todd mumbled as he chewed. "I'll make you a meal you won't forget, my praying mantis pal. Maybe Spam fried in lard covered in more lard. Yummy." He turned back to the window and scanned the neighboring playground and empty street before his gaze skipped across the sunflower-yellow hatchback parked on the lawn below him. His eyes rose to study the skyline, hoping to see smoke from a chimney fire, before a nagging at the back of his skull made him look at the car again.

The car sat exactly as he remembered—at an odd angle, half on the grass, half on the sidewalk, with a cracked windshield and a front end crumpled against the concrete wall the car had attempted to run over. The driver's side door had been bent open far past what should have been possible, giving him a full view of everything inside the car, including the dead body locked under the driver's seatbelt. Todd leaned closer to the glass and narrowed his eyes.

The monster had really gone at the driver, removing most of the flesh on one leg from the calf all the way to his groin. Any remaining meat had dried to a dusky-black bark in the hot sun. Todd studied the man's skull, remembering the fearful, ravaged expression on the corpse right after he'd died, as if the man's terror hadn't been able to escape his corporal husk. The eyes had been the worst, wide and bulging over a mouth frozen in a scream. But the birds had taken care of those long ago.

Todd froze. Unease spread up his spine as he leaned closer to the window. "Where the hell are the birds?" he muttered.

He looked toward the no-longer-recognizable body of a dog that had died outside their home months ago. The murder of crows that feasted on the bones, that never let a day go by without picking at tiny scraps of flesh as if they devoured a T-bone steak and not something dank and decomposing, were gone. Dark bones and rotting flesh lay on brown grass completely devoid of scavengers.

Something had scared them away.

Todd dropped his burrito and moved to the end of the table. His eyes scanned the wall of windows that extended from his kitchen and through the living room before he began walking down them. Dead bodies, of both the human and animal kind, lay out in the open, in cars, and hanging halfway out broken windows like an all-you-can-eat scavenger's buffet.

But there were no birds.

He swiveled around and held his breath. Although he'd heard movement inside the building at the beginning of the apocalypse, he'd heard nothing in months. And now, even though he hoped to hear the same, it was different, unnatural, a warning of a predator in the midst. Todd's mouth soured, as he was sure the gazelle's did before it was attacked by the cheetah hiding in the weeds. He licked the salty sweat from his upper lip and stepped closer to a window.

"Okay, I give. What are you doing now, Todd?"

Todd wheezed out a barely contained scream and jerked around with his hand clenched against his chest. He quickly let go and swiped his arms across his face in a giant *x* before he brought his finger to his lips.

Gordon, for once, listened and shut his mouth. He crept forward until he stood over Todd. "What's going on?" he whispered, his breath blasting Todd's face.

Todd scowled and jerked his head away from the offensive air before responding. "Something's changed. The birds are gone."

Gordon stiffened and stepped back from the living room windows. He tiptoed past the half bath in the entryway to stand before the front door. With his hands pressed into the wood of the two-by-fours crisscrossing the doorframe, he peered through the peephole.

Todd chewed his nail and watched Gordon. Their apartment was one of six populating three floors, each with the same configuration as theirs. Outside their door was a long, windowed hallway that led to their neighbor's apartment at the other end. In the center of the hall was an elevator and stairwell that led down to the first floor or up to the third. If anything was coming for them, it would be through that door. The hairs along his back rose, and Todd rolled his shoulders.

Gordon turned and shook his head, but they both knew the serenity outside was deceptive. Much like the deep, dark depths of a pond where a crocodile waited in ambush, the monsters could still be waiting to make their move. Worse was knowing they didn't take hostages. They killed, they ate; they ate, they killed. There were no survivors in altercations with the black devils.

Todd backed out of the light on shaky legs while casting his eyes between the four windows in the living room. Nothing moved on the street or in the trees. No leering black face grinned from the dark cover of the forest, nothing crawled along the bricks to peek into the windows with glowing red eyes, but that didn't mean they weren't out there.

Todd's foot slid off the sloped edge of the living room carpet onto the wood of the entryway. He froze for a second before he twisted to peer down the hallway that led to the bedrooms. Daylight faded to nothing at the end of the hall, leaving the last section in utter blackness. Black monsters lived in blackness. A sense of impending doom, of the certainty that something had broken into the bedrooms, assaulted Todd.

Something thudded in the apartment above them. There

was a moment of chilling silence before Gordon's voice sliced through the tension.

"It's probably the Kimbles," Gordon whispered.

Todd swallowed and remained silent. They hadn't heard anything coming from the Kimble's apartment in over three months. No whispers or movement, definitely no thuds. If a monster had gotten into their apartment, what's to say they weren't in this one?

Todd twisted his fingers together and breathed deeply. He looked at the bathroom door, and a vision of himself settled safely in the small room popped into his head.

There was water and a toilet, but no food. His lips parted as his hand dropped down to his considerable stomach and gave it a gentle wiggle. He might be down three sizes, but he was still large. He'd read somewhere that death by starvation was a slow process. Considering his bulk, he might be able to survive a month or two. Definitely long enough to know if anything hid inside his apartment. He took a step toward the bathroom, only to be stopped by a high-pitched Gordon-esque squeal. Todd slapped his hands over his ears and glared at his roommate.

Gordon's wide eyes glanced back and forth between Todd and the bathroom door. He raised his arms into the air and said, "Are you kidding me? Your once-a-week constitutional has to happen now?"

Todd flushed and gave one last longing look at the door. "Shut up," he muttered. He crept toward the bedrooms, stopping every few feet to listen. Dark tendrils of fear crawled up his back like fingers against his spine, sending his emotions into overdrive. The certainty that something stalked the apartment grew stronger.

He paused as he reached the edge of the kitchen and the beginning of the hallway. His shaking hand reached out and grasped the edge of wall separating the kitchen from the hall.

Timidly, he pulled himself forward with his hand, not really wanting to progress further, then let out a deep breath. He yelped as something grabbed his elbow and squeezed.

"What do you think you're doing?" Todd hissed, suddenly realizing his bladder had grown heavy in his abdomen. He glanced at the bathroom door before returning his gaze to Gordon.

"Sorry. I wanted to tell you I got your back." Gordon stood behind him with a long black umbrella swung over his shoulder. A fluorescent yellow duck with giant googly-eyes stretched across its surface. "I didn't mean to scare you," he said, running his hand through his comb-over. Gordon pumped the umbrella up and down in the air and nodded encouragingly. The googly-eyes wiggled in their plastic bubbles.

Todd started to snort but stopped. A long steel spike stood out from the top of the umbrella, like a dagger. "Where'd the umbrella come from?" he whispered.

Gordon looked at him for a second, as if he couldn't understand the question, before he dropped the umbrella to his side to examine the black fabric. "It was in the closet," he said, looking back at Todd. "I don't know how it got there."

Todd chewed his lip a second before asking, "Was there another one?"

Gordon shook his head no.

Todd scratched his head before stepping into the kitchen. He pulled a frying pan off the drying rack next to the sink and hefted the weight in his hands. "Hmmm?" he said with a glance at Gordon.

Gordon smiled and nodded so hard his comb-over flopped off his scalp and hung from the left side of his head.

Now, where do we start? Todd wondered, turning back to the hall. On the left was his room with a Jack and Jill bathroom that connected the third bedroom, which was their considerable pantry. Directly across from the third room, and on the right side of the hallway, was Gordon's room.

The sound of breaking glass split the air with a sharp tinging that made his balls shrivel inside him. He jerked his pan up and let his eyes flick between the rooms. He wasn't sure where it originated from.

"I—" Gordon started.

"Shhhhhh," Todd hissed and twisted around to scan the kitchen and living room. He listened for a second before whispering, "We should have boarded up the windows when we did the door."

"I agree," Gordon answered. "I think the noise came from upstairs."

It could have, but Todd wasn't so sure.

Todd glanced into the darkness and felt his stomach twist in dread. The doorways to Gordon's room and the spare room were hidden in the shadows, completely concealed from where he stood. His eyes flicked toward the light switch for a second before he stepped away from the wall. Somehow, announcing his arrival seemed like a bad idea.

His heart thundering in his chest, he crept to his room with his frying pan held in front of him. His room remained silent, but his sense of unease persisted. Todd grasped the knob. Not sure if he should push the door open slowly or throw the whole thing open in a fast swoop, he hesitated. Todd was suddenly struck with the need to giggle, wishing he'd thought this out better.

"What are you doing now?" Gordon whispered in his ear.

Todd giggled when Gordon's breath touched the side of his face. He slapped his lips shut and turned wide, terrified eyes toward Gordon. "I don't know," he whispered.

Gordon nodded. "Okay. That's fine with me. Take your time."

Take my time? Yeah, that sounds smart. Todd leaned against the door with his shoulder and grasped the doorknob. His head bobbed with his indecision, then he turned the knob and jumped into the room with his weapon arm raised. He whipped around and scanned the tall shelves brimming with cans of processed food, smacking the side of a shelf with his pan. It wobbled, and Todd flung himself forward, using his own body to stop his precious cache from hitting the ground. The boxes slid against his chest before he shoved them back onto the shelf.

Gordon came inside and shut the door behind him. He wrinkled his nose and pushed his comb-over across his scalp. "Ugh. How can you sleep with this filth?"

Todd rolled his eyes and stepped forward. "They aren't going to bite you," he hissed.

"Not in the literal sense, Todd, but they are the proverbial wolf in sheep's clothing, which is why I could not allow your food to be in the storage room with my stuff. Just you wait—"

"Shut up, Gordon! The food in these cans might kill you slowly, but those monsters will eviscerate both of us like dead fish. Would you rather die like that?"

Todd watched Gordon's lips pucker as if he debated the merit of each option. "Are you kidding me?" When Gordon opened his mouth to respond, Todd raised his pan in warning, then waved it toward the back of the room. "Check the goddamn window, Gordon!"

Gordon's eyes widened. "No."

"Yes," Todd snapped back.

Gordon shifted from foot to foot, glancing between Todd and the curtain. When Todd waved his hand in the direction of the window, Gordon hunched over with his shoulders pressed inward and drew the umbrella against his torso until his face rested against the duck. He sucked his lips into his mouth and shook his head.

Todd sighed and moved away from the rack. He ran his hand along his stomach and tried to calm the rumbling happening within. His bowels bubbled and groaned loudly. He glanced at Gordon and wasn't surprised to see him casting disdainful glances between Todd's stomach and the food stacked on the shelves behind him.

Todd stopped walking and jerked his head back in incredulity. *Are you serious? You are worried about my diet now?*

Gordon caught his look and turned his head skyward to study the swirls in the ceiling. His arms relaxed, and he turned slightly, as if he found something interesting above the bathroom door.

Todd turned away and inched forward, his shoulders tensing the closer he got to the dark-blue curtain blocking the glass. He pulled the edge of the curtain out of the way and peered down at the common area built into the center of the square building. The courtyard looked as it always had, a sad little island of dead grass and dying trees surrounded by concrete and windows. Nothing moved. Todd let his shoulders drop, and the curtain swung closed.

The door leading to the shared bathroom stood on his right. Behind the wood, he heard the steady hum of their generator. Todd opened the door and peered into the darkness in alarm. Although no window could mean no monster, the lack of light could also hide many monsters. Todd slammed the door and stepped back into the bedroom.

"What are you doing?" Gordon whispered over his shoulder.

Todd glanced at him and shook his head. "I don't want to go in there."

"It's just a bathroom."

"Then you go in," Todd snapped.

Gordon's eyes bulged as he shook his head. "It's fine. Take your time," he said, crossing his arms over his chest.

That's just great. Todd glared once and turned back to the door. He took a deep breath, shoved the door open, and ran his hand along the wall. His hand flapped around the wallboard searching for the light switch. *No, no, no,* he thought as he shoved his arm further into the dark.

Where the hell are you? Somehow, although he'd been in this room a thousand times, he couldn't find the switch. He pulled his hand back and found the toggle. The light shot on, displaying nothing unusual.

Todd wiped his hand across his forehead and pushed the long strands of sweaty hair away from his eyes. He tiptoed past the bathtub, toilet, and small solar generator to stand with his ear pressed against the door to the third bedroom. He was still in that position when Gordon tapped his shoulder.

"What?" Todd whispered.

"How can you hear anything over the generator?" Gordon yelled. He turned and pointed at the little red engine running against the wall. His eyebrows rose in response to Todd's glare.

Todd shoved the door open and stepped into the room. Rows of metal shelves filled the large space. He glanced at the back wall, noticing nothing had disrupted the shelving units positioned by the windows, then toward the long walk-in closet in the back. With Gordon following behind him, he worked his way through the inventory labyrinth until he stood before the door that opened into the hall. He pressed his head to the door and listened for a few seconds before pulling the door open. Light from the storage room lit the once-dark hallway, displaying nothing but beige walls.

Todd stepped into the hall and faced the door to Gordon's room. He shivered, rubbing his arms where it felt as if beetles crawled under his skin. "What if we are overreacting? I don't hear anything, do you?" he asked, turning around.

"And if you think about it, I never saw anything outside, either." The self-serving part of him gained more ground, turning his gaze to his already checked, verified, and completely monster-proof room before returning his attention to his roommate. He grinned, then licked his lips nervously. It was wrong, but he'd already done his duty. It was time Gordon did his job and checked his own room.

Gordon blinked in confusion, then shook his head. "You saw something outside."

"I did not."

"Yes, you did. That's why we are searching the house armed with weapons." Gordon thrust his umbrella into the air.

Todd's eyes flicked between the duck umbrella and pan. He snorted. "Weapons? You remember when I told you we should buy a couple guns? 'Noooooo, they're dangerous,' you said. What are you going to do with your umbrella? Flap the hood at the monsters and hope they react like a bunch of geeses?"

"Hey, you wanted one." Gordon stepped back and jabbed the pointy tip at Todd, "You asked me where I got it." He took another stab and grinned when Todd flinched.

Todd lashed out with his pan. It clanged against the metal on Gordon's umbrella before returning to its spot in front of his chest. "I only asked to make you feel better. You look ridiculous."

Gordon curled his lip in a snooty snarl. "Look who's talking, you pudgy—" His eyes widened, and he suddenly seemed to be choking on his words.

"Are you okay—" Then Todd heard it—a muffled noise coming from somewhere behind him. He licked his lips and clutched his pan tighter before stepping closer to Gordon. "Gordon," he whispered, "what is it?" He didn't want to turn around. Not right now.

Gordon leaned to the side and peered behind him. His umbrella lowered to the ground. He answered with an unintelligent gurgle.

Todd's back stiffened as a shiver crept up his spine. He pulled his lower lip into his mouth and chewed on it anxiously. "It's not in your room," he belted out suddenly. "I'm sure it's outside. Why don't you check this time? I'll even give you the pan." He thrust it forward, knocking Gordon in the chest.

Gordon's eye's widened even more before a high-pitched giggle escaped him. He took off down the hall, his umbrella bouncing along the ground in time with his tiptoe prancing steps. He turned his head to peer over his shoulder at Todd, then slipped into Todd's room and shut the door.

Todd giggled nervously in response and turned to face Gordon's room. He swallowed once, squared his shoulders, and stepped forward. As he hovered on the outside, squeezing his hands around his pan's handle, he talked to himself, telling himself the noise had come from outside the building.

"There's nothing behind the door," he said, breathing deeply. *Nothing at all but a few clumps of GMO-free wheatgrass and long-limbed lima beans bouncing around the room in a sacred dance.*

He giggled again before sucking his lips into his mouth. It had happened: he was losing his mind. He held his breath for a second before letting the hot air out. *I can do this.* Todd wrapped his hand around the bronze knob. "One . . . two . . ."

Something slithered behind the door, the sound marching up his spine as if the monsters themselves stroked his back. The sound stopped for a second, leaving the hall in deathlike silence, before resuming its slow progression along the floor.

Wings, Todd thought, recalling the monster he saw climbing the outside wall a few months ago. *It can't open them, and they are dragging on the floor.* He let go of the doorknob, banging his pan against the wood in the process.

Movement inside the room intensified, and Todd's imagination took over. He saw the ebony monster rushing across the room, its knuckles thumping along the floor. Its nails scratching a path down the wood. Then something banged on the door. Something large enough to make the door quiver in its frame. Putrefaction flooded the hall in a foul cloud.

Todd stumbled back and peered over the top of his pan at the floor gap, at the dark shadow that crossed in front of the thin light before retreating and coming back. The room went quiet, and Todd held his breath. He waited, scared to stay, but terrified to move.

A long black finger slid out from under the door and ran along the floor before pulling back inside.

Todd stepped backward.

Four more fingers emerged from the crevice. Long, with more knuckles than possible, the black scales along the tops gleamed in the light as they stroked the wood. They suddenly curled and dragged their nails along the floor, their needle-sharp tips creating long spirals of golden oak in their wake. The sound of shredding floor increased as more fingers slid out of the darkness. Suddenly they grabbed the bottom of the door and yanked it back in its frame with a loud bang.

Gordon squealed from the room down the hall.

Todd sprinted to his room, a piercing shriek following him the whole way. The sound seemed to come from nowhere and everywhere all at the same time, surrounding him in a disconcerting embrace. Todd swirled to find the source, only to realize the sound came from himself. He closed his mouth, stumbled to a standstill before his bedroom, and twisted the doorknob. The door refused to budge. "Come on, Gordon!" he yelled. At Gordon's silence, he turned and raced back the way he'd come.

The monster hissed when Todd drew close, and more fingers slid out from under the door. They were a swarming pile of ebony fingers, each tipped by long, deadly nails. A few scraped, others curled, some beckoned him to come inside.

Todd tried not to think as he ran for the storage room. Tried to forget the dark scales and bright-red eyes of the monster that had feasted on the man in the yellow car months ago. Tried to forget the long dagger-like teeth that had filled its mouths. *No need to pee now*, he thought with a giggle as hot wetness slid down his leg. His legs almost buckled when a thick, cold voice floated through the air.

"I can smell youuuuuu," the monster growled as something heavy slammed into the door. The creature screamed, and the door began to shake within the frame.

"No, no, no!" Todd shrieked as he ran through the storage room and into the bathroom. He slammed the door before turning the little lock and stepping back.

"Nuh uh," Todd muttered, remembering he hadn't locked the storage-room door. He wasn't going back out there. No way, no how. He twisted the doorknob to his room, but, like on the other door, the knob refused to budge.

"Gordon. It's me. Let me in." He waited a few seconds before smacking the door lightly. "Gordon! It's me!" He turned and stared at the door behind him. *Would I hear anything if the monster made it to the spare room? Do its fingers have the dexterity to turn the knob?*

The blood drained from his face as he pictured the many knuckled claws reaching under the door. He raised the pan in his hands and turned to his bedroom. "I'm going to bust the door down, Gordon. Let me in!" He heard Gordon shift behind the door.

"How do I know it's you?" Gordon's squeaky voice asked.

"Who the hell could I be, Gordon? Let me in before I

shove every bit of canned meat down your green-loving throat!"

The lock clicked softly, and the door opened. Gordon backed up as Todd bolted inside. He locked the door and turned around.

"Are they in the apartment?" Gordon stood before him, wringing his hands together nervously.

Todd nodded and stared at the bedroom door leading to the hall. A shadow moved across the space beneath it. He sucked in a strangled breath and raced to the shelves. Grabbing boxes of canned goods, he made a wall, stacking them hazardously one on top of another. Gordon caught on and began stacking cases against the bathroom door. Neither spoke or acknowledged each other as they worked. Ten minutes later, the doors were fortified, and both men stood together, flicking their eyes between the two barricades.

"You should change," Gordon whispered from behind Todd. "I think you urinated."

Todd glanced at him before looking down at his pants. "I did," he whispered. "That thing spoke to me." His eyes narrowed, and he waited for Gordon's taunting response.

Gordon pursed his lips, then nodded. "Yep, monsters. I'm not surprised. Probably polyglots—all of them. Glad you didn't die."

Todd stared at his roommate in surprise before he shook his head and walked to his dresser. Once he was done changing, he sat on the edge of the bed with Gordon. Hours passed in silence.

"We should move the cans into the bathroom so we have a toilet. I've got to pee," Gordon said, breaking the silence.

"I'm not going in there."

"I don't have to go," Gordon responded. He crossed his legs and squeezed them together as he stared at the door leading to the hall.

Todd suddenly sighed. He hadn't finished his burrito and was hungry. He couldn't seem to get the thought of chorizo out of his mind. Unfortunately, he couldn't make another one without visiting the kitchen. It had been his last one ever. His eyes moved from the door to the cans surrounding them.

After a few minutes, Todd got up and strode to the boxes still on the shelves and pulled a can from each. He studied them a second before raising his head. His smile spread as he caught Gordon's suspicious eyes. *Payback*, he thought.

"Vienna sausage or Spam? What's your poison, Gordon?"

Gordon's nose wrinkled for a second before his face relaxed and his shoulders slumped. "Spam," he whispered with a loud sigh. "Maybe we'll poison the monsters when they eat us."

DORIS AND ERVIN

MURDER SWEETENS THE BLOOD AND STRENGTHENS THE LOVE

THE CAVE

"Doris, I think they're back." The small black demon shifted positions in the narrow entrance to their cave, the ebony claws on his hands dragging down well-formed grooves etched into the rock. He leaned forward and drew in a deep breath of the cold, earthy scent of their home. The large bat-like wings on his back twitched before flattening along his spine. "Yes, I can smell them. It's faint, but I know it's them."

His crimson-skinned wife gave a noncommittal grunt from where she sat against the wall. Her dark black hair hid her face when he glanced her way, but he could tell she wasn't really listening. He leaned further into the dark and breathed in again. "Yes!" he yelled, tilting his head to watch her out of the corner of his eye, "I smell them!"

Doris tossed a chopped mushroom into a bowl before grabbing another. "What is that, Ervin? You smell? I don't think you smell. But it has been awhile since you had a bath."

Ervin swiveled his head in her direction and scowled. His

wings flared in agitation before settling back into place. "I didn't say I smell, Doris. The humans. They smell."

"Oh. Well, of course they do, dear. They are animals. Filthy creatures who slather their bodies with disgusting, unnatural scents. Think they'd know with all their fancy buildings and technology how much easier that makes them to hunt."

"They don't know they are making it easier because they don't know they are hunted, Doris." Ervin sighed and turned back around. "You've never understood them, dear, but I forgive you. It's enough that you live the lifestyle for me."

He smiled suddenly and turned away from the doorway to shuffle forward into the light of their fire. "I can't believe they are back. It's been so long. I'd assumed they'd given up exploring this area. I'm glad they haven't. There's more than one, you know."

The sound of the knife striking the cutting board paused as Doris's head rose from where she'd been hunched over her bowl. Her nostrils flared before she resumed her preparations. "How many are there?" she whispered, her voice thick with want.

"Oh, not many, but more than one, I'm sure of it." Firelight flickered across his ebony form as he stretched his arms above his head and sat on a long rock. He went to work at his teeth with a long black claw before peering curiously at what he found. "It's been ages since I've actually seen a human," he said, flicking the food to the floor, "which is probably for the best. I find their fragrance distracting enough. A visual might make my urges impossible to ignore, and we wouldn't want that."

His stomach chose that moment to fill the cave with an angry rumble. His forehead crumpled, and he wrapped his arms around his waist. "Are those mushrooms almost done? I'm a tad hungry." He looked away from her bowl to her face.

"Or should I hunt something up? Remind you of how demonly I can be?" he said with a waggle of his eyebrows and a flex of his spindly arms.

Doris laughed softly from where she sat.

"With your stealth," she teased, nodding toward his rumbling stomach, "I think the cave critters are safe. I'm not sure you'd be able to catch a fish trapped in a pool, must less a human."

Ervin snorted and waved his hand in the air. "I'm out of practice, Doris, but these old bones haven't forgotten what they were designed to do. I've just chosen to underutilize my unique skills." He waggled his eyebrows at her suggestively.

She laughed, and silence descended on the room.

Ervin stretched his fingers a couple times before stuffing one in each ear. His face relaxed into a mask of pleasure as he scratched and dug at earwax.

Doris glanced at him before speaking. "Maybe," she said, "a tiny cheat wouldn't be so bad. You'd feel so much better with something more substantial than mushroom soup—"

"Doris!" Ervin rolled his eyes while his fingers continued exploring his ear canals. "Have you forgotten why I'm here?"

Light flashed on the cave walls off the knife Doris suddenly waved in the air. "Of course not! I'm not saying we should kill them. Just cut off an arm. Or . . . or . . . something smaller. A finger. Maybe two. Just enough to round out the broth. They won't miss them. They have ten, you know."

"Of course I know they have ten. What do you think I've been doing for the last hundred years?" Ervin shook his head and wagged a finger at her. "We mustn't ignore our ideals, Doris, or what kind of naturalist would we become? Nothing but liars!" he said, slapping his hand on his thigh. "I get enough flak from my family as it is. Every letter they send implies we cheat. Last month's letter from my brother made me so mad I almost attacked the courier while he waited for me to write back! Wouldn't that have been a problem? Who knows how much the next demon would charge to deliver our mail if they knew we killed the previous one." Ervin kicked at a small rock and watched it roll across the floor. "No, as tempting as they are, we should leave the humans alone. We've survived this long on our principles; I'm sure we can last the few hours it takes them to wander the tunnels."

He sighed softly as a dreamy look came over his face. "I do wish I could watch them explore the cave-in that bumbling way of theirs, but I find their scent too seductive in my old age and don't trust myself to get close. My interest in their behavior and habitat is not enough to keep me away. It's been so long since I've savored their flesh . . ." His voice faded away as he got lost in thought. The grumble of his stomach brought him back, and he patted it appreciatively. "See? My body knows what it wants. Let me cut even one, and I don't think I could stop myself from killing the bunch. It's safer if I stay in here."

Doris gave a soft chuckle and returned to preparing dinner. "I give, my love. Just tell me, how do you expect to keep them away? Eventually they will find the entrance to our little home. What then? Can we eat them then?"

Her husband pursed his lips in thought. "Of course not. We'll have to move." He sighed. "I've tried what I know. Obviously, the line of dung I left at the topside entrance didn't work. I guess I'll try making them more smelly.

"Didn't think that would ever be necessary," he muttered as if to himself.

Doris laughed and dropped her mushroom knife on a stone shelf. She picked up the bowl and moved to the small pot of water boiling next to the fire. Squatting, she stirred the soup before turning her onyx eyes toward her husband. Life normally gleamed in their depths, sparkling like dark shards of diamonds in the firelight, but her eyes seemed dull in her worry-filled face.

Her husband had grown thin to the point of emaciation during their time with the humans. Bones jutted out from his hips and chest in sharp points while his once-muscular arms and legs were little more than sticks. The high cheekbones and brow ridge she'd once found so attractive had become painful to look at. His ears, not overly large, appeared gigantic on his starving frame.

Doris tapped her spoon on the edge of the pot and let familiar questions fill her mind. Questions she was unable to brush away, not while staring at a demon who was but a sliver of what he'd once been.

Whatever possessed him to attempt this lifestyle? Why'd he given up his home, his comfort, his health for no return? Why didn't they just visit the human side like normal demons on vacation? The answers still eluded her even after all this time. He'd come no closer to explaining his reasons yesterday than a century ago when they'd planned their move to this place.

She wiped a tear from her eye and sighed. And why did she stay? She could always go home; she still had over a century of life left. Could find another mate, settle down somewhere warm and above ground. Have little ones to love. Her eyes flicked to Ervin, and her shoulders fell. But she wouldn't have him.

"You should clean up, hon," she said, standing. "DETH will be here soon. I've decided to make something special for our guests. I'm going to forage for some of those crumbly spores you enjoy so much."

Her husband grinned at her, his white teeth suddenly obscene in his shrinking face. "Can you believe this is happening, Doris? My life work—coming to fruition. Finally. Do you like their name? DETH: Demons for the Ethical

Treatment of Humans." He sighed and stood, dragging his hand across his gleaming head and the two short horns protruding from his skull. "I think I'll bathe. Maybe shine my horns." He smiled at Doris and gave a suggestive thrust of his hips. "I may want to celebrate tonight, if you are willing."

"It's been awhile," Doris said with a snort. She stepped closer to him and slid her substantially larger body against his in a hug—her scarlet against his ebony. Her heat against his chill. Different breeds from opposite ends of Hell. She'd loved the contrasts when he'd sauntered up to her in that bar so long ago. So bold and confident she'd want him. So brazen. So secure in thinking his diminutive size wouldn't be a hindrance against his competition. He'd fought so boldly against her other suitors. And she'd been impressed.

Ervin nipped gently at her neck.

She hissed at the sting and snuggled closer, momentarily forgetting where she'd been going before the sharp feel of his bony breastbone against her ribs brought her back to reality. She drew a sharp nail down his arm and watched his skin shiver under the onslaught. "I'm willing. Once your guests leave, we'll have some fun, my bony little demon."

Ervin laughed and drew away. "Enjoy searching for your morsels," he called after her.

Doris gave a quick wave and left the room for the inky darkness of the cave system. The air grew cooler the further she moved away from her home, and she shivered before settling down to all fours.

Thirty feet from their den, the tunnel disappeared into the darkness of a large dome cavern. The earth fell away, leaving her with the option to climb up higher or crawl down to the cave floor. Reaching the vast expanse, Doris used her claws to move up to one of the many connecting tunnels leading to the outside. She circled the opening, sniffing and listening, before crawling inside to hang from the ceiling. She stayed there for a minute before dropping to the floor.

She stood in a crouch, her shoulders bowed in and knees bent, and tilted her head toward the far end of the tunnel. Light, if there'd been any this far down the cave, would have reflected off the armor-hard red skin covering her muscular frame and off the short, sharp spines flowing down her back and ending at the tip of her long, thin tail. She smiled wickedly, her large breasts rising as she took in a deep breath and extended the long claws that capped each finger. She swayed as her tail flicked back and forth, slowly agitating the still air in warning.

Doris couldn't smell the humans like her husband, but she could hear their movements in the tunnel ahead. Like a beacon beckoning her forward, the sounds called to her, tempting her to give in to her base desires. She often wished for the hunt and dreamed of the catch and subsequent slaughter while relaxing at home. With prey so close, she allowed herself to become lost in her tortuous thoughts for a few minutes before reality settled against her like a heavy, wet blanket. Her tail dropped, and she retracted her claws. As willing as she was, she couldn't do it. *Ervin would know*, she thought as she dropped to all fours and continued forward.

Voices rose and echoed through the tunnel as it narrowed to a four-foot diameter. She crawled to a large rock partially blocking the passage and peered over the top into a small cave created by three converging tunnels.

Her nostrils flared. Ervin was right. The humans that stood facing each other smelled delectable. With three of them in such a confined space, there was no way he'd have been able to control himself. As it was, she fought her urge to jump over the rock and eviscerate them all. Doris forced herself to focus on the woman speaking.

"Look," she said while directing everyone's gaze to a map

illuminated by her headlamp, "if we continue in this direction, we'll have to descend almost forty feet to the cave floor. I doubt Ferguson and Beatnik would have attempted a rappel with such a young novice."

"No shit, Jane," one of the men beside her muttered before shaking his head. The raspy sound of him scratching the stubble on his chin filled the cavern. "How the fuck are we sure we haven't passed them already? In this darkness, we could be standing beside them and not even notice. Maybe we should return to their logged path and check it again, Mitch."

"It's been done, Jerry," the man said from beside him. He shifted slightly. "Twice this week."

At Jerry's scowl, Jane stepped forward. "And we'd have seen them, Jerry. Our headlamps are giving off more than enough light to see their bodies—" Jane's eyes widened, and her hand flew to cover her mouth. "I'm sorry—"

"Damn it, Jane," Jerry answered.

"I didn't mean to say that," she whispered, touching his arm. "I don't think we'd have missed them though. I just—I think you're tired, Jerry, and getting a little agitated. Maybe you should head back to the hotel and rest. Twelve searches in twelve days is exhausting work. Mitch and I can handle the rest of the search on our own."

Mitch nodded in agreement while Jerry's jaw clenched. "He's my friend, Jane, and I don't give a shit about how tired—"

Doris stopped listening and turned her eyes to the second man. He was tall, bulkier than most of the cavers she'd seen, with dark hair that curled around his ears and the slightest hint of stubble on his chin. Tasty flesh bulged slightly on his stomach and around his neck. Juicy. Fatty. She licked her lips and leaned forward.

The man stayed relaxed and calm, even as Jerry's voice

rose. He replied, his deep voice entering the conversation but never rising above a low timber.

She liked the way he shifted and responded within the group as the conversation continued. There was strength in his bearing, cunning in the way he tipped his head and watched before speaking. He was the alpha. Instinct had her leaning forward as hormones flooded her veins, sending heat through her in a powerful surge. He was the one she wanted. Her claws involuntarily clenched against the rock and sent pebbles scattering onto the floor.

The man's head swung her way.

Doris sank down behind the rock as light illuminated her tunnel.

"Did you hear that?" the woman asked.

"Yes," Mitch said in a low voice.

The small chamber became silent. Doris heard their heart rates increasing as an intoxicating tinge of fear scented the air. She swallowed the drool filling her mouth and forced her tail to remain still. Seconds passed before Mitch spoke.

"Well," he said, "it's not a cave-in."

"Could the noise have been Ferguson?"

"Jane," Jerry grumbled, "don't be silly. A small tremor, animals—anything could have made those rocks fall. If it were John, or Beatnik, we'd hear more than just a few pebbles falling."

The light vanished as Mitch turned away. "Out of curiosity, did either of you research this cave before we came? Not the maps, but logged visits, missing reports?"

Doris peered over the rock at the humans again and watched Jane and Jerry shake their heads.

"This cave system," he continued, "is immense. There are portions that have never been touched, never explored. Pristine rock that's never been seen—"

"We don't need a fucking geology lesson, Mitch," Jerry grumbled.

"Hear me out, Jerry." He reached into a little bag strapped to his chest and pulled out a folded piece of paper. Flipping it open, he moved it into the light. "It's rather famous, actually. People from all over the world come here to see the striations and rock formations. And the injuries-to-activity ratio has been acceptable, fairly normal—until the last few decades.

"In the last thirty years, seventeen climbers have disappeared. Ten of those disappearances have occurred in the last three years. Ten. And they've never been found. Cavers report weird noises, seeing strange things moving in the dark, and feelings of being watched."

The three studied the paper in silence for a minute before Jane spoke in a hurried whisper. "Missing people are not uncommon, Mitch. People fall, get wedged into crevices. Inexperience leads to mistakes, and after that book came out, all kinds of weekend hikers think they can cave with the rest of us—"

"Jane —"

"And," she continued, her voice rising to normal volume, "there was that earthquake a few years ago. Maybe a shaft has opened up that we don't have mapped, and people are falling into it."

Mitch crossed his arms and seemed to ponder her idea before he shook his head. "No, that still doesn't explain why no evidence has ever been found. If these were inexperienced hikers—and they aren't, just look at the names on my list—they'd have left something for us to find. Something that shows they'd been here."

"Oh please. What are you trying to say, Mitch?" Jerry, who'd wandered back a few steps down the other tunnel, turned to face him, reaching up to twist his headlamp downward as he did so. His fists balled at his side as he stomped forward. "You trying to scare us?"

"No," he answered, "of course not. I'm saying there's something strange going on here. It's unusual for so many cavers to go missing without a trace. No helmets, cams, lines, or harnesses are ever found. Much less bodies. It's not normal to find no evidence at all. Where are the bolt anchors? Ropes? Anything that would indicate where the hikers had gone? If we had some of those, we could track people, but there's nothing."

Jane wrapped her arms around her chest and glanced around, her headlamp flashing light across the gray stone surrounding them. "To be honest," she whispered, "I've heard things. If it wasn't for Ferguson gone missing, I wouldn't be here."

"Jane," Jerry snapped. "What the hell are you talking about? This is no different than that kid who went off trail in the park last summer."

"It sure is. We knew going into it that we'd probably find the boy." She swallowed and chewed her lip. "Everyone knows," she whispered, "we probably won't find Ferguson."

"Oh, Jesus Christ." Jerry suddenly stepped toward Mitch and flung his hand in the air. "Was this your point, Mitch? To fuck with our brains while we search for my fucking friend?"

Doris licked her lips before drawing her tongue over her long teeth. Aggression scented the air, sending curls of excitement through her torso and into her primitive glands. Drool filled her mouth and dripped out the edge of her mouth. She needed this. Wanted it. Missed causing harm and carnage. Watching the two men study each other under the dim light of their headlamps was the next-best thing.

Mitch stood silently staring down at the littler man—doing nothing. *Hit him*, Doris thought. *Hit him hard*. She sucked back the drool hanging from her lip and swallowed.

Humans were an odd bunch. In Hell, a fight would be over and done with in the time it took for these people to size each other up. What was the point? Someone would die. Someone would live. Get it over with. It was the reason she and Ervin never fought. Why take the chance one would have to kill the other? No, they found other ways to work out their problems besides fighting.

She leaned forward excitedly when Mitch opened his mouth. "Do it," she hissed so softly no one heard. One word and the smaller one would be pushed over the edge—fists would fly. Blood would boil. Her eyes shifted to Jane when the small woman moved.

Jane reached out and gently touched Mitch's arm before letting her hand drop to her side. Their eyes met, and Mitch closed his mouth.

Doris growled to herself as Mitch folded the paper and placed it back in his bag.

"Nope," he said, setting his hands on his hips. "Forget I brought it up. I just find it mighty peculiar." He nodded his head toward the tunnel in front of them. "Let's keep going. We know this path will eventually lead to the cavern. I think Jane's correct and they wouldn't have descended, but we can check the walls for cams or any indication they came this way. If we don't find anything, I say we turn back and try one of the other tubes. We'll search each one connected to the north entrance. Descending will be our last resort."

As Jerry's shoulders lost tension, Doris's excitement fell. She scowled and sank to the ground. There wasn't going to be any blood. Or even words. Mitch had squashed those dreams.

Why am I surprised, she thought as she ran a hand over her face. Lately, she'd been thinking a lot about disappointment. How it had followed her to this foreign world and didn't seem to be leaving anytime soon. When she'd agreed to move to this dank cave, she hadn't realized they'd spend the rest of their lives here. Why would she have? Ervin was always on some crusade or another, and they never lasted long.

Closing the slavery corporation on Fire Crest Road had taken six months. Six months to disband a successful company and free three hundred slaves. There'd been banners, balloons, and parades when the iron doors had opened and the slaves had marched their way to freedom. They'd carried her Ervin on their shoulders like a hero, not quite understanding what they were doing, but excited by the cheers surrounding them.

She and Ervin had moved soon after.

Doris flicked a rock away from herself. She had to admit, their quick move wasn't by choice. They'd essentially fled for their lives from the angry horde.

How was Ervin supposed to know slave demons had the intelligence of dung beetles? They'd wandered the streets like the reanimated dead. No will to survive, no will to die—just walk, walk, walk until heat exhaustion had dropped them where they stood. Not once had the slaves asked for help.

Ervin's success became an odorous disease-producing path of decomposing corpses. No one had been happy. They'd been lucky to get out alive.

And then, she thought with a chuckle, *there'd been the fight to save the mammoth tooth butterflies on Blood Creek Ridge*. Took two weeks and one of the buggers chasing Ervin down the hill, with his Save the Butterflies banner snapping in the wind behind him, before he'd abandoned his endeavor. She'd never forget the "I was wrong!" he'd screamed as he'd run. Doris chuckled again. It ended up there was a valid reason for the planned extermination of the blood-sucking butterflies.

Maybe she should be happy nothing egregious had occurred here.

But then again, if something did, they could go home.

Doris stood and walked through the cavern where the humans had been. She took a deep breath, relishing the lingering odor of the humans, before leaving the area through the tunnel on the right. After twenty feet, she returned to all fours and continued through the narrowing passage. She moved with the twists and turns, taking auxiliary tunnels down and to the side, tunnels she was sure the humans didn't know existed, until she pulled herself over a narrow ledge into a hidden cave.

She slid into the soft dirt and stood. Here, in this dark place, she could make out shapes and shadows but nothing else. She couldn't see clearly in the dark like her husband, which wasn't surprising. She should have been living on the crimson stretches of scorched dirt in Hell, along the Bandol Peninsula, bordered by lakes and rivers of burning lava, where the sun only set for two hours a night. Bright light and heat were what she craved. Not the cold and darkness that existed deep within the earth. For this reason, she kept candles made of fat, as well as carbon steel fire strikers in holes throughout the cave system. Doris removed a set and dragged the metal along the walls until sparks flew. The candle she held beneath the steel flared to life.

Doris kicked a stray hardhat out of the way and let the glow lead her deeper into the cavern. The further she walked, the more often the light reflected off dusty old helmets, bright safety patches sewn into ripped clothing, and mounds of climbing gear stacked along the walls.

Doris shoved a teetering stack of gear to the floor. Soon she wouldn't have room to move, much less room to store more gear.

Doris stopped before a large stone blocking the tunnel and stretched upward to where a small space existed between the ceiling and the boulder. Using her claws, she dragged herself into the opening and exhaled everything from her lungs. She shimmied through the tight channel without breathing, pushing the candle ahead of her. A few moments later, her fingers found the edge, and she was able to drag herself out.

Shadows created by the candle flickered along the rock walls and narrow stream running through the cave. Doris sniffed the air as she headed toward a large boulder she'd chiseled into a level platform. She loved the sulfuric tang that mixed with the icy scent of the stream and the pungent bouquet of ripe fungus and rotting flesh that hung over everything. Together, they reminded her of home. All except for the cold. That was one trait she could do without.

Doris grabbed a bowl she'd created by grinding out the inside of a rock and headed to the water rushing alongside the far wall. Dark, it glittered under the glow of the candle. There was something ominous about the flowing blackness, the way it slid like a snake under the rocks at the end. And she used to be scared of its dark intent. But she'd swam it enough to know there was nothing scary in its depths. Nothing but more cold.

She slipped her toe into the frigid water before drawing it back. She hated the cold. The way it rose up her skin in icy tendrils, painful in its progress. But her mother's words stopped her from running away: one did what one must to survive. This task was necessary if she wanted to keep her precious Ervin alive. Taking a deep breath, she stepped into the flowing mass and let the current carry her the three feet to the opposing wall. She grasped at the rocks and pulled herself up.

Doris shivered and made her way to a rocky area covered in algae. Among the green slime were nestled small, red balloon-like fungus that clung together as if one organism. Using her claws, she ripped them from the rocks, making sure to leave a few from each colony to encourage more growth in the coming months. Once done, she slid back into the water and let herself drift to a shallow area of the stream.

Water slid down her skin and puddled in her steps across the cave floor. Her body shook, and her tail lashed angrily in the air. *I hate it here*, she thought suddenly. She hated the cold. The dark. The wet. Her eyes flicked to her bowl when she grabbed the candle. She hated the fungus.

Once DETH promoted her and Ervin's successful lifestyle, there was no telling how many demons would follow them to this place. And then Ervin would never leave. Would never want to go home and eat the flesh of the weak. And he'd die. Maybe not soon, but eventually his self-imposed starvation would kill him. Only her deceit kept him alive now.

Unless . . .

Could she do what she was thinking to the demon she loved? Destroy his belief system, cast him as a failure, to save his life?

Doris chewed her lip and made her way across the room to a shadow along the wall. Veiled in darkness, the opening to the adjacent cavern was hidden unless you accidentally walked into it. She'd found it in just that way while exploring.

The cold dampened the scent emerging from its recesses. Even so, she knew what lay inside, and breathed deeply to receive more of the intoxicating scent of decaying flesh. With her long tongue, she licked her lips.

This place would make her husband angry. Remind him of what he couldn't have, couldn't do. He thought it evil to kill humans. As the lesser species, they weren't equipped to fight demons, which made them an immoral kill. But he'd happily kill weaker demons. She'd never understood his logic. Especially how killing humans doomed her soul.

She didn't believe in the gods like he did. Didn't believe

she had a soul. But he did, and he desperately wanted her to travel with him to Hal'mal, the place of the gods. But she didn't believe, no matter how often he explained it.

Doris passed through the entrance and set her candle on a small ledge she'd carved in the wall. She walked down the length of hanging carcasses to the back of the cave. *This one*, she thought as she ran her hand down the mottled flesh, *had been a fighter*. He'd clung to the cave walls longer than the others, desperately waving his weapon at her, as if he had a chance. His strength would nourish Ervin best.

Using her longest claw, she sliced paper-thin pieces of flesh off the dead man and let them fall into the bowl of bulbous fungus until she had a small stack of fragrant morsels. She hummed a child's lullaby to herself and made her way back to the main chamber.

I could do it, she thought as she spread the meat on the level stone. She picked up a cleaver and began dicing the slices into tiny pieces. Put just a tad too much meat into the fungus. Just enough for DETH to realize her husband lied.

And how much was too much? *This much*, she wondered, pushing the food into a small pile. *Or maybe a little less*. Doris slid her fingers into the slimy pile and brought them to her nose. She breathed in their fragrance before slipping them into her mouth.

Still savoring the taste, Doris used her knife to scrape the meat to one side. She dumped the orange fungus onto the spot where the meat had been pulverized and began dicing the large pile. Once the right size, she slid the mushrooms into a pouch she had tied around her waist. The meat went into a hidden inner pocket in the same pouch. There was no need to be caught with the meat if her husband fancied a look at the fresh morsels. Occasionally she'd had the nagging feeling he knew what she'd been up to. That he'd learned of all the bodies, had scented the kills upon her skin. But so far, he'd said nothing. Not even when he'd asked to have a fresh piece of fungus, and the pungent scent still clung to its surface.

Still, she wondered.

Doris heard them long before she entered the tunnel to her home. Their unknown voices mingling with her Ervin's familiar tone. One guttural and deep, another high and whiny, echoing in the cold cavern. She paused, still clinging to the cave wall, and took a calming breath. Would she do it? Could she do it?

She didn't know. Doris dropped to the floor of their tunnel and rose to a stand. She reached down and caressed the pouch around her hip. Would he hate her if it happened? Let her remain in his life?

Every step toward their cave had her vacillating between yes and no. Each answer revealing personal questions she hadn't considered. Ervin might forgive her for her indiscretion, believe her betrayal an accident. But would she then be able to live with herself? And if he didn't forgive her, and she was cast aside, could she survive without him? All alone?

Unable to answer these questions, she chose to let what happened happen. If her hand made its way to the secret pouch, then it was meant to be. If not, well, she still had her Ervin until he wasted away to nothing.

Doris stopped outside their cave and prepared herself for meeting the new demons by rolling her shoulders back and stiffening her spine. Weakness among demons was asking for domination. Not something she'd willingly give.

Her steps echoed hollowly in the room as conversations stopped and eyes stared at her from the sitting area.

"There you are, my dear," Ervin said as he shuffled toward

her. "Our friends, Allocias, Andros, and Vendriss have arrived." He reached down and took her hands between his, patting them softly. "Put your pouch down, get cleaned up, and I'll introduce you."

Doris nodded before making her way to the trickling stream on the far wall. She removed her bag and slid her hands into the cold water pooling at her feet. As she washed off the dirt and grime, she listened to the conversation happening behind her. To the voices mixing with her husband's, flowing and interacting, revolving around humans and the human world. How nice it was to hear demon voices. To hear something from home. The conversation was almost enough to sway her into believing she was where she should be. Almost.

The others paused their discussion as she approached. She smiled brightly and slid to a stop beside her husband.

"This is Doris," Ervin said as a way of introduction. His chest swelled as he slid his arm around her waist and pulled her in tight.

She smiled and nodded to each of their guests. "Welcome to our home."

"You've been on quite the adventure, Doris. Traveling through the seven ascensions to get to this realm, living with humans in an environment so contrary to the Bandol Peninsula. You must have a tale or two to tell."

Doris studied the short, green-scaled demon who'd spoken. He reminded her of a gargoyle with his large nose, bumpy toad-like skin, and large yellow eyes. Not something to fear unless asleep, nightmare demons, nevertheless, made her skin crawl. She resisted her urge to back up and plastered a smile on her face. "Storytelling is not my thing," she responded, unsure whom she spoke to, and unwilling to ask, "but my husband has many tales to tell."

"Many to tell, indeed," Ervin said with a wave of his hand.

"But none would have been possible without you by my side. You are the reason I still live." He kissed her gently on her cheek. "Why don't you finish dinner while I begin the interview?"

"Okay." Doris went back for her pouch and made her way to the pot of boiling water and mushrooms. She tasted the broth, adding salt and herbs to the water before raising her eyes to her husband. She watched as she stirred and reached into her pouch.

Like an electrical storm, her Ervin was alive and filling the air with unbridled energy. His arms moved like lightning as words exploded out of him in quick and descriptive prose. His voice danced, rising and lowering in crashing waves while he painted pictures of what he'd seen and learned. Happiness, pride, and wonder exploded out of him, bringing him to life. The two nightmare demons listened raptly, their faces beaming, hands twisting together, excitement filling their eyes. The dark shadow of the third demon paced silently behind them. Doris studied the outline of his large frame before looking down at the soup.

Would she do it? Could she? Again, Doris questioned her motives and considered the repercussions. She chewed her lip for a moment, then sighed. There was only one answer that made sense. Her fingers rubbed the human flesh between them, sliding against each other with silky smoothness, before slipping out of the secret pocket and into the pouch of fungus to draw them out.

"What," a silky voice hissed from behind her, "do you have there?"

Doris jumped. There was danger in that voice—in its tone, its intent. She could feel it burn its way inside her with those five little words. *Run*, her instincts ordered, and she reacted without thinking.

Her heart pounding, Doris rushed to the other end of the

fire and turned in a defensive crouch. She stared at the mysterious demon from where she stood. At the large, spiraling horns atop his head and the glimmering diamond-like sparkles that swirled across his ebony skin. He was skinny but imposing with cords of sinew and muscles flexing with every movement he made. Piercing deep-red eyes met her own as the cloven-hooved male moved closer. His nostrils flared.

"What," Vendriss whispered, "is that smell?"

Doris swallowed and pulled her hand from the pouch. She held it up, opening her fist to show the diced orange fungus. "Plants," she said, hating the way her voice trembled, "for the soup."

The red eyes narrowed as the demon stepped toward her. Doris involuntarily retreated. She stopped when her back pressed into the rock wall. "Just mushrooms." Her head twisted up to keep eye contact with the approaching demon. "Nothing more." Menace swirled around her, the emotion cold and sharp, tangy against her tongue.

Fear twisted in her gut, forced her to cringe even as her claws extended and adrenaline filled her. Conversations disappeared, and nothing existed except the tall, dangerous demon before her.

His hand reached out and wrapped around her fist. He pulled her toward him and up while he lowered his head to sniff her hand. His horns, so long and sharp, slid by her face and she flinched.

"Lies," Vendriss whispered. He drew in another lungful of air before reaching out a long black tongue and running it along her fingertips.

Doris shuddered and tried to draw back, but she couldn't pull her fist from his hand.

"Putrefaction. Death. I know the scents of the dead and hunted."

"No," Doris said, pulling more urgently against his hand, "The mushrooms are unique to here. I find them in the cave. They smell like death, but they are not.

"I swear," she whispered, her eyes frantically looking around, suddenly noticing the silence was real, not just in her head. The two nightmare demons stood across the room, not moving, just watching. Huddled together in the darkness in rapt attention. She flicked her eyes right and saw her Ervin creeping toward her, his wings relaxed, his eyes gleaming. Observing. Evaluating.

She swallowed.

Hunting.

She'd been wrong to bring the human flesh here. He meant to protect her, and he would die. He was too weak to defend her now—nothing like the courageous young demon who'd fought her suitors when they'd been young. His death would be her fault.

"I swear," she begged, peering imploringly into the demon's eyes. "He's done nothing wrong. He's a believer. He had no part in this."

The demon smiled, displaying the long, sharp gleaming teeth within his mouth. "You lie," he hissed leaning closer, his hot breath stroking her face. "I can smell death on you—scenting you like perfume. He would have known.

"You've brought me here on false pretenses. Forced me to travel when travel was not needed. Forced me to endure the company of those blathering idiots for no reason."

He leaned closer, and she sensed the hunter within him. She knew it had awakened and wanted satisfaction just as hers had wanted Mitch to hit Jerry. The difference being there'd be no Jane patting Vendriss's arm to calm him down.

Doris dropped the mushrooms and slashed out with her free hand.

Pain exploded in her neck as she was suddenly hoisted

into the air and pressed into the back wall. She couldn't breathe. Not with the hand wrapped around her throat and squeezing. Doris clawed and scratched, trying everything she could to get away, but the world continued to darken as the hand squeezed tighter. She pulled her legs up and tried to release her tail from behind her. It quivered, smacking ineffectually against the stones with her own body acting as a trap. Through the fog consuming her mind, and the sound of her blood rushing in her ears, came a blood-curdling scream.

The hand fell away, and Doris dropped to the rocks. Air burned its way down her throat and into her lungs. Her mind cleared, and her first thought sent fear through her heart.

Ervin.

She pulled herself up and twisted around. Her husband fought Vendriss in the corner of the room, stabbing at the demon with his silver knives. Doris watched him jab and twirl away with his wings wrapped around himself in a protective shield. Vendriss screamed and slashed with his claws. They ripped at Ervin's rotating body, and crimson slashes appeared in her lover's flesh.

Doris struggled to stand up. She held the wall and sucked in lungfuls of air to combat her wavering vision. The darkness and pounding in her head eased with each breath. Across the way, she could see the nightmares watching from the sidelines. She turned back to the fight and stepped away from the wall.

A war cry exploded out of Ervin, and his knives flashed. The dance continued with Vendriss and Ervin alternating moves. Back and forth they went, moving around the room in a fast rotation. Neither making substantial progress toward the death of the other, until Vendriss threw himself forward with his head lowered. He missed his mark and aimed again, stomping his foot once before attacking.

Ervin flew up, his wings opening in a majestic fan, before

he somersaulted and landed behind the giant beast. He sliced his knives across Vendriss's back, filleting the flesh in cross-sections. Blood spurt in all directions, coating the floor beneath the demon as his back arched and his arms flung wide. Then Vendriss bellowed. Ervin jumped forward, stabbing repeatedly into Vendriss's sides.

Doris ran toward the fight. At the last second, she dived to the ground and slid across the floor to get below his waving arms. Her tail, poised behind her as she slid, rose up like a striking cobra and sliced across his abdomen. Doris twisted to her knees and came to a stop once she'd passed him—in time to see his intestines drop to the ground.

Ervin reached up and grabbed Vendriss's magnificent horns from behind, pulling his head back before slashing his throat. Then he released the demon and stepped backward.

Vendriss gurgled and stumbled forward a couple steps. He swayed and slowly fell to the floor and didn't move again.

Doris stood as Ervin shuffled toward her.

"You okay, dear?" he asked while dropping his knives onto the floor. He patted her arms and shoulders gently before tilting her chin up to look at her neck. "Tsk, tsk," he said, "you are going to have bruises, dear."

Doris ran her eyes over Ervin, noting every little cut and bruise on his body. "Open your wings," she instructed, moving behind him. She ran her hands over the leathery structures, sighing at the bloody slashes decorating his skin. "Ervin," she whispered.

"I'm fine, Doris. Dealt with worse." He closed his wings and turned, taking her hands in his. "Are you okay?"

Doris started to answer but was interrupted by the sound of a clearing throat. Ervin dropped her hands, and both turned to face Allocias and Andros.

"Good show. Good show," the short, green-scaled demon

she'd talked to earlier said, stepping closer. "Quite entertaining, don't you think, Andros?"

"Indeed, it was," Andros responded, "but it is getting late, and we really should get this interview moving. We've spent far too much time getting to know each other and not enough picking your brain. Figuratively, of course."

Allocias laughed and shook his head. "Although, I wouldn't call it time wasted, Andros. Being candid with our new friends, I don't know how much longer we could have put up with that arrogant ass. Maybe not as bloody or exciting as your physical fight, our fantasy of his domination in the nightmare realm has kept us entertained for days. In the waking world, I'm not so sure we could have bested him, but thankfully, that's no longer a concern. Now that he's gone, we can enjoy our travels. Maybe see more of this beautiful world before we head back to Hell. You did us a favor."

Andros gave his friend a sly smile. "Terrorizing him would have been enjoyable. But you are correct. A physical altercation would have ended badly, I think." He turned to Ervin and Doris. "Let's get to business, shall we?"

Later, wrapped in furs atop their bed made of feathers and leaves, Doris snuggled closer to her favorite demon. "What a day," she mumbled, kissing him lightly on his horn. She ran her hand along his hip in loving strokes.

"Yes. Turned out nicely, didn't it?" He mumbled, half asleep.

Doris thought back over the day and shrugged. She wasn't sure how she felt. The interview had gone well, but they'd had to kill one of the interviewers. And she'd come dangerously close to ruining Ervin's life work. Ruining her relationship. And they were still here in this dank cave. But on the good side, they did have demon meat and she wouldn't have to kill any humans while it lasted. At least the visiting demon they'd killed had been the largest one. That was lucky. Doris sighed. "I suppose so."

"All those infuriating letters," Ervin said, his voice thick with sleep. His fingers stroked her skin lightly, his breath warmed the spot between her breasts. "Took so long selecting the right interviewers. Needed one who wasn't smart enough to recognize the scent of their own dung to make it work. Another who could—there had to be one who figured out the truth. Then getting them to come was another challenge. I wasn't sure it would work."

Doris's hand stilled. "What?" she whispered.

Ervin snored softly against her chest.

She ran her tongue against her lip. She'd thought it odd the society had found them in this isolated cave system on the human side. Only the occasional letter to and from Ervin's family kept them involved in the demonic world, and she'd figured his family had approached DETH, but maybe she'd been wrong.

"What were you saying, Ervin?" she said with a gentle shake of her husband. "About the letters?"

Ervin grunted softly before repositioning himself against her body. "Shouldn't be eating morsels," he grumbled before letting out a soft snore.

He continued to mumble between his snores, but no matter how hard she listened, Doris couldn't decipher anymore. Finally, she laid her head, heavy with confusion, down on her pillow. She felt loved. And sad. And caught like a child with their hand in the cookie jar.

Morsels. Soul. Soup. He mumbled.

Maybe her Ervin had known all along and found a way to stop her without confronting her. Maybe her Ervin was smarter than she thought.

THE REAPER

AND HIS GRIM DESIRES

IT WATCHES

The grim reaper walked around the body with his hands clasped behind his back, his tattered cloak barely moving in the still air. It was dark except for the moonlight streaming through the trees to reflect off the curved steel blade of the scythe holstered on his back. Occasionally, he peered up at the cars driving on the Twenty-Eighth Street Bridge, but for the most part, Laurant's gaze remained focused on the glowing corpse. She'd been beaten then slashed with a knife. He squatted to inspect the blood seeping into the soil. "They really should have used more restraint," he muttered.

Using a skeletal finger, he turned her lifeless gaze toward him and stared into her dull eyes. He shook his head in disappointment. Both her eyes were red from ruptured blood vessels, which diminished the beauty of their mossy-green irises. *What a waste,* he thought, scanning the ravaged skin on her cheeks and neck. *There's got to be something usable here.*

He moved down to her feet and let his gaze slide up her legs and narrow waist, over the arm crossing her chest to her shoulder and the arm flung behind her head. A splash of yellow caught his attention, and he leaped over her torso to yank her hand into the air. As her body rose, her head fell to the side, and congealed blood dropped to the ground with a loud plop. Smiling, he removed a knife from his pocket and flicked it open. He hummed as he sliced the flesh off her forearm.

He shook the pilfered chunk, then examined it again before leaning close and blowing a frosty breath along its surface. The dirt and grime crystalized, then fell away in a delicate shower. He pushed the frayed sleeve of his cloak up his arm.

"This is perfect." He placed the girl's flesh atop his blackened forearm and shifted it around. After making sure the edges lined up with the deep brown skin he'd already attached to his bicep, he removed a threaded needle from his pocket and began to sew.

"Beautiful," he whispered when done, admiring the yellow sunflower tattoo that now wrapped about his forearm. It tingled where the nerves were reanimating and growing—connecting the new patch of flesh to his deadened skin. With this addition, he had five pieces. Not even close to enough, considering his goal.

The dry black skin over Laurant's empty eye sockets drew together, and he dropped his arm. Something watched him. His head rose to peer around the small clearing. The same sensation had occurred twice yesterday while he'd been working. He kicked at a dirty needle lying next to the girl's body, then returned his annoyed gaze to the darkness.

His lip curled. He had an idea what it was and why it was here, but that didn't alleviate his irritation. If anything, it made it worse, as he didn't think following him was warranted. He'd taken responsibility at his last performance review for how much his dallying was skewing the department's soul-retrieval numbers. He may not have improved yet, but it had only been a month—it was way too soon to be shadowed. He tugged at the threadbare remains of his black cloak and squatted next to the body.

I always get it done eventually, don't I? I don't need a babysitter.

Sullen, he let his hand go ethereal and drop into the girl's chest. His fingers wiggled in the cold shadow he felt inside until they banged against something small and hard. After a gentle pull, the soul began draining out of the human's tissue and into the soul stone in much the same way blood flows through veins to the heart. He pulled harder. "Hurry up," he grumbled, turning to study the inky darkness behind him.

The glow around the body vanished as the soul stone came away from its corporal remains with the wet, sucking sound of release. He stood and dropped the stone into a pocket, then drew the transparent gray figure that'd risen from the corpse to his side. As they walked, the six stones within his shroud clinked together loudly.

He glanced at the spirit. "I know. I know. Your soul isn't the only one in my pocket, but, believe me, it's nothing to be concerned about. I'm just a little behind in dropping them off." He tilted his head so he could show off the pilfered skin on the lower portion of his face. The heavy jowls were not the look Laurant originally wanted, but flesh was flesh. And life felt good. Slightly disappointed at the spirit's lack of interest, he kept talking.

"I've got a few personal errands to run before I take you to the underworld. Important stuff." He considered the spirit in earnest, ignoring its blank stare. "I'm on a mission, you know. A scientific expedition of discovery that my boss knows nothing about." The spirit turned its focus to Laurant's pocket. Laurant idly stroked the flesh covering the lower half of his face.

"Yeah," he continued. "I want to try something new, even if only for a short while. I figure I'll cover all my exposed bits and take a walk on the living side. No more hiding in the shadows like some Peeping Tom watching the humans go about their lives. Nope. I'm going to walk on the boardwalk, maybe dip a toe in the ocean, and try ceviche." He looked at the spirit beside him. "Do you know what that is?"

The spirit had faded to a muted version of what it had been: trees were visible through the edges of its body while its center glow had dimmed considerably. It opened its mouth and moaned silently for a second before returning its gaze to his pocket.

Laurant sighed and turned away. This was why his quest was so important. If he had flesh, he'd feel comfortable sharing his hopes and dreams with a human. A boy. A girl. Maybe someone old with exciting life experiences to share. And maybe, just maybe, he'd never feel the need to confide in a lowly spirit again.

For a spirit couldn't think or speak. It couldn't hear him, much less understand him. It was nothing more than a physical manifestation of the soul particles being left behind. Those remnants always formed a spirit body and attempted to follow, which was why this particular spirit couldn't keep its eyes off Laurant's pocket. Unfortunately, spirits weren't strong enough to keep themselves formed for very long, and it was only a matter of time before they faded into nonexistence.

And here he was talking to one. *So pathetic.*

Laurant looked at the spirit again. "Did you know your soul is a soft yellow? You were probably a good woman, even if you did die in a drug den. It's obvious you weren't a true believer, either. Those souls glow with this bright light . . . ," Laurant went quiet, then shook his head. "It's hard to describe. It's so brilliant it makes my head hurt."

By this time, the spirit had faded to nothing more than a

dark shadow and no longer looked at him when he turned her way.

"Not that I see well," he said, indicating his empty orbs. "Mostly I see in grays with splashes of color: red is vibrant, yellow is bright, white glows. Of course, I see nothing with these empty sockets. My vision just comes to me. But you can see why I'm looking for eyes. I don't want to scare the living when I make my entrance." He paused before continuing. "I suppose I could wear sunglasses."

The spirit vanished with a sudden pop of displaced air. Laurant studied the spot it had vacated and shook his head. "And now I'm alone," he muttered, turning his focus to the faint premonition of death brewing in the distance. Its pull was undeniable, and he let himself be drawn toward it. He had a soul to collect and more flesh to gain.

He hummed as he stepped off the narrow path leading down to where the girl had died and onto the sidewalk. Even though it was late, the city streets were still brimming with commuters heading home or out to dinner. Those on the sidewalk slid out of his way when he drew close as if a sixth sense told them they were somewhere they shouldn't be, close to something they shouldn't touch.

Laurant suddenly came to a halt and turned to peer behind him. An unfamiliar sensation made the skin along his back crawl as if someone ran a finger up and down his spine, tracing a road to its end before reversing and returning the other way. Uncomfortable, he shifted his back and studied the dozens of humans crowding the small boulevard, moving around him like a rushing river around a seven-foot-tall boulder. He yanked his cowl down and turned in a slow circle. His black skin stretched taut over his skull and across the empty orbs of his eyes. It wrinkled around his nasal hole as he breathed in the stinging scent of exhaust and humanity. The flesh sewed onto his lower face twisted with his snarl. "Who do you think you are? I can feel you watching me—"

He stopped midgrowl. What if his boss had found out about the souls, and it wasn't a fellow psychopomp following him, but the head honcho himself? The Pusher of Papers.

The Destroyer of Dreams.

My God. He can't find out. He'll ruin everything. Turning quickly, Laurant yelled, "I'm doing my damn job. Stop following me!"

Pigeons burst into the sky as silence descended to hang over him in a heavy shroud. The humans close to him raced away, and the sidewalk surrounding him emptied. Laurant ran his hands down his cloak and retreated a step. If anything, his outburst had made the unnerving sensation more intense. He wondered for the first time if he was wrong about what followed him.

Laurant rolled his skull along his neck and latched on to the familiar pull of impending death. It tugged at his core, reminding him he had a job to do, giving him a reason to escape.

"I've got to go." He turned away and replaced his hood. The tattered strips of cloth at the bottom of his cloak flowed in the air as he hurried down the street. The people around him became blurs he slid through without thought. Through everything, he could feel the mysterious eyes watching him, probing his form, running down his back and across his shoulders as if the watcher could now keep up with his swift pace. Periodically he glanced behind him, but whatever followed never exposed itself.

"I don't know what you are," he muttered, trying to muster a bravado he wasn't feeling, "but you better knock it off."

Death's call guided him through the city and down a long freeway. He sped through the human realm without his typical interest, only able to focus on the constant feeling of being scrutinized. A breath seemed to caress his body, causing his new skin to tighten painfully and the hairs to stand at attention. Laurant glanced at his forearm in wonder, enjoying the strange sensation while simultaneously despising it. This wasn't what he'd anticipated, this flow of life moving over him so freely without his consent, and he suddenly wanted it to end. All of it.

He thought for a second, then slashed his hand through the air, creating an inter-dimensional portal. About ten feet tall and oval, the rift in space looked like a shimmering pool set over the cityscape, blurring the city lines and lights, while still allowing them to be visible. Through this doorway was the Nether—a place that existed between the dozen dimensions like the frosting between layers in a cake. With a last glance behind him, he left the human realm. He did not close the portal but stood slightly off to the side and waited.

Almost nothing existed in this realm: no roads, no trees, nothing but a fog that settled thick around Laurant and the shimmering doorway. His shoulders hitched uneasily as the minutes slid by, and nothing came through. Only one explanation made sense. The watcher was not a reaper. He chewed his lip and considered what it could be, before wondering why it followed him in the first place.

His compulsion tugged at his subconscious, and he let the matter drop. He had a job to do, even if he wasn't doing it correctly. Procedure instructed him to deliver souls to their final resting place within thirty minutes of a human's demise. So far, nothing untoward had happened to the soul stones he carried—not even the one that had languished in his pocket for almost two days. But what if he was making a mistake? He slowed when his compulsion directed him out of the Nether and back to the human dimension. Waving his hand, he opened another rift and walked through the new portal.

The preternatural silence of the neighborhood made him pause. It felt as if the air itself had ceased conducting sound, like the neighborhood had died and become a tomb with walls made of towering structures of brick and glass and a hard asphalt laid floor. Nothing moved. Nothing breathed. Even the apartments were dark on the lower levels, with only a few sickly yellow glows coming from behind thickly shaded windows. As he watched, the lights went dark one by one until only apartments high above continued to shine. Further down the street, two humans dashed out of a doorway and raced away from him. They turned down the nearest cross street and vanished. Laurant strode forward in slow, measured steps.

He stopped before an alley steeped deep in shadows. Inside, he counted six doorways, each lit by a small incandescent bulb barely strong enough to illuminate the doorstep below. Between each sat a large garbage dumpster, five in total. These receptacles created shadowy spaces of utter blackness that completely blocked any light coming from the fixtures above. He inched past the first doorstep, then found himself hurrying through the darkness to the next lit area. Embarrassed, he stopped to roll his neck along his shoulders. He looked up, studied the shadowed brick walls, then returned his gaze to the alley.

For the first time in centuries, he didn't want to collect the soul pulsing weakly in the darkness ahead.

For the watcher was back and felt more substantial than it had before. He could almost pinpoint it now, back there in the darkness, throbbing with a dark energy that tainted the air with a malignant desire that even the humans could feel. But unlike them, he couldn't run or hide. He had a job to do. Laurant squared his shoulders and moved forward past one dumpster, then another, through darkness that seemed to be getting thicker with every step.

"I am the darkness," he snapped, unnerved by being unnerved. He lived in the underworld and wasn't scared of its inky shadows and creepy trees. Of course, that was a solitary existence, but here . . .

Here, he was not alone, was he?

The watcher's eyes were running down Laurant's body with increasing intensity—its gaze almost searing his new flesh where it touched. He couldn't explain how it had gotten here first, nor how it knew where he'd be before he'd known. He swallowed, then ran a hand down the sunflower tattoo before reaching back and retrieving his scythe from behind his back.

His arms shook as he hoisted it in front of him and hurried to the last circle of illumination that stood between him and the body. Tiny hairs on his new skin rose and caught on the fibers of his cloak while a strange knot grew inside his belly. It burned and made him want to listen to the internal voice urging him to flee.

"Fear," he whispered in sudden understanding. It was a word discussed in the quiet of the break room when there was nothing else to do but wonder at the quirks of the living. What did it feel like? Why was it bad? What caused it? As his fear mounted, he realized he knew the answer to one of the questions—fear was like falling down a cliff and not knowing what waited for you at the bottom.

Laurant licked his new lips as a shiver made its way through his arm, leg, and face, through every piece of flesh he'd stolen. *Fear*, he thought again.

Something moaned in the darkness, and his skin puckered in response. "What do you want?" he asked, leaving the safety of the light.

Darkness swooped in, surrounding him until he could see nothing. His sight adjusted slowly, revealing glimpses of the brick walls and piles of garbage in small shadowy frames while continuing to hide his elusive stalker. His fear intensified.

Laurant listened to water dripping in the distance. To a muffled bark coming from one of the apartments above. A car roared its engine in the streets, and from far away, he heard someone cough. But nothing came from near him.

"Okay. Calm down, Laurant." He ran a hand over his scalp and let out an angry huff. "There's nothing here. Just get the soul and leave." Three steps in, another moan assaulted his ears.

He whipped around and dropped his cowl. He could feel eyes scouring him from head to foot. Touching. Sampling. Rolling over him much like the eyes of a beast searching for the most tender morsel before it attacked. Vulnerable and exposed, Laurant's breath quickened, and he tapped the handle of his scythe against the filthy ground. It smacked into something soft, and he shoved it aside. A diaper fell open, and he drew back in horror. Grimacing, he pushed the diaper away.

Something tickled the new flesh on his thigh.

Stroking up, then down. Wrapping around him in a tender embrace.

Laurant screamed and repositioned his hands. He swung his scythe low and tight, the sharp edge flashing as it arced toward his leg. It connected with a painful thump, and Laurant flung his head back with an inhuman cry that sent birds erupting into the sky. Vermin scattered, surging from the garbage bins to race down the alley toward the street. Dogs howled, and a homeless man already hunkered down for the night in a nearby doorway curled into a tight ball and prayed.

Panting, Laurant dropped his head, and silence descended.

Nothing moved.

He shifted and noticed the plastic hanging from the end of his scythe. "It's just a bag," he whispered, pushing it off. He breathed in and out slowly. A bug landed on his chin, and he swatted it away before gingerly raising his robe to check his injury. A cut ran across the pale flesh attached to his thigh. He ran his fingers over the wound, then examined them for blood.

Something moved, and he eyed the darkness suspiciously. He felt a presence looming over him, but he was alone. He rubbed the goosebumps erupting on his arm. "Just get the soul, Laurant. Then get out of here."

The bugs were back, crawling across one side of his new chin before moving on to the other. It almost felt like a person tapped his face. Laurant brushed them away, then flipped his scythe over and used it like a rake to clear a path to the body.

Something touched his arm.

He spun. Breathing in, he noticed an ozone scent to the air behind him that hadn't been there before.

Get the soul.

He hurried to a large mound of black plastic lying a few feet away. His hand went ethereal as he crouched, but instead of plunging into the body, he stopped and let it hover an inch above the corpse's still chest. His compulsion directed him to finish the job, but something more powerful stopped his hand from continuing the task.

It was his need to become human. Beneath his hand was flesh covered by nothing more than a thin sheet of flimsy plastic. It was another step toward his ultimate goal of a better life. Laurant glanced behind him. Seeing nothing, he pierced the bag with his fingernail and dragged it downward.

Something shoved him forward.

Laurant flung his arm out and caught the ground before he face-planted. His hand curled in the dirt as a cold presence bore down on his back. Fear spread out from where it touched him, crawling up the curve of his spine and over his shoulders, soaking deep into his bones, settling into its new home like an unwanted squatter. Laurant jerked upright and screamed.

The weight fell away with his movement. The fear released him.

He panted and twisted around. There was nothing behind him that could have caused him to fall, but something had pushed him over. A bug landed on his face, and he swiped it away. Another came, and he swatted at the air. His breath caught when his hand touched something icy and substantial but with some give. The fear returned, then vanished when his arm continued its downward course.

Laurant stood with his scythe gripped tightly in his hands. Whatever had been standing beside him was gone. He probed the alley until he reached the far wall. There he focused on a small pile of rubbish stacked in the corner. *Could something dangerous be that small?*

"Mine," a cold breath breathed across his ear.

Laurant screamed. The ghost vanished, but not before it tapped its fingertips on his cheek in a way that sent ripples of understanding through him. There'd never been any bugs, just this ghost.

"Mine," it hissed again, reappearing at his side.

Laurant swung his scythe wide. His blade sliced partway through the ghost's middle before he drew it out. Stumbling back, he stared at the ectoplasm leaking from the split edges in wispy lines, scenting the air with more ozone.

"No," Laurant whispered. Ghosts were not the same as spirts. They were vicious. Dangerous. Creatures even reapers avoided. No one knew where they came from, nor why some deaths created ghosts while most did not. Ghosts always appeared as they'd been at death but with a luminescent glow.

This ghost was large, with excess fat jiggling over its pants and rolling along its neck as it thrashed about. The long hair of its mullet floated in the air like a hairy halo around its head. The ghost's writhing slowed as the two sections drew together. The ghost's pronounced jowls gave a last wiggle.

Laurant touched the stolen flesh on his chin. "I know you." The last time he'd seen the ghost, he'd been a human and lying dead atop a dirty mattress in a filthy apartment, staring into oblivion.

The ghost lumbered toward him. "Mine," it growled before leaping.

Laurant turned ethereal and spun in a circle, stepping through the dead body wrapped in plastic. He swung his scythe into the ghost's shoulder, then yanked the blade downward through its chest, splitting the ghost in half. He pulled his scythe away and stepped back.

The ghost's body fell to the ground in two mounds.

Laurant's grin faded as the ghost reformed and hauled itself up.

"Mine," it repeated.

"I'll keep doing it," Laurant hissed. "I'll keep dicing you into smaller and smaller pieces. I have all eternity."

The ghost screamed and lunged.

Laurant scrambled backward until he smacked into the wall. He shoved at the ghost. Its fingers touched, stroked, then finally grasped at his chin. Sharp nails dug into his flesh, sending pain rippling through Laurant's face. The ghost's scent filled his nose, and an almost debilitating fear pulsed through him. "Stop touching me!" he screamed, understanding the fear came with the touch.

Fiery pain radiated from his chin to his scalp. Dropping

his scythe, Laurant grasped the ghost's hands and pulled. Cold ectoplasm chilled his fingers, but the ghost refused to release him.

Instead, he yanked Laurant away from the wall and shook him back and forth.

With each reverse in course, Laurant could hear the sound of stitches ripping. Could feel the flesh separating from his own skin. He tried to escape but couldn't. At last, the flesh gave way.

His chin fell to the ground in a twisting mass. It turned black, its movements slowing until they ceased altogether. Foul fluid leaked from the edges and made its way down the asphalt. The ghost stood over it.

Laurant darted to the side and watched the ghost sway back and forth with glazed eyes.

Laurant's hand fluttered to his face. He ran his nails down the hard skin below his cheekbones and across his shriveled lips. He'd lost his sense of feeling. The ghost's gaze grew sharp, and he realized the fear hadn't left but still lay curled inside him in a bubbling mass. "I need to get back to work," he whispered.

The ghost didn't respond.

"You have your chin. You don't need me anymore." Without a response to stop him, he turned and ran to the body. The ripped plastic had fallen open to reveal a young man of about thirty. He had beautiful smooth skin and thick dark hair. Laurant glanced up, then returned his gaze to the corpse. After moving the plastic off to the side, he studied the body more closely. Maybe Jowls had been an aberration, as no other ghosts had appeared and he still had four pieces of flesh sewn to him. Laurant smiled, then shifted his shoulders. He could feel the ghost watching him. "You can stop staring at me," he said, turning around. "I gave your chin back, didn't I?"

But the ghost wasn't paying him any attention at all.

Laurant whipped around and studied the darkness for a dim glow. "Wait," he said, throwing his hands forward when he found the malevolent glowing eyes in the shadows. The ghost's lips rose in a snarl, and Laurant squeaked.

"I got it. Don't worry. I got it." He dropped his scythe on the ground. Patting his body, he tried to remember what he'd taken from the dead girl, but he honestly couldn't recall if she'd been the one at the hospital or the one in her room. It's not like he'd looked *that* closely. It was just flesh, for God's sake.

His eyes suddenly widened, and he jerked his robe up. He'd forgotten about the tiny square sewn to his stomach. With the cloth balled in his fists above his navel, he could see the little diamond glimmering in his belly button. *Well, its belly button,* he thought after glancing in the ghost's direction. "It's only four stitches!" he explained, dragging his nail across the first one. His hand shook so much he stabbed the small bit of flesh instead of cutting the thread. "Come on!" He flinched and tried again.

The ghost groaned, and Laurant fought off an urge to scream as he pulled and yanked, popping apart stitches as quickly as he could until there was only one left.

Then something tackled him from behind, and he flew to the ground. Rolling to his back, he pushed against the ghost straddling his chest. His fingers fell through it. "Why can't I grab you?" Laurant yelled, twisting to the side. He stumbled to a stand and raced for his scythe. Another ghost materialized beside him and bit down on his extended arm.

He screeched and smacked at its head. The ghost chewed faster, twisting back and forth like a dog with a tug toy. Stitches popped, and pain streaked up Laurant's arm. "Take it! Take it!" he screamed as it ran off with its prize.

More ghosts came. They clamped onto their stolen flesh

as he fell, scratching and digging, damaging his desiccated hide in their zeal to retake what was theirs. The air filled with the sounds of the struggle—thumps, and moans, as well as tearing flesh. Ozone smothered the smell of garbage beneath it.

Then it was over. Laurant lay curled in the fetal position with his arms wrapped around his head. Slowly he raised up and peered around. At first, it was a soft awareness barely scraping his consciousness, then his compulsion broke through his shock like a wielded hammer, pounding through his center to remind him he had a job to do.

The five ghosts hovered over their decaying body pieces, not moving, not moaning, just watching as he rose to a stand. Bending down, he retrieved his scythe and twisted his hands around the handle. How was he supposed to reach the body with all these ghosts around?

His gaze stopped on a ghost that no longer watched him but had lowered itself to a crouch and stared intently at the black sludge that had once been a piece of flesh.

Laurant took one hesitant step toward the ghost, then another. His breath quickened the closer he got. He was almost past it when the ghost erupted upward in a snarling whirl of fists and teeth, all semblance of safe and nonthreatening gone.

Laurant screeched and jumped away. Then he turned to face it with his scythe raised.

The ghost was again crouched and staring at its sludge.

Laurant's brows furrowed. He studied the others, then returned his gaze to the one crouching. Why had it lost interest? More importantly, why had it suddenly attacked him at all? He tapped the handle of his scythe on the ground, then moved closer.

It didn't respond.

He inched closer. He was less than two feet away now.

Close enough that he could see the individual hairs floating in the air about its shoulders. Could smell the rot of its liquifying flesh. He wanted to stop but couldn't.

It raised its head and glared.

He lifted his leg to take a step, and it hissed through bared teeth. When it started to rise, the fear coiled in his belly billowed outward and told him to run. Instead, he lowered his foot. He had to know. With a pained grimace, he shoved his scythe into the sludge.

The ghost flew upward and landed on top of him. Laurant screamed as it scratched at his face. "I'm sorry! I'm sorry! I'm sorry!" he shrieked, rolling away. It vanished, and he dropped his head to the ground. Blowing out, he pulled himself up. Now he knew it wasn't him that set it off, but his proximity to its body part.

The ghost was once again crouched on the pavement, seemingly oblivious to his existence.

"I'm not going to touch your . . . puddles." He slid carefully between the two ghosts before him. Twisting sideways, he shimmied past another with his scythe clutched to his chest. Finally, he was through them, and Laurant holstered his weapon and hurried the last few steps to the body.

Then a glowing hand grasped Laurant's sleeve.

His back arched with fear. He twisted and tried to pull free by ripping his arm from the ghost's grasp. It held on, and he swung out with his free hand, which sliced through the ghost as if it didn't exist. The ghost moved with him when he spun again. It didn't attack, but let him drag it with him around and around the body. Panting, Laurant drew to a stop. He stared into its silver eyes.

The ghost moaned. The burnt skin on its lower face cracked open, and ectoplasm oozed and rolled down its chin.

"I remember you." He'd retrieved the man's soul yesterday at a building fire on Sycamore. None of his flesh had been usable. "You shouldn't be here. I didn't steal anything of yours."

The ghost continued to moan and clutch at Laurant's arm, then it tilted its head and peered at his pocket.

He blanched. *I've got his soul stone.*

Laurant brought his hand to his forehead. Fluttering strips of black hung before his face, blocking his view of the ghost. He drew his hand back and stared at the mangled skin dangling from his wrist and arm, revealing the ivory bones underneath. He'd been shredded.

He sighed and dropped his arm. "It's all my fault," he muttered, meeting the ghost's eyes. "I know what I need to do."

The ghost released him and went to stand with the others.

It had been twenty-two minutes since the human at his feet had died. Laurant turned and squatted down. "Welcome, newly deceased," he said, pulling the spirit from the body. "Don't worry. It won't be long until you are in your final resting place."

He glanced up when he stood. The burnt ghost shuffled about the alley unencumbered by a sludge puddle, while the others guarded their dissolved flesh.

He turned back to the spirit. "So, want to hear a story about how ghosts are created?" He slipped an arm around the spirit's shoulder and started walking. Their forms began to fade as they transitioned to the underworld. "I'll tell the story quickly so you can hear everything. But be warned, it's one hellova scary tale."

THE TRANSFORMATION

A SLOW AND LONELY METAMORPHOSIS
OF BEING

1
MAGGIE

Maggie's eyes flew open as her body arched upward on the bed. Memories flashed through her mind in colorful displays: the dirty brown wood peeking through the flaking white of her home's exterior, the bright yellow of the long grass in the yard, the emerald water of the creek across town. She screamed when pain followed, sharp and hot, piercing her eyes as if thin needles were being inserted through them into her brain.

"Sarah," she groaned when her sister's laughing face slid into view. Sarah's visage danced away, retreating into the distance with her arms twisting above her head, her long golden curls bouncing against her back. She peered over her shoulder at Maggie, a teasing smile curving her lips upward before she disappeared behind another memory.

"No," Maggie whispered before dragging in a shuddering breath. She wanted her sister here, holding her hand, caressing her head. Maggie's back arched again as she clawed at the blanket. Lightning burned beneath her skin, arcing its way along her ribs toward her spine. The pain increased when she inhaled and lessened when she exhaled. With each breath, the torment came and went like a rushing tide.

What's happening to me? Why—

She cried out and pressed a hand to where her heart jerked in her chest. It pounded once beneath her palm before quivering weakly and growing still.

Was this dying? Was her body failing and her mind rotating through her memories before they went with her to heaven? She ran her hand over her motionless chest while suppressing a sob. Nothing there—no throbbing, no pulsing, no beating. Then it started, delicate movements much like the first tentative kicks of a baby, soft against the inside of a womb, missed until they happened too frequently to ignore. Then the faint flickers vanished as her heart revved into overdrive, beating her to death with each powerful thrust against her rib cage. Maggie clutched the cloth over her breasts, desperately wanting the painful pummeling to end.

She focused on the memories that continued to bombard her: her brother's birth, a day at school, the taste of sweet cream on a hot day. Random recollections in no particular order—one minute she was ten and hanging laundry, the next a toddler eating berries with her four siblings, then at an unknown age with her mother hovering as she ran a cold cloth along Maggie's forehead. Here the memories seemed to pause, just for a second.

Maggie's eyes opened, and she let her hand fall to her side. She breathed in and out, counting her breaths as she tried to ignore the feeling that she should know this memory. Her heart now beat strong and steady.

This was her room. She recognized the pitched ceiling that slightly sagged in the center where water had seeped through the roof in years past, and the layers of circular stains proving it would continue to do so year after year until the tiles were replaced. These were her walls—a familiar off-white in desperate need of repainting, especially the one across from the window where it received the most sun and appeared a washed-out yellow.

It was her room, but somehow not. Her bottom sank in the mattress where it should. Her head rested on a soft pillow she remembered. Her sister's bed sat two feet away from where she expected it. Still, she couldn't shake the feeling that this was not her room. That she'd woken in an alternate universe where things were not quite what they seemed. That maybe this was a dream.

Maggie shifted on the bed and breathed in. The tang of burning firewood filled her nostrils and brought about thoughts of snow and cold and snuggling under covers with hot stones at her feet. She sat up and twisted to the side to peer out the window above her sister's bed where a bright-blue sky met her gaze. There was no snow, but somewhere a fireplace was lit.

She closed her eyes when memories of working in the field under the hot sun pushed forward. She remembered sweat rolling down her spine and through her hair, occasionally falling down her forehead into her eyes, making them burn from the salt. The feel of feathery carrot tops stroking the palm of her hand was just as vivid, as were the greens of the climbing beans and lettuce, and the red of the peppers. But the recalled scent of soil and tangy tomato bushes vanished when she breathed in the harsh, acrid smell of the fireplace. Her eyes opened. The memory seemed to be from yesterday, but it was not summer, no matter how real her memory felt. Not with the smell of woodsmoke in her nose.

Maggie exhaled slowly and forced herself to relax. "I'm on my bed," she whispered as her fingers played with the scalloped edges of the cloth at her wrist, "wearing my Sunday dress." She glanced down at her feet. She was missing her shoes and socks, but her toes weren't cold. As a matter of fact, they ached. She squeezed her feet, then burrowed them in the mattress, rubbing them against the rough wool of the bedcover. The pain increased until her feet burned, until flames seemed to be licking her soles in ever-increasing laps. Maggie's face contorted into a scowl as the heat crawled from her ankles to her knees, cresting in an undeniable urge to stand. She flung herself off the bed, and the feeling vanished.

Maggie stepped across the cold floor, and her room melted. The white walls slid downward, every discolored spot and break in the plaster flowing together like a watercolor sprayed with a fine mist of moisture. The off-white marbleized with the discolored yellow and brown in the plaster, the blue from the sky outside the window joining in wet lines with the window frame's cream.

Once the furniture color merged, the world began to spin —every color spreading and mixing, swirling in psychedelic rivulets until nothing had form or texture. She couldn't distinguish walls from floor, windows from furniture. Up became down, and the acids in her stomach churned. She moaned and considered laying down before deciding against it. What would happen if she touched the colors? Would she remain herself or be absorbed into the mixture and cease to exist?

Then the world went black. Fear spindled inside her as a pin-sized light flared on her left, growing until it bathed the hall in dusky shadows. Walls returned. Soothing. Familiar. She could now make out the large ornate mirror covered with a scrap of black fabric before her.

Maggie brought her hands to her face and screamed. She shouldn't be here. Shouldn't be in the hall outside her room. She scanned the inky darkness surrounding her before shuffling in a slow circle. A strange glow lit the Victorian-style dresser in front of her, while everything else in the hall was cloaked in shadows. Shadows that grew thicker the further away she looked until there was no definition in the gray blobs.

Even her bedroom door, looming three feet behind her, stood dim and dark, shaded as if she viewed it through a thin fog. She raised her arm, noticing how two feet made her hand softer on the edges, less defined than it should have been, as if her cells were dissolving in the darkness or becoming one as the paint had done in her room.

Maggie jerked her arm back to her chest and peered around. Here may not be safer than her room, but as long as nothing came crawling from the shadows, she'd stay rooted to this spot like a tree to the earth. Maybe she'd wait here for this nightmare to end.

A low sound escaped the back of her throat. The shadows were moving, thickening and darkening further down the hall, growing larger and moving toward her, absorbing the little light that existed. They slid across the ceiling and floor, traversing the walls and over her head until everything was the same shade of black and coated in ill intent—a greasy otherness that made her skin crawl. From what she could tell, the house was gone, nothing discernible except the hazy outline of her bedroom door that was rapidly fading away. Then it, too, vanished, sliding into oblivion until there was nothing. "This isn't real," she mumbled with a shake of her head. The nothingness surrounded her now, with only a thin circle of light encapsulated her and the dresser. She inched closer to the piece of furniture while wrapping her arms around her stomach.

Three feet wide and considered so ancient her great-great-grandmother had called it old back in her day, it was not special beyond it being a family heirloom. It wasn't made of rare material, even though the lighter striations in the walnut seemed to glow under the unnatural spotlight, making the bottom portion more beautiful than usual. The mirror on top was hidden beneath wispy strands of black lace made from fibers so fine the cloth resembled black spiderwebs when held up close and had to be folded multiple times to completely hide the mirrored surface.

Her eyes ran down the edge of black cloth, sliding to a stop on a tiny sliver of uncovered mirror. An unnatural brightness beckoned her closer to peer at herself in the reflective surface. "Dear Lord," she whispered, tracing the contours of her cheek with a finger. Not only was her skin too pale, too young, too perfect, but the imperfections that had become so ingrained in her self-image to be overlooked were glaringly missing now. Her finger shook as it ran along her brow where a three-centimeter cut had healed into a smooth white scar when she was seven. No hair had ever grown there again, something her mother said gave her face character, and her brother called a flaw. For ten years, it had been her brother's go-to insult when they fought, but he couldn't do that now. The defect had vanished along with her chickenpox scars, the freckles across her nose, and the minuscule scar beneath her chin.

She drew her hand back to hover in front of her face. The skin glowed with an eerie light. Not enough to see by, but enough to make the surrounding darkness seem darker than it should. She leaned closer to the mirror and pulled her lower lid down to display her glowing eyes.

Unholy. At the thought, a breeze seemed to float across her ear, tickling her skin with coldness.

"No," Maggie whispered, jerking her arm back down to her side. The mirror no longer felt safe but like a harbinger to something evil with a message she wasn't understanding—and wasn't sure she wanted to. There had to be more clues somewhere. She shivered and turned toward stairs she could no longer see. Her eyes darted, then shifted to the front before she took a hesitant step forward.

The light and dark swirled together in a monochromatic wave, her circle of illumination blending into the darkness in golden streaks. Maggie shut her eyes with a groan. *Breathe*, she told herself. Seconds later the movement ceased, and the heaviness that had invaded her brain vanished. She cautiously peeked from beneath half-lowered lids at the familiar dark wood beneath her feet.

She swayed, clutched the bench beside her, and glanced over her shoulder and up the stairs to where she knew the mirror sat. Again, she'd been transported somewhere other than where she'd meant to go. Again, she felt tendrils of fear unfurling inside her. She swallowed and shuffled in a small circle until she faced the opposing wall.

She stood in the foyer, next to an oak bench and across from a two-foot-tall wooden cross nailed high on the wall. Like before, the brightness of the room only extended so far, dimming the further she looked as if the air was compressed, darkening until she could barely make out anything a mere six feet away. The nebulous shapes in the hazy kitchen to her right matched the stove and table even if they weren't clear, but to her left, the sitting room was an absolute black that concealed everything. Even more baffling was the crisp line at the entrance that somehow appeared darker than the room.

Maggie glanced at the line and blew out. She didn't know what to do and sat on the floor with her head resting against the door, her eyes creeping back to the line before moving to the cross. Within moments, her legs began to ache, the feeling intensifying and culminating in her kneecaps.

"No," she muttered, shifting her legs around. The movement didn't help; it seemed to inflame her nerves until her skin burned and her muscles twitched. Maggie growled deep in her throat and leaped up, but the not-quite pain persisted, and she knew she had to move. But moving meant spinning, and spinning induced nausea.

Her knees throbbed demandingly.

It had to be done, whether she wanted to or not. Maggie gritted her teeth and took a hesitant step forward, relaxing when the world remained static—the walls solid, the lighting the same. She didn't know what it meant and looked around. Where was she supposed to go? Dismissing the kitchen, she glanced at the front door where dim light flared in the crack surrounding it. Although a welcoming contrast to the murky ambiance of the rest of the house, it was not enough to stop her from turning toward the shadowy sitting room she felt compelled to investigate.

With every slow, hesitant step forward, her heart rate increased.

The darkness in the room responded by growing less opaque, fading from the center outward, revealing tall unidentifiable shapes in the hazy gray that didn't match the cupboard, the couch, nor the rocking chair that should have been inside. She reached the entrance to the room, and the fading stopped at a dim twilight, a murkiness that left her with the ability to make out shapes but without enough light to see all the way across the room. Maggie tapped one finger against the wall and listened to the deafening silence. Not a sound came from inside, not a whisper of movement.

Her eyes trailed down to the line, which had not paled but appeared more distinct with the floor visible behind it. Should she do it? Within that room might be the answers she needed. Impulsively, she stepped forward, shuddering when her foot crossed the line, and dread slid across her tongue like a sour wine, leaving a bitter residue that made her gag. Her stomach turned, and she yanked her foot back to the safety of the entryway. She scraped her tongue against her teeth before spitting on the floor.

"Hello?" No one answered, and she raised her voice and called again.

A tiny dot of light popped into existence behind the shapes. Brighter than a pinpoint, but not bright enough to expose more details, the light revealed more shapes posted about the room. Peering closer, she noticed their edges weren't sharp, but hazy, and appeared to be leaking into the air like smoke.

Maggie backed away.

Her mother's sob came from the sitting room. "Mama?" Maggie whispered.

Hinges squeaked behind her, and an unnatural light flooded the foyer, casting her shadow across the floor where it ended abruptly at the line. There were her legs and the beginning of her torso, but that was it, as if she didn't exist beyond the divide.

Maggie turned and raised a hand to shield her eyes from the sun coming through the front door. A brittle wind blew across the tall Indian grasses in the front field, sending their brown lengths toward her in a crackling wave. Closer. Closer. Then the wind entered the house in a gust and blew her long hair behind her, filling her body with warmth, filling her with calm. Maggie closed her eyes. She wasn't so dense she didn't understand the symbolism being sent her way. Outside to the light meant safety, to the dark meant something altogether different. She thought of nothing for a second, her breath low and shallow. The answer was in that room and not outside, she was sure of it. Her mother and family would know what was happening.

"I'm sorry," she whispered, opening her eyes. She needed to see this through. Maggie's hands twitched once at her side before she returned to the doorway and stepped across the threshold into the dark.

Blackness encircled her in a cold embrace as the light from the entryway vanished. Warmth fled while the feeling that she chose wrong intensified. She stepped forward, studying the two curtains drawn across the room's windows, leaving only faint candlelight for illumination. The room seemed larger than she remembered, but then the furniture wasn't usually stacked along the wall, leaving the center empty of everything but the shapes she'd seen from the foyer.

Although beeswax and woodsmoke scented the air, there was an unpleasantness that caused her to recoil and wrinkle her nose. A memory came to her then, invading her thoughts in little snatches until she recalled where she'd smelled it before. "Aunty," she whispered, remembering the homely but kind woman. She'd lived with them for many years, unable to find a husband of her own, and when she'd gotten sick of consumption two years ago, she'd been moved downstairs to this room to convalesce. When she'd died, the medicinal cherry scent of Ayers Cherry Pectoral and the stomach-churning bouquet of regurgitation and loose bowels had stayed behind, and that is what Maggie smelled now. Maggie studied the far corner but couldn't tell if a sickbed hid in the darkness.

"Mother?" She clenched her hand painfully tight. This wasn't what she expected. "Father? Where are you?"

She crept further inside, her steps slowing as she approached the first dark, nondescript shape. It stood alone, separate from the group crowded at the front. Slender tendrils of semitransparent smoke floated out from the shape's edges, while the rest was completely opaque. The shape shivered, wisps waving in the air for a second, and the shadows enveloping it faded, revealing an old man with a back curved like the top of an *s*.

"Mr. Hammond," she breathed. He lived two miles down the road and rarely came to town, much less visited neighbors. She knew he hated to be touched, hated to be noticed, and wanted nothing more than to be left alone with his dog.

The town considered him odd, but she'd always liked him. She enjoyed how softly he spoke, how gently he treated his animals, the small smile that flitted across his face when he thought no one watched. She'd taken care of him when no one else would—bringing him milk and eggs and sometimes chopping his wood when he'd had none.

The pastor, who had met with him privately every week, had recently placed a bench outside an open church window so he could worship with the town without having to come inside the church. The last few sermons, she'd taken to sitting alongside him, and he hadn't seemed to mind. She'd gotten the distinct impression that he had appreciated her company, even if he didn't voice it.

Maggie studied his bald head and milky eyes before moving down his body. He looked frailer than she remembered, his face gaunt, his arthritic, knobby fingers more skeletal as they worked his hat between them. She found it difficult to look away from the ripped seam along the elbow of his Sunday shirt, sure it hadn't been there the last time they'd met. She glanced up to his face again, suddenly worried. Why did he look like this? Why hadn't she fixed the rip?

"Mr. Hammond?" she whispered, growing cold when he failed to respond. She stepped in front of him and waved a hand before his face. Besides the delicate quiver of his lips, he didn't move. Then a tear slid down his cheek while his cloudy blue eyes continued to look through her. Maggie's hand fell to her side, and she turned away, shaken.

The darkness at the back of the room was broken by a small glow that created outlines of the shapes standing before it. At least twenty hovered in a group, the scene reminding her of people surrounding a fire before the last embers burned down. What were they doing?

Maggie moved closer.

"You do not have to see."

Maggie stiffened and looked around. The words had reverberated through her head like her own thoughts, but in a deep male voice. She studied the darkness, the shadow too far away to discern. "Who are you?" she whispered. In answer, warmth spread through her veins, traveling from her head to her toes. She rejoiced in the comfort, briefly forgetting her plight until the voice invaded her thoughts again.

"Your way is forward, outside this house, not to the past. Trust in me. Let me guide you."

Maggie awoke from her daze with a jolt. The past? A heavy weight settled upon Maggie at the words. What past could the voice be speaking of? The only one she knew included her mother, father, and family. She swallowed and looked down at her thin arm then her hand. Her nails were perfect pink ovals, her skin blemish free and soft like a baby. There were things she'd been ignoring—her glowing eyes, her skin's lack of imperfections. The mourning cloth. "Is that me up there?" Her chest throbbed in sudden agony. "Have I died?"

"Answer me," she whimpered, "or I'll find out for myself." She waited, but the voice didn't respond. Maggie wiped a hand across her face. "I'll figure it out myself then."

A brush of warm air flowed across her skin when the voice returned. "Trust in me. Go back to the door."

Maggie considered the words thoughtfully. Trust in me, the bible said. Trust in me, her pastor said. But why? Why should she do that when she didn't know who spoke to her now? What if the voice was the devil? What if this was just a dream?

Maggie strode forward, watching the misty shadows fade from the nebulous shapes as she approached, revealing more friends and neighbors from town. Although no one acknowledged her, they responded as if they sensed her among them, shifting to the left and right, creating an empty path for her to walk, closing behind her as if she'd never been. She passed them by until a familiar woven cap came into view. Her heart fluttered in her chest, and she hurried forward to grab her friend's dress. "Milly! It's me—" she cried before stopping.

There was a baby cradled in Milly's arms. Delicate. Young. A newborn. Its cheeks moved as it sucked on its tiny fist. Dark lashes stood out against its pale skin. It smelled of life and cookies, and she couldn't help but lean forward to breathe its scent in. The baby kicked suddenly, and a strong male hand shifted into view to cup its tiny feet. Maggie followed the hand to where Randall Bealey stood beside Milly, his brown eyes sad and downcast, peering at Milly in concern. Pain ripped through Maggie's chest, and she clutched Milly's dress tighter.

"I missed your wedding," Maggie whispered in sudden understanding. "Or did I forget it? I don't remember being sick." She swallowed the lump in her throat and peered down at the baby. "You were pregnant." They'd had plans to get married together, raise their kids together, grow old and support one another. None of that was happening now. She didn't even know the baby's name. "I'm so sorry, Milly."

Maggie tore her hand away and stepped back. Panicked, she turned in a circle. "I need to see them!" she screamed suddenly, turning back to the front. "I need to know they are okay."

There was no comforting air when the voice spoke again, just an inexplicable urge to obey. "Trust in me," it said. "Do not continue."

Maggie fought her urge to turn and stared into the distance. "No," she said before she rushed through the remaining rows of mourners without looking at those she passed. When the last row parted, she stumbled to a stop.

"Four children, not five," she whispered through the tears

sliding down her cheeks. Her throat grew sore, and her vision blurred. The voice came as if from a distance, intrusively pushing her anguish aside as if it didn't matter.

"This is not your place. There is nothing but pain here. Do not continue."

"I'm already here!" she screamed back, wiping the tears away.

For the first time, she noticed Pastor Markem's voice rising and falling, the words sending shivers through her body even though they remained unintelligible and garbled as if she listened to him from the bottom of a pond.

Her family stood stoically against the wall, their gazes fastened on the pastor even though she stood mere feet from their faces. She studied them in their Sunday best: her sister's beautifully bouncy curls, the rare dark eyes of her youngest brother, the path of tears on her mother. *They seem okay*, she thought with a sob. Walking forward, she placed her head against her father's chest and cried. The scent of the cherry tobacco he smoked mixed with the subtle hint of dirt and dust that came from working a farm. She ran her hand down his vest before pulling away and stepping back.

"I'm so sorry," she sobbed. She'd left them but had not gone to heaven nor hell. She had to be in purgatory, destined to be tortured by her family's memories for eternity.

"You can't do this!" she cried. Throwing her head back, she screamed and spun around. "Why?" she directed at Pastor Markem. "What have I done?"

Her gaze flitted behind him to the small casket against the wall. Built of knotty pine, it glowed a blondish white in the gloom, almost seeming to float because of the shadows cloaking the table that held it up. Shakily, she moved toward it, glancing up accusingly into Pastor Markem's eyes before taking a step past him. He'd not told her of this option—

doomed to walk her home, able to see her family, but unable to communicate.

A weight descended her calves and into her feet, pressing her downward as if she wore lead-weighted shoes. Each step became more difficult, each step a little heavier than the one before. She jerked her leg up and grimaced. Over her harsh gasps, she heard the voice speak.

"Why do you continue when I cannot protect you from what you learn? Trust in me. Abandon your quest."

"Why should I?" Maggie asked, raising her foot again. She couldn't stop now. Wouldn't.

She was close, two feet away at most, and pine scented the air, mixing with the beeswax and sickness in an oddly spicy way that burned her nose and throat. From here she could tell the coffin was well made, the seams sanded down so there were no rough edges to catch on, the outside smooth and soft looking. Maggie cried softly, knowing it had been handcrafted with love.

She could no longer raise her feet but slid them forward centimeters at a time. It was like slogging through the thickest mud and with every slide becoming just a little more bogged down. She cried in frustration as her calves burned and feet throbbed. "Let me pass!" she screamed, the casket almost close enough for her to touch. She stretched her arms out and lurched forward, collapsing against the side. Below her fingers, she saw a blue blanket.

Her fingertip brushed the soft cloth, and time paused. Her legs no longer hurt, nor did the air burn, but mentally she hurt more than she ever had before.

She caressed the shoes someone had tried to painstakingly make new. The creases webbing the thick leather had been waxed to make them less obvious, the small gash in the right instep had been patched with a small row of stitching. She wondered if socks had been stuffed in the toes to make them fit her much-smaller feet or if they'd bothered trying to make them fit at all.

She swallowed, and her eyes moved up the blanket-covered legs, over the smooth expanse of a stomach, to the small bump of her chest. Here she paused, unwilling to raise her eyes further. Her chest grew tight as a sob escaped her. Then she followed the blanket to where it ended.

Her grip tightened on the pine when she swayed. The white collar of her Sunday dress, delicately edged in hand-stitched pink roses, was stark against the blue of the blanket and grayish tinge of her dead flesh. She stared at the obscenely sharp angle of her protruding collarbone. "No," she whispered.

Knowledge came back in a rush: memories of being sick, of pain and sweat, of not being able to hold anything down even though her stomach cramped with hunger. She remembered the long nights of agony. The sweet relief of sleep when the cherry medicine hit her tongue.

"I am sorry," said the voice in her head, "I can no longer protect you from what is about to happen."

"From what—" she started to ask when a coldness invaded her core, piercing her stomach like an icy shard. She groaned and doubled over before standing upright. "Why are you doing this to me?" she whispered. She glanced down at her hand where it felt like something crawled beneath her skin.

With her ignorance stripped, she suddenly saw who she really was, watched as death consumed the life still existing in her ghostly flesh, stripping it from her cell by cell. The hand she rested against the wood grew translucent before the skin drew tight against her tendons and bones. The fat between the two layers dissolved, removing the vestiges of youth that had smoothed the flesh along her limbs when alive, revealing veins that bulged like dark webbing. There was a slight pull as her lips dehydrated, shrinking tight against her teeth.

"No," she groaned, her withered vocal cords making her voice raspy. She removed her hand from the casket and touched her face. Her skin felt dry, her eyes more sunken, her cheekbones sharper than they were before. A crinkling noise drew her hand to her hair, which she brought forward to inspect. The blond curls were now white, and they broke away in brittle strands at her touch.

Her lungs inflated on her last breath and moved no more. Her heart beat one last time then went still. Maggie raised her eyes, set deep into a face cadaverous and ghostly, and turned away from her casket.

Her father stood with his hands clutched together before his stomach—locked in an embrace that left them red and twisted. He stared into space, not at the coffin, not at the wall, but seemingly at something far from where he stood. In dreams and memories, she assumed, anywhere but at the body lying before him.

Her mother lunged forward a step and threw her hands to the sky. Her red face turned upward, and she screamed.

Maggie rushed toward her and felt the world tilt to the side. She screamed as she transitioned, knowing she'd recover somewhere other than where she wanted to be. In the kitchen, upstairs, in the root cellar? Was this her new life? Never reaching her destination? For what end?

When the world stopped spinning and sounds made their way through the silence, she was no longer in her home, but standing outside it. A bird tweeted, wind swished through grass and leaves, and the air smelled of dirt.

Her eyes, once a brilliant blue like the sky on a clear summer day, opened. Now milky with death, they gazed across the landscape. She was truly alone.

2
TONY

Tony closed his eyes and breathed deeply, reveling in the heat of the campfire smoke as it settled in his lungs. A minute passed, and his lungs burned, but still he held his breath, savoring the heady feeling of detachment and lightheadedness from delaying his exhale. When the need to breathe became unbearable and dizziness settled behind his eyes, he blew it out, his head falling back against his neck in defeat.

He should have let his younger brother, Leonard, cough on him when he had the chance. He should have leaned in close when Leonard had begged for his help between coughs and nose blowing. Instead, Tony had kept his distance and agreed to everything he'd asked just to get away from his infectious ass. And now he was stuck camping with a bunch of boys.

He was such an idiot.

He hated camping. Hated the way tree limbs rustled in the wind, camouflaging potential predators at minimum, moaning like a lost soul at worst. Then there was the campfire smoke that burrowed into everything, bonding with the fibers of his clothes, the proteins in his hair, the cloth of his car. He'd have to detail his car when he got home, spending money he didn't have. And then there was the créme de la créme: burying his shit in the dirt with a shit-covered shovel he'd have to carry out in a shit-coated bag.

Shit.

Tony opened his eyes and peered at the red-tinged sky. Soon he could order the kids to their tents, and peace would again be restored. Until then, he'd let them talk. About what, he wasn't sure. He'd ceased listening when the option to have his nipple twisted off or be kicked in the balls came up during a wild game of Would You Rather. He couldn't remember being so disgusting when he'd been a kid. But then again, he'd been working through his own issues at the time—

A loud squawk jolted him to attention. He turned quickly, noticing his nephew's normally bubbly smile had shriveled to a thin white line, and red had crept up his cheeks in a splotchy rash.

"That's not true," Bobby snapped, glaring at his best friend through the smoky haze drifting upward from the campfire between them. His pale blond curls flopped about his ears as he shook his head. "You don't know everything."

"I know you're a baby who still believes in ghosts," his friend retorted.

"I'm not a baby. I'll be eight in two weeks, Joe, just like you. You didn't become a grown-up when you had your birthday last month."

"I'm old enough to go through Miller's Maze by myself. Are you?" Joe's fat lips curled in a sneer as he leaned forward and jabbed a bony finger at Bobby. "Or are you too scared of ghosts to even try?"

Tunnel vision narrowed Tony's focus to the angry visage of his nephew. Words continued to fall while small fingers pounded the air, but nothing registered but the one word. *Ghost* reverberated about his skull, filling his stomach with dread, holding his breath hostage as he clutched the log beneath him.

Through his detachment, he noticed his nephew leaping up and taking a step toward the fire. "You—" came from his nephew as if from afar. The next words flitted away before Tony pulled himself from his stupor and stumbled to a stand. Tony grasped his nephew's scrawny bicep and dragged him back down to the log. Anger replaced his fear. "That's enough, Bobby," he snapped, his voice hoarser than he expected. "Stay seated, or go to bed." He made eye contact with Joe and snapped his fingers before pointing at the log behind him. Joe sat on his log.

"But—"

"I said that's enough, Bobby. You know the rules. No horseplay around the fire."

"You know," came a nasally voice from the other end of the log, "my momma says ghosts are made up. Just like Santa Claus and Jesus." Pauly gave a matter-of-fact nod of his head as he crossed his hefty arms over his chest. "And don't get me started on the Tooth Fairy or Easter Bunny."

Tony rolled his eyes as screams erupted from the other boys. *Oh, dear Lord.*

"Don't you say that! Jesus is our Lord's son."

"Santa Claus is so real! I got a train set from him last Christmas. I'm hoping for a bike this year."

"Mike Zimmer said he saw a ghost in Palmer's field last summer—"

"You are going to hell, and I'm telling my dad when we get home!"

"Stop!" Tony roared, glaring at the boys through the

smoke. "Everyone be quiet. I don't want to hear any more about Jesus or Santa Claus or ghosts. Does everyone understand me?" He ran his hands through his thick blond hair. "This is supposed to be fun. Not some kind of fight club."

"But Uncle Tony—"

"What did I say, Bobby?"

"But they don't believe in ghosts, Uncle Tony. They say I'm a liar. You need to tell them what you saw. Tell them how the ghost killed aunty so they believe me." His nephew's voice lowered, quivering slightly as he whispered, "I'm not a liar."

The crackling fire and steady hiss of wet logs thundered in the sudden silence. An owl hooted in the distance as something small scuttled through the bushes beside them. Five heads twisted away from Pauly to stare at Tony in expectation. No one said a word. No one seemed to breathe.

Oh, Bobby, Tony thought, wrapping his arm across his stomach. Sourness bubbled in his gut as memories long ignored attempted to break into his consciousness. With a quick shake of his head, he readied himself to take a stand. There was no way he'd go back to that horrible place. To those memories that had tortured him for twenty-one years. He'd let the scene around the campfire play out and hope for the best. With enough support from him, his nephew needn't fall into the same self-loathing he'd experienced when he'd been bullied.

Bobby had fallen silent beside him. He sat with his shoulders rolled forward and his head hanging down, appearing only a portion of his normal size. Tony's resolve broke when he saw his nephew's small hand surreptitiously wipe his face before falling back to his lap. He'd spent a decade in that same withdrawn position, with no one to talk to, condemned a liar and freak. Crying. Alone. Reaching over, he squeezed his nephew's knee in understanding.

"Bobby is not a liar. He tells the truth." His voice faltered as he met the eyes of the boys around the fire. "I'm going to warn you now, this is not a happy story with a happy ending. You won't be laughing when I'm done. Are you sure you want to hear it?"

With six heads nodding their confirmation, he began.

3
MAGGIE

Trees moved in the breeze, the sound of their leafless branches rubbing against one another filling the air. It reminded her of the spring winds and the chirp of crickets, of things she didn't know she'd ever experience again, of life. With a conscious expansion of her lungs, she breathed in the cold, let it caress her throat and settle in her lungs, then turned toward the house she'd spent her life in.

She gazed at the white two-story gabled house and traced each window, the chimney, and the covered porch before letting her gaze settle on the rocking chair on the front deck. How often had she sat shucking peas at her mom's feet while her mother rocked back and forth?

"Goodbye," she whispered. There was nothing for her here. No one to talk to. No one to hold. And the pressure was back, building behind Maggie's kneecaps like expanding marbles, imploring her to move. Soon she knew the ache would become unbearable when the request changed to a demand. Might as well leave now.

She walked down the dirt lane that led to the forest, studying the land as she went, memorizing every bush and rock she'd ever jumped, kicked, or trampled in her seventeen years, somehow knowing she'd never be back. When the road ended, she hesitated before continuing down the deer path that meandered through the trees and neighboring meadows. Within hours, she'd left all she'd been familiar with behind as the forest turned to pasture, and the path dwindled to nothing. She stopped.

"God," she whispered, pushing out the breath she'd been holding, "don't forsake me." She listened for the voice, but it never came. Sighing, she let the urge to walk guide her and continued through the pristine field.

She considered her life, wondering what she'd done to warrant abandonment on Earth. Her church said nothing of being a ghost. They spoke of heaven and hell, light and dark, and earning your place in the afterlife. Had her life deeds been so neutral that she deserved this nonexistence? Of limbo? She shook her head. She wasn't without sin. This could be her purgatory where she waited for purification. It might not match her pastor's depiction, but how would he know for sure until he died?

Only one question remained: how long would purification take?

Time passed, and Maggie's questions remained unanswered. Eventually, they ceased to matter as the years and miles grew. Her senses faded, her thoughts ceased, and she found she no longer cared. There was no cold when sleet fell from the sky. There was no warmth when the heat waves of summer appeared above the ground. Decades in, when the cool wetness of autumn phased into the harsh cold of winter and the water along the lake froze, she no longer noticed. Colors faded into various versions of black. Deep blues were a dusky gray, yellows and oranges were the palest ash. Some colors were no longer distinguishable from one another. The sun became nothing more than a brightness that faded every night into nothingness.

It seemed she was stuck in this world. A world where the cold was not cold, hot was not hot, pleasant smells were no longer pleasant, and beauty was only as deep as her willingness to accept a pale and lackluster world she could not enjoy.

She walked from one city to another over years that seemed to pass in the blink of an eye. Sometimes her steps moved her much farther than they should have, while other times she seemed to wander the same long road, staring at identical fence posts and wheat until she thought the images had been burned onto her retinas. Frequently, a step not only passed over miles of ground but time itself as years were skipped in a single motion. She watched the transition from horses to buggies to eventual cars and planes with an ebbing sense of wonder.

Nothing touched her. Nothing mattered.

She had walked, forever alone, not expecting things to change. But today, something surprising happened. Today, for the first time in centuries, her urge to walk the road ended. Today, she stepped through a white picket fence outside a tall pale house and knew her trek was almost done when the sky melted, her stomach sunk into her chest, and her world spun in shades of black.

Watching the gray swirls, she wondered if knowing she was dead was the reason she lived in a soundless gray world. Or was it the passage of time itself that had made her senses fade? The most troublesome thought was that she'd insulted God and had been abandoned.

The spinning ceased, and Maggie's wondering stopped. She found herself sitting on the floor instead of walking a new path, and she wasn't quite sure what to do about it. After a moment of consideration, she squeezed her arms tight around her calves and raised her head from where it rested atop her folded legs.

High on the wall behind her, two narrow windows glowed a faint gold, letting in rays that warmed the steps descending to her left and the three steps in front of her that led upstairs. She sat on the landing that faced the set of stairs leading up to the next floor.

Her brittle white hair floated skyward when she moved, framing her emaciated face in a shining cloud that undulated as if alive. She pushed the annoying strands aside and peered cautiously over her knees before her shoulders lowered in disappointment. Varying hues of gray still surrounded her as they had for centuries. Coming inside hadn't fixed anything —hadn't released her from the life she lived, hadn't returned the senses she'd lost.

Raising a bony white hand, she splayed her fingers into the sunlight and stared at fingertips that tingled with the softest hint of heat. Excitement made her mouth fall open, anticipation made her roll her arm over and thrust it forward. The sun touched her palm, brightening the lines under her knuckles before kissing the soft pads of her fingers. Even so, there was no warmth but on the tips, and that was faint. Her face crumpled as she drew her hand back into her lap. Her sense of touch had faded to the point where it almost didn't exist, becoming another piece of herself lost except as a hazy memory.

She stared up at the window and tried to remember the last time she'd been inside a home. Tried because her memories were slowly evaporating from her consciousness like water from a tall, thin glass on a warm summer day. Already a half-empty vessel, she feared what she'd become when her memories were no longer linked by the fragile threads of thought necessary for keeping everything in order. What she'd become when there were no more moments to forget.

When had she been born? Why was she alone? What had happened to her? Maggie no longer remembered answers to these questions but recalled the feel of her first kiss, how the boy's soft lips pressed against hers and left the faintest hint of mint on hers. But what was his name? Why did she struggle to remember her mother's face and the sound of her voice while her pastor's visage still retained vivid blue eyes above a hawkish nose and a long, twisted mustache? She could still remember how his voice echoed through the church and thundered against the walls. But she couldn't remember the smell of the exhaust filling the street outside this home—the place she'd been a few minutes earlier.

Maggie turned to stare through the soft morning light at the empty wall before her. And she waited.

Maggie tracked time on the landing by the passing of the sun and the illumination of the wall opposite her. The white paint blazed with the afternoon light, dimmed with shadows that moved with the descending night and warmed with the calm that came with the morning. Over and over, the cycle repeated itself while she waited for the urge to walk to return.

And while she waited, she pondered her new situation, going back to a thought that had plagued her during her first decades as a ghost but had long since been deemed a waste of time. Why was she here? She'd spent so long following the command to walk that she'd forgotten how to think for herself. Maybe she should be doing something other than waiting.

She rose slowly. The voice that had accompanied her on her first day had long grown silent, but maybe it would speak now. "What do you want me to do?" she asked. There was no answer, and her shoulders fell. "That's what I thought," she muttered. Maggie took a step with her head cocked to the side. She waited for the sucking pull of quicksand to let her know she was going the wrong way or for instructions to enter her mind. When neither happened, she tapped her fingers against her leg before climbing the stairs. She paused, then and headed to the right to a set of open dark-gray double doors.

She dragged her bare foot along the thick gray carpet covering the floor and wished she could feel the pile beneath her toes. More luxurious than anything she'd ever seen, it reminded her of the wolf pelts her brother sometimes brought home. *Had brought home*, she reminded herself. By now, her brother was long dead, buried in the field with the cherry trees, as most of her family were.

How things had changed since she'd been alive. The rough flooring with its splinters and knots had been replaced with material that didn't quite seem natural, like this room with its stark white paint and trim, four colonial windows along the one wall, and a large vestibule to her right. It was all beautiful and much more luxuriant than anything she'd seen when she'd been alive.

Maggie ran her finger along the smooth wall as she walked, remembering the rough feel of her own room, the faded yellow and brown stains along the ceiling, the cold that seemed to seep through the walls throughout winter. She doubted that would happen here.

She glanced down when the floor changed from carpet to something smooth and slick. Not wood or like anything she'd seen before, but white and striking where it butted against the black cabinet. The cabinet was missing its top, and long wires dangled from holes in the ceiling and wall. A door was missing from the small room off to the side, and a strange hole sat in the floor. She peered down it curiously before walking back out to the hall.

She stopped, sudden unease making her pause. She'd hoped to find people when she'd entered the house. To see them, hear them, maybe exist in their lives, if just as a shadow. But there was nothing here, not a whisper of life or crumb of humanity. Not even furniture for her to explore. While outside, she'd lost the hunger for living she'd once had, having existed in a perpetual state of limbo for so long, but with the prospect of experiencing more so achingly close, she found the idea of returning to life in a vacuum terrifying. *This*, she thought suddenly, *is worse*. No wind, no trees, not even a bird to watch. An empty, sterile prison.

Steps flashed by as she hurried to the lower level. She stopped at the bottom and spun in a circle. The living room to her right was bare. The kitchen comprised of nothing more than wires and pipes jutting from the walls and half-finished cupboards sitting in a corner. The house was deserted.

"No," she cried. She wanted to feel the throb of anxiety that should have been coursing through her veins, anything to tell her she wasn't empty. But there was no pounding, no physical response as she looked. She realized she was as empty a husk as the house. Only when she stopped to face the front door at the bottom of the stairs did she let out a soft sob.

She remembered once finding a young deer struggling to survive in the cold snow. Its mother lay dead beside it, struck by one of the mechanical monstrosities she saw driving the roads. Close to death, it breathed heavily while laying on its side with every bone in its small chest visible. She'd cried then, even if her eyes produced no tears, and wondered why she'd been left here if she couldn't help the starving fawn. Like then, she wondered if the voice in her head was not the voice of God, as she'd originally thought, but of the devil, and this was her personal hell. Unable to help anyone. Unable to help herself. Stuck.

Maggie grabbed for the doorknob, and her hand passed through the metal, clenched in a fist that should have been clutching steel.

"No!" she shrieked as she rushed the door with her head lowered. She'd go through the door, as she'd done to so many cars and pedestrians, and be free of this hell.

The world spun much like it had in the beginning. But it was white merging with white, with small slashes of gray instead of the kaleidoscope of color from before. Once the walls settled to their static place, her mouth fell open, and her hands unclenched. She'd been returned to where she started on the stairwell.

The reality of her situation sunk in—she'd come in from the road to an emptiness even more bleak than before. She turned to a corner of the landing and lowered her head to her chest while facing the wall. Her brittle white hair fell forward, covering her face as her eyes closed, the white strands no longer floating.

4
TONY

Six small faces leaned toward Tony excitedly.

He licked his lips and considered how he'd start. "I was young when it happened," Tony began. "Four, almost five. My dad died in a car accident six months before, and we —my mom, baby sister, and I—moved in with my grandparents. I didn't understand what was going on and was excited about the move. My grandfather and grandmother were everything to me." He swallowed and shook his head. "I didn't realize my father wasn't coming back."

Tony stared into the fire as his memories swirled around his head like broken film from a movie. He didn't want to organize them, much less put them into words. Years had been spent with a therapist, first trying to come to terms with his memories then eventually trying to forget them and move on, and now he was dredging them up to share.

"The house was three stories tall, similar to the house Pauly lives in now. My grandparents had just moved in a month before, so it was new to all of us. They took one of the bedrooms on the second floor, while my mom, sister, and I had the small bedroom on the first floor. It was safer for me since I wouldn't have to use the stairs."

He glanced around the campfire and smiled through the smoke. "The backyard was awesome. It's the kind of backyard I want if I ever have children. It had a huge pool, a tree with a tire swing, and lots of room to run. I loved that backyard . . ." His voice faded as he let his eyes drift back to the fire. Sweat broke out on his upper lip. When he spoke again, his voice was hoarse and low, deep with despair.

"That's where I first saw her: the ghost that killed my sister."

5

MAGGIE

Maggie came to slowly, not sure how long she'd been standing in the corner but feeling like she'd woken from an extended break. She raised her head and stared at the wall in front of her, letting her eyes trail over the many bumps incorporated in the drywall. She wasn't tired but couldn't say she was refreshed, either. She was just awake.

She rolled her head along her neck and waited for the compulsion to walk to take over, but nothing happened. There were no tingles in her feet, no ache in her knees. Nothing at all to explain why she'd been brought from the darkness back to hell.

"Let me be," she said with a sigh.

Was that to be her life now? In and out of wakefulness for no known reason? At least while asleep she didn't think about what she missed. But when awake . . . Maggie raised her face to the sunlight and closed her eyes. She fantasized about the warmth caressing her skin while she stared at the golden glow on the back of her eyelids, hoping to remember what it felt like to bathe in the sun's rays. After a minute of pretending, she turned and climbed the steps leading to the second floor.

The bare wall was blank no more but decorated with pictures across the whole expanse. Over a dozen frames in various sizes made of thin silver, thick gold, or dark black with tiny inlaid roses held pictures of people Maggie didn't know. There was no rhyme or reason behind the selection or placement, but somehow the display worked like a bouquet of mismatched wildflowers. Maggie chewed her lower lip, unable to look away. A young girl and boy being wed, standing before a white arbor dripping with grape vines. Then another where they knelt at the foot of the priest, dressed in their finest. Followed by them dancing under bright lights while people cheered. And the largest of them all was of a baby cradled within the married woman's arms.

A memory roused in the dark recesses of Maggie's mind, something about the baby's round head and the way it was held within the crook of the woman's arm brought it forward. Soft wispy hair, delicate toes. The clasp of a hand around a foot.

"Millie," she whispered. Her best friend's face appeared at her name. Angelic and beautiful, always with a smile on her face. Except for that last day. She was long dead, but she'd once had a baby like this. Had experienced life to its fullest. Had experienced love and loss. Death, Maggie knew, was not the worst that could happen to a person. Not living was.

She smiled suddenly and grasped at her midsection. Pain simmered in the pit of her stomach, something different, new. Her memories were also returning, and she wondered what it meant. Was her trial almost over? She looked down the hall to the left where a table with a plant stood in the corner against the wall. Across from the table was a set of stairs she surmised led to a third floor. Maggie peered to the right and noticed a comfortable-looking chair in the once-empty bedroom at the other end of the hall.

She walked toward it, her eyes touching everything, each item making her stomach churn a little more. I could have had that. The twist to her gut at the unbidden thought wasn't as welcome this time. Her brows furrowed, and she continued into the bedroom. The same gray carpeted the floor, but a luxurious white rug covered the area beneath the bed and the two bedside tables. Slippers lay before one, a book atop the other.

She'd slept through their arrival, but it was obvious someone had moved in. If she could see them, maybe there'd be a connection, a reason for her being here. Maybe the void would return and guide her again.

With a last glance in the room, Maggie turned and headed downstairs.

She found the kitchen had been finished with white cabinets, dark countertops, and gleaming new stainless-steel appliances. Dirty dishes sat in the sink, and a soft rug lay on the floor. She grinned and drifted closer to study items on the counter. Her fingers traced a dirty dish before moving to a glass vase. Flickering movement on the other side of the sheer curtain covering the window caught her attention and she looked up. Vague shapes were outside, sitting on a deck. Without a thought, she ran to the French doors and stood with her hands pressed against the glass.

Outside the window, an older gentleman reclined in a lawn chair next to an older woman. He twirled the fingers of her hand between his while she laughed and stared into his eyes. He said something, and she threw her head back and pulled her hand away. There was a connection there, something deep and meaningful that Maggie could feel through the expanse separating them. She stood oblivious to anything else until the lady raised her hand to wave at someone across the yard.

A small in-ground pool, surrounded by slabs of concrete, stood between them and the little boy standing in a sandbox. He stood frozen, staring not at his grandparents but through the doors at Maggie with eyes wide with fear. A small dark stain spread across his pants and down his legs. Then his mouth opened, and he screamed.

Maggie backed away from the glass, and the boy moved with her, twisting his torso and his head as he strained to see where she'd gone.

He can see me, she thought as her hand fluttered to her chest. Her gaze dropped and locked onto her hand. She held it out in front of her and swallowed.

He can see me!

Brownish-gray mottled flesh was pulled taut over bones and sinew that ended in fingers too long, too narrow, too boney to be anything but claws. Her shoulders hunched as she turned and hurried to the stairs. She stopped when her reflection popped up in the mirror across the way.

She took in her darkly veined skin, sunken eyes, and sharp cheekbones before moving to her hair. She touched the brittle strands that floated around her face as if alive. They broke and fell toward the floor, exposing more of her already spotty skull. A crusty patch of dead skin flaked off her face and floated downward under her watchful gaze. She looked like a monster. A monster with a bad case of death.

The floor vibrated, and she glanced behind her in time see a hand pulling the patio door open. She raced into the living room, turning into the small room at the back of the first level. There was only one thought in her head: *He can't see me. Not like this.*

Open suitcases lay on the floor. In one, tiny baby clothes mingled with boy-sized shorts and T-shirts. In another,

Maggie

flowery skirts and delicate tops lay folded in perfect squares alongside shoes and sandals. Her eyes scanned the toys scattered along the ground with horror.

"Not here," she whispered. Maggie turned and noticed the bed.

A baby slept in the center. Her chest rose gently as she breathed and blew air out of softly puckered lips stained a soft pink.

Maggie stepped closer. Pink. She could see pink. Maggie bent down and breathed in the soft scent of talcum powder and life. A groan escaped her as a tear slid down her cheek. It had been so long since she'd seen color, smelled anything. She felt more alive than she had in a long time.

She reached out a hand and tried to touch the baby, but it passed through her cheek in a cold rush. The baby shivered and stared at her with wide eyes. She drew her hand back and let it hover over the baby's lips. The baby twisted and slid a pale tongue out.

6

TONY

"I remember everything," Tony said, wringing his fingers together between his knees, "and I really shouldn't. I was so young when it happened." He swallowed and stared at the golden embers floating above the fire. If his memories from those two days had floated away like this ash, his life would have been completely different. And if not different, at least peaceful, empty of nightmares and anxiety.

"Uncle?" Bobby whispered.

Tony glanced his way and continued. "My parents sent me to a therapist after I saw the ghost, and again anytime my nightmares returned. Some might call me a frequent flyer," he said with an uncomfortable laugh. None of the children responded, and Tony cleared his throat. "My doctor says I remember the experience so vividly because we are evolutionarily programmed to focus on the bad, that those who are attuned to the negative tended to live longer. It's a survival skill. I don't know if he's right, but I can't seem to forget what happened, no matter how much I try."

Tony looked at Pauly, who sat across the fire, his thick red hair blazing in the firelight. "What your mother believes is wrong, Pauly. God exists."

"But—" Pauly started.

"No," Tony interrupted. "Just listen." He considered his words. "The ghost wanted my sister. I don't know what she planned, but she was always trying to touch her and pick her up." Tony shook his head and tapped his foot against the ground, then continued. "It was God who sent an angel down to take my sister to heaven, Pauly. God who protected her by not allowing the ghost to steal her away. Without his help, I don't know what might have come of her."

Frankie, with his missing front teeth and ceaseless exuberance, bounced on his log before asking, "It was a girl ghost? What did she look like? Was her skin falling off? Could you see her bones?" His eyes widened as he grinned excitedly at everyone.

"That's a zombie, not a ghost!" Joe said with a roll of his eyes. "Ghosts look like fog with bright, glowing eyes. Even I know that."

"No, they don't," Tony snapped. He flushed when Joe leaned forward and bowed his head to stare at the ground. *Dang it*, Tony thought, deflating. *This isn't Joe's fault.* "I'm sorry, Joe," he said, his voice lowering. "I shouldn't have yelled."

"It's okay," Joe grumbled, running his foot through the dirt at his feet.

The fire popped and sizzled in the accompanying silence. Tony wrung his hands together, considering what to say next.

"Tony," Kyle asked from his spot beside Joe, "did your therapist believe you? My mom is a psychologist and says people who believe they've experienced the supernatural are delusional. That they create stories in their head and can't tell they aren't true."

Tony looked up, his lips pursed his lips in sudden understanding. That was why Dr. Kirken often sat silently staring at him when she thought he wouldn't notice. She obviously knew of his past, what with small-town gossip traveling like grass seed in the wind. He'd always felt funny around her, and now he understood why.

"No," he answered. "They didn't and still don't. Four different doctors gave the same explanation: I was young, feverish, and hallucinating. My mom says I only had a cold, but the doctors never believed her."

Kyle crossed his arms over his chest. "And you don't believe them."

Tony smiled. With his serious face and button-down shirt, Tony could easily see Kyle following in his mother's footsteps when he got older. Maybe listening to his story would help him trust and believe in his patients. Maybe good could come from this.

"No, I don't, Kyle. They didn't see the ghost or what she did." How he wished he hadn't either, but the past couldn't be changed. His sister was never coming back. He swallowed and closed his eyes. "Ghosts are not what you see in movies. They are so much worse. Let me think for a minute."

Tony stood and paced a couple steps away from the fire before returning to the log. It was hard to breathe. The air around the campfire was hot and uncomfortable, but he wondered how much of his discomfort was caused by his story. He stood silently with his arms crossed, staring at the flames.

"Are you ready, Uncle Tony?" Bobby's eyes gleamed in the light. He gave an encouraging nod, his eyes flicking between Tony and his friends in a subconscious reaction to the long pause.

He's worried they'll get bored, Tony realized. *And if that happens, they'll pick on him again. A situation I well remember.* How many times had a joke or story saved him from his bully? Too many times to count. He ran his hand through Bobby's hair and sat back on the log.

"The ghost was skinny. No—worse than skinny. She looked like a skeleton wearing skin as clothing. Her eyes bulged in their sockets like glowing white eggs. I don't remember her having any color in them. They were just—" he paused. "White—almost silver.

"They were always watching me, tracking me through the house. Mostly from the landing leading to the second level. Whenever we met, she screamed, her cheekbones jutted out like knives, her chin narrowing to a sharp point. When she pointed her hands at me, I noticed they were claws with long, sharp fingernails."

Tony shuddered and ran his hands down his arms. The darkness around him seemed to draw closer with each sentence, the fire dimmer. But that was in his head, not real. He tried swallowing the lump in his throat, finally giving up and clearing it with a guttural hawking noise until he felt ready to speak. "Ghostly white, her skin looked thin enough to rip with my finger. It seemed . . . dry. Like she hadn't had any water in months. Large flakes of skin, some of them the size of dimes, hung off her cheeks, her lips, her skull. Dark purple veins bulged beneath her skin like roads on a map. They were everywhere." Tony's voice ended as he chewed his lip.

"Her head was the worst," he said. "Most of her hair was gone, leaving her skull bare and mottled with brown and pink patches. What remained was bright white and grew in clumps all over her scalp. It floated in the air as if a breeze blew around her even when the air was calm. There always seemed to be a cloud of falling hair where ever she went.

Funny thing is, I saw them fall but never found hairs anywhere. Even when I watched where they fell and searched for them later. It was as if they disappeared once they left her head. But I know I saw them break and fall."

The sound of a rock smacking the fire broke his concentration. Tony glanced at the shower of hot embers floating skyward before turning to Joe. "Joe?" he questioned. "Do you think that's appropriate?"

The boy responded by spreading his long, skinny arms before him. "But that was so stupid. She's a ghost, Tony. You can't touch a ghost."

"Hey! He was only four, Joe. He didn't know—"

Tony hushed Bobby with a gentle touch to his knee. "I know that now, Joe, but at the time I was hoping to find evidence to give my mom so she'd believe me."

Marcus spoke from the other side of the fire. "Did you ever find any, Mr. Arles?"

Tony glanced his way and smiled. No matter how many times he'd asked Marcus to call him Tony, he insisted on calling him by his last name. The politest boy he knew, he was also the biggest jock and most athletic at the school. Strange combination when he remembered his younger years at school.

"No. Nothing. Although, there was one situation no one could explain." He hesitated, then shook his head. "I don't want to tell you about that yet. I think it's best if I start at the beginning and the first time I saw her.

"I'd been in the house for about a week. Mom was at work, and my sister was asleep in our bedroom. My grandparents had taken me out back to play where they could watch me. They'd bought me a bright-red ball the size of my head. It bounced on anything, including the grass. I was watching it bounce away from me when I felt her eyes."

The hair along Tony's arms rose as his mouth suddenly

became dry. He licked his lips before continuing. "It was if someone had taken ice and dragged it down my spine. I knew I was being watched, but at first, I couldn't pinpoint from where. I walked around the yard staring at the fence and through the trees. My ball was forgotten as I searched."

Tony's voice became labored, changing from his normal pitch to one much lower. He stared into the fire, lost in the memory, no longer aware he was speaking.

"I remember my grandmother calling me, and when I turned to her, I saw the ghost watching us from inside the house, through the back door.

"She floated above the floor, hunched at the shoulders with her eyes peering intently toward me. I could feel them piercing me, burning me with their hate. Beneath the long white hair that floated around her head, she grinned evilly."

His voice hitched. "I was terrified and couldn't stop screaming. It took my grandpa picking me up and carrying me into the house to calm me down. I couldn't walk myself. I couldn't make myself go into that house. So he picked me up, wet pants and all."

Someone snickered, and Tony heard someone whisper, "He peed himself!" Bobby yelled at them to shut up.

Tony ignored them. "They didn't understand. I couldn't put into words what I'd seen. I just cried as my grandfather took me to my room. When we were outside the door, I heard something. A groan. Like the zombies you see on TV. So I turned, and I saw her. She was reaching for my sister with her hands outstretched before her, on the verge of pulling my sister to her chest. I could see it in her eyes, in the brightness gleaming from inside her. She was stealing my sister."

Tony let out a sob and brought his hand to his mouth. He felt his nephew's hand as it touched his leg.

"You don't have to go on, Uncle Tony. It's okay. You don't have to say anymore."

Tony wiped the tears off his cheeks and looked around. Most of the boys stared into the fire, not willing to meet his gaze. But a couple glanced between each other and smirked.

"No," he said, sitting up straighter. "You want to know what ghosts do? Then I'll tell you. No one is lying here."

7
MAGGIE

Maggie shuddered and moved her hands down to pick up the baby. A muffled sound twisted her head to the side where she saw the boy.

Her mouth opened, and she gave a mournful cry. "I won't hurt you," she cried as she flung her hands before her. The cloth at her wrist caught her eye as it waved gently in a breeze she could not feel. She glanced down at her feet, which hovered centimeters above the floor. She'd never cared before, but knowing what he saw hurt more than anything. She was nothing but a ghostly monster in his eyes.

The boy's mouth opened in a scream as tears rolled down his red face. He bawled, clutching the arm of the old man who'd lowered himself to his level and desperately tried to calm him down.

Maggie screamed in shame, her mouth opening like a dark hole in her white glowing face before she rushed down the hall and flew past the people blocking her way. The old man looked up at the air vent before returning to the boy who followed her with his eyes.

The old woman came rushing around the corner with a

wet rag held in her hands. Words Maggie could not hear fell from her mouth beneath eyes opened wide in confusion.

As their forms collided, easing through each other as if neither existed, a cold shock zipped through Maggie's body. She turned her head toward the woman and watched her steps falter—as if she, too, felt the contact—before she continued to the man, who now clutched the little boy within his arms, hiding him from her view.

Maggie ran up the stairs to the large bedroom on the second floor. She twisted her fingers as she turned in a circle. Where could she hide? In the bathroom? The door was closed. The closet was large and quiet, not a place a young child might play, but the thought of hiding away in the silence where she couldn't see made her cringe. Instead, she hurried to a dusky-colored high-back chair placed in the corner. From behind it, she could watch the hall for the little boy, see the elders go about their daily life, and keep the tiny one innocent. Maggie's shoulders lowered, and she leaned her head back against the wall. She watched wispy strands of hair float around her face sadly. The boy would be damaged. Possibly scarred for life after what he'd seen. There was no need to damage him more.

8
TONY

"The ghost had heard me. I must have pissed her off because she flew toward me with her hands extended like claws. They clasped and unclasped in front of her, tipped in long, sharp nails. I thought she was going to grab me instead of my sister, and I clung onto my grandpa. He couldn't see her, and he wrapped his arms around me, protecting me without even knowing what he was doing. But it was enough because she didn't get me.

"She screamed the whole time. A warbling moaning sound that sends chills through me to this day. Look." Tony held up his arm and twisted it around. The firelight illuminated the short blond hairs covering his skin, showing how they stood at attention.

"I'm not making this up. The ghost was there. And she was trying to take my sister when we walked in." He kept his arms raised until everyone had come around to look them over. Once they were seated, he lowered his arms to his knees.

"She flew right through us. You know how they say it gets cold when a ghost is in the room? It does. The air was absolute ice. I could see my breath for a second before she disappeared."

He stopped talking and ran his hands over his forearms.

"Did you see her again?" one of the boys asked.

Tony looked up and nodded slowly.

"She hadn't gone far. I was too terrified to go into my room, so my grandpa carried me upstairs. She was waiting for me."

9
MAGGIE

Maggie's eyes flicked to the hall where a shadow grew on the floor. The person walking up the steps moved slowly, pausing now and then before advancing another step. Maggie swallowed and watched the old man cross the stair landing and pull himself into the hall. He turned her way, revealing the little boy held in his arms.

"No," Maggie cried as she stepped out from around the chair.

The boy's head lifted, slowly turning from where it lay on the man's chest. His mouth opened in a scream as his hands clutched at his grandfather's shirt.

No choice, she thought as she ran for the door.

The man advanced into the room, his mouth working as he struggled to keep hold of the boy, who now struggled within his arms. He stumbled to a stop when the child lurched upward and tried to crawl over his shoulders.

Maggie moaned and turned away from the terrified child. She couldn't run through him again. She raced to the bathroom door, swinging her arm out to enter the wood before her face did. To her surprise, her hand slammed into a tall table lamp and sent it flying through the air. The shock sent needles of coldness racing up her palms. Maggie gasped but continued forward through the door. She thudded to a halt against the wall of the stair landing. Maggie froze with her hands pressed against the wall beside her head. She'd been returned to where she'd started. Again. She was never leaving this place.

The urge to sleep rushed over her, filling her limbs with heavy warmth that slightly tingled and threatened to pull her to the floor. She chose to follow it this time, wishing that she'd done it before.

Maggie relaxed against the wall. Her eyes closed, and she slept.

10
TONY

"I remember it clearly," Tony croaked out, "and I know this didn't happen by accident. She tried to kill me." He pulled his shirt up, showing a long, thin scar where the skin puckered in odd waves from his highest rib to the middle of his back. He pulled his shirt down and continued.

"As soon as we entered the room, the ghost screamed and attacked. I tried to get away but wasn't fast enough. She threw a lamp at me, and the metal plug at the end of the cord scraped my skin. The scratch burned with cold and didn't heal the way it was supposed to, even after a month of ointment and bandages. The doctors had no idea why.

"My grandparents couldn't explain the flying lamp. Even after I told them it was a ghost, they didn't believe me. They never . . . they never explained it."

Tony swallowed and lowered his shirt. "The ghost was real. It tried to kill me and my sister. I prayed every day for God to help us. I wanted him to take us away like he had done my daddy. Anything to keep us safe from the ghost."

He shivered and stood up. He didn't notice the silence around the fire as he gathered wood. Nor how it continued even after he'd added logs to the pile. No one spoke while they waited for him to continue.

"She didn't go away," he finally whispered. "She just stopped moving. I didn't see her every day, but when I did, she was in the corner of the stairwell facing the wall. Not breathing. Not screaming. Just standing there. It freaked me out." Tony swallowed hard while he stared into the fire. The worst was still to come.

11

MAGGIE

"Shhhhhh, little baby," Maggie crooned, glancing furtively over the bassinet and into the backyard. She studied the boy, who played ball with his grandparents along the back fence, before leaning down and tracing a skeletal finger along the baby's flushed cheek. The pink of the girl's skin against the gray of hers. Depressing. "It's okay. I'm here."

Pooled tears rolled down the baby's cheeks to puddle along her collarbone when she twisted her head to peer up. Her delicate lips trembled for a second before they spread, and she gave a happy gurgle. Plump fists waved in the air as she kicked her little legs.

Maggie giggled and moved her finger to the baby's hand. She felt nothing when the baby's fist passed through her own. Nor could she hear the baby, but the remembered sound from her past left her feeling light and happy.

"I know," she whispered, not able to look away, "life is hard." How long had she been this way? Trapped in this prison? This hell? What had she done to deserve this? "I've done nothing," she whispered, dropping her hand to run it along the blanket over the baby's chest. Her fingers passed through the soft material with a slight tingle.

Maggie licked her lips and drew her hand back. The urge that made her wake and creep down the stairs had returned and now commanded her to pick up the baby. To hold it. Love it.

But how? She looked into the backyard again, worried the boy would turn and see her. But he remained focused on his game.

The baby coughed, and Maggie dropped her gaze. The little thing was sick with fever, her eyes glassy and hot looking, but still she gave a big gummy smile.

"I want to hold you, too," Maggie said. Her mind returned to the incident from the last time she'd been awake, and her fingers curled into her palm. She'd moved that lamp. Not intentionally, and not with the intent to hit the boy, but she'd done it. Her fingers unfurled as she bent forward and moved her hands to the sides of the bassinet. They slid toward the baby and didn't stop, bumping together in her center.

She stood in frustration. Something inside her said she could do this, she just needed to try again. Jaws clenched, she leaned down and directed every thought into grasping the baby. Into putting her fingers around the baby's warm back. Into making it happen. Memories of the way it should feel flooded her. How heavy babies were. How they flopped like flour in a sack, their weight in her arms solid but at the same time flimsy. *I can do this*, she thought, curling her fingers under the baby's waist. Weight filled her hands when she lifted, and she smiled.

The baby squealed and grabbed for Maggie as she was raised higher.

Maggie laughed but didn't let her focus waver. Her hands tingled with the strain of being corporal, her fingertips practically on fire. "I've got you," she whispered.

The baby sucked contentedly on her fist while staring into Maggie's eyes, and an understanding passed between them. Trust, love, the knowledge that this was how it should be. *I'm okay*, Maggie thought before the baby suddenly jerked and twisted to the side.

Maggie jumped in surprise as the feeling in her fingers vanished. Her concentration broken, she scrambled to catch her, even as the baby slid through her grasp. "No!" Maggie yelled, desperately grabbing at the baby falling into the bassinet. Her fingers passed through her form, swishing back and forth as if through air.

The baby hit the blankets and howled, her arms stiffening in angry protest.

Maggie screamed. She'd had her. Had connected after centuries of being alone. Her hands curled into claws at her side. Whoever had interrupted them needed to pay. Needed to feel her anger. Her rage turned her to the sliding glass door, and she bellowed in rage.

The small boy quailed for a second before jumping forward and pounding even harder on the glass. His eyes wide, filled with terror, a steady stain spreading down his legs. The glass quivered under his onslaught and shook in the frame. "Leave her alone!" he screamed.

Maggie flew forward, fury making her blind to what she did. Her arm lashed out, smashing into the glass with a bang. Spiderweb cracks spread as the glass shattered.

A small splat of blood bloomed on the glass where the boy's small hand had been pressed.

Maggie drew back in horror as her anger vanished. What was she doing? Who had she become? With a sob, she turned and ran toward the protection of the stairs.

12

TONY

"She attacked the baby while I was outside playing baseball with my grandparents. Even now I have a hard time enjoying sports because of that day. Even though I know it's irrational, I expect bad things to happen while I'm having fun." Tony stopped talking and stared into the flames. It seemed odd that such a beautiful day could go so wrong. He glanced down and ran his foot through the dirt.

"She had my sister grasped in her claws when I saw her through the sliding door. I ran over as fast as I could and banged on the glass." Tony's brow's furrowed. "Which, oddly enough, seemed to scare her. She dropped my sister, then turned on me."

Tony looked up and met the boy's eyes one by one. "She flew at the glass between us and shoved her claws toward me. The door shattered, and my hand was cut. My grandparents came running at the noise, and the ghost disappeared."

He held his hand up to the firelight, turning it so the boys could see the long dash that ran across his palm. Once they'd all sat back, he lowered his hand to his lap and continued.

"By this time, I wouldn't stay in the downstairs bedroom.

Nor would I sleep in my grandparent's room. We had no other options and moved into the third-floor bedroom. It was a girly room, decorated in pink with pink roses on the wallpaper. I hated that, but there was room for the three of us, and I'd never seen the ghost up there. I felt safe, or as safe as I could knowing the ghost was standing on the landing."

13

MAGGIE

The familiar pangs returned to her legs as Maggie woke from her sleep. How long she'd been down, she didn't know, but the sun had descended as the hall was dark. A soft glow from down the stairs indicated a light had been turned on to keep the darkness at bay. She stepped away from the wall and stretched her legs. They wanted to move almost as much as she wanted this experience to end. As she walked across the dark flooring to the set of stairs ascending to the next level, she remembered what had happened before she'd closed her eyes.

Maggie peered over her shoulder to the double doors securing the old man's room. Was the boy in there? Was he having nightmares as he slept? She hoped not and returned her gaze to the stairs. A sudden realization made her twist around in surprise.

A path of shiny footsteps showed everywhere she'd stepped, from the landing to where she stood now. They lay frozen and sparkling, slowly evaporating one at a time until no evidence of her passage existed. But they'd been there. Maggie smiled as her foot rose.

"Move quickly."

A familiar warmth flowed over her body, and Maggie raised her eyebrows. The voice had abandoned her after that first day, choosing to remain reticence as she traveled. Not answering questions. Not giving direction. Not helping her when she'd lost all hope. She'd begged, she'd pleaded, and finally she'd stopped asking. And now it was back. Maggie's hope mingled with fear. Did this mean she was done, or was she on another path to another test she'd eventually fail?

The stairs leading to the third floor let out a strangled screech as her foot settled against the wooden step. She closed her eyes and pressed downward until she'd elicited another groan. Her heart didn't beat, but emotions exploded inside her. There was sound.

"You are almost there. Look ahead."

Maggie opened her eyes to stare at the halo of white light surrounding two red doors at the top of the stairwell. Not gray, like everything else she saw, but bright-red doors with shiny silver knobs. The light splayed across the doorway like a spotlight and beaconed her forward. It pulled at her, as if strings attached to her chest slowly reeled her through the inky darkness of the hall. Maggie didn't notice the air growing colder, nor the way the walls turned white with frost as she passed. She noticed nothing but the color of the door and the thump of a heart she'd long forgotten.

Thump, thump—each beat sent a ribbon of excitement through her. Her mouth hung open as her hands clenched at her sides. Delicious warmth eased from her center into her extremities as the vitality of youth returned to her skin, filling her with a lovely glow. She raised a hand flushed with life in front of her as the entrance neared.

Her fingers slid through the beautiful door as if the wood didn't exist, as if she did not exist, even though she could feel her heart beating within her chest. She watched her hand disappear beyond the wood. Excruciating but exhilarating pain moved through the limb as she continued walking forward, mingling her ghostly form with the wood until she'd passed and came out the other side. She let out a low moan and rolled her head along her neck. Luxurious golden hair sprouted on her head until it cascaded down her back, caressing her flesh in silky waves. Agony and excitement, things she hadn't felt in centuries, colored her cheeks a delicate pink.

Maggie opened vibrant blue eyes surrounded by thick lashes and smiled. She found herself in a short hallway decorated with delicate wallpaper covered in pale pink and red roses. Thick pink carpet covered the floor and a small night light lit the room down at the end. She didn't notice the bed in the corner because she was preoccupied with an impulse to hurry to a white and blue bassinet sitting in a small alcove off to the side. A mysterious light from above bathed the area in a heavenly glow. Without meaning to, she began to hum a soft lullaby.

14

TONY

"The day my sister died," Tony choked out as a tear appeared in his eye, "the ghost was more substantial than normal. I'd passed it a few times and seen it move and twitch even if it didn't look at me. It had scared me, and somehow, I'd known it wasn't a good thing. The ghost was coming back.

"So, I prayed every chance I got. I asked God to protect us. To not let the ghost take either of us. I placed Saint Barbara, the patron saint of protection, on the dresser next to our bed. I did everything I could think of to keep us safe. I wrote promises and begged for protection . . ."

Tony brushed the tear from his cheek and chewed his lip. "And it worked. Not exactly how I wanted, but it worked.

"Late that night, I wasn't surprised when I heard a moan coming from downstairs. I wasn't surprised when I heard the steps creaking outside my room. I rolled over and prayed. I begged that he take us before the ghost made it into the room. I begged for his help until I couldn't beg anymore."

15

MAGGIE

Sparkly white frost grew along the walls like a creeping vine, extending icy tendrils across the roses and over the ceiling and floor. The spidery webs crackled as they grew, and the temperature of the air dropped. White crystals dusted the carpet as they followed her path to the other side of the room.

Something moved among the yellow covers on the large bed when she passed. A small figure twisted around as a puff of breath crystallized over the pillow.

Maggie smiled and peered down at the baby within the bassinet. Reaching out, she rolled the infant over and stared into her sightless eyes. Her hand trailed along the baby's pale, cold form before Maggie leaned down.

Her lips puckered, and she blew a soft breath across the baby's face as her hand pressed gently into the motionless chest. There was a moment of stillness, and then a soft twitch under her hand.

The baby girl's left arm rose as her head twisted to the side. Her eyes, a light blue like the sky on a hot summer day, blinked as her lips twisted up in a smile. Her arms, flushed pale pink with blood, pumped rapidly up and down as she let out a little squeal.

Maggie felt something, a stirring she couldn't remember feeling before, as her heart clenched and a tear filled her eye. Bending over, she picked the infant up and pulled her to her chest. Her gaze never left the small form in her arms, or she would have seen the infant still in the bassinet. She breathed in the soft scent of baby and curled herself around her form.

"You are not alone," she whispered as the baby cooed against her neck. "I am here."

The rushing wind she'd become accustomed to intensified, flowing over her skin and through her cells in a warm caress. She gasped at the sensation and let out a small sob as a white light shot down from the heavens above her.

"Bring her home." As the voice spoke, Maggie could feel a pull directing her upward.

"Father," she said softly, tilting her head to peer into the light. Pastor Markem had been right. The heavenly gate was bathed in white.

Maggie rose, completely unaware of the little boy screaming in the bed behind her.

Tony stared at the pale angel hovering a foot above the ground. At the way her filmy dress spread around her as if a breeze caught the edges and pulled the fabric in all directions. At the blond hair floating around her head like slowly whipping arms of an octopus as she looked into the sky. At the rapture consuming her face. In her hands, he saw his sister, squirming and laughing.

"The baby," he screamed as his breath spread around him in a wide frosty plume. "The angel's saving the baby!"

His mother jerked awake next to him. She shivered before reaching out and grasping his shoulders. "Wake up, Tony, you're dreaming." She pulled him roughly to her chest as he continued to scream. "Shhhhhh . . . honey, you are going to wake Anna. It's just a dream."

Tony struggled and jerked his head around. The angel and Anna were floating up, the movement of her hair and clothing reminding him of swimmers moving through a pool. "Look!" he yelled again and pulled away. Tears began rolling down his cheeks as he raised a finger and pointed to the angel, whose upper body had already disappeared through the ceiling. "The angel's got the baby, mama!"

"Honey, shhhhhh. It's okay. Look, I'll go get Anna." His mother tried to stifle a yawn before covering her mouth and letting it out. She shivered again and hurried on tiptoes to the bassinet. When she reached the tiny bed, she screamed. Her arms lifted her lifeless daughter to her chest as her heart bled.

Tony wailed with her as he watched the angel's feet disappear through the ceiling above him. With their departure, the room warmed, and the frost melted.

16
TONY

Tony swallowed. "I saved her," he whispered. "I prayed to God to come and save her from the ghost, and he called her home. He sent an angel through the door, one dressed in white robes with long blond hair streaming behind her. She grabbed the baby and carried her to heaven. I saw them rise through the air and vanish."

The fire crackled and sputtered, but the boys were silent. Tony stared into the flames and remembered the angel as she'd carried his sister away. He remembered feeling relieved until his mother began to wail. Then sadness had consumed him. He'd been responsible for his mother's anguish.

"Did the ghost come back?" a quiet voice asked from across the fire.

Tony look at Pauly and smiled. "Did I see her?" he asked. "No, but she was there. Watching. I could tell because her coldness froze the floor and our breath. It was colder than when we'd run into her the first time. I think she was angry that I'd outsmarted her. That God had won."

He smiled sadly. "Yes, God won, and my sister went to heaven."

ACKNOWLEDGMENTS

I want to thank my husband for always being there for me. Without him and the encouragement of my daughters, my aunt, and my mother, I would have kept my stories to myself and never attended my first critique group.

Andi and Erika, without you to bolster my confidence, I wouldn't have been brave enough to put my stories into the world. Without you, I would have stopped long ago.

Thank you, Christine, for always being available when I needed a laugh. You are my twisted sister and friend for life.

Thank you, Carol, Georgeie, Greg, James, Jim, Karla, Kim, Komiko, Penny, and Sherry for reading through my manuscripts, offering advice when needed, and giving me the chance to learn from you. Your knowledge and wisdom in writing were instrumental in my finishing.

Special thanks to my editor, Kari Filburn at Line by Line Copyediting, for holding my hand during the process. She was a wonderful editor.

ABOUT THE AUTHOR

Ever since she was a little girl, Jessie McClure has daydreamed about odd things like aliens terraforming Earth and demons who wear assless chaps. Into adulthood, her vivid imagination has caused her more than once to dash from the light switch to her bed like a terrified child. As she tells her children, she's not scared of the dark, but rather what her brain thinks lives within it.

In her forties, Jessie began sharing her stories with her family. When they suggested she write a novel, she wasn't sure if her first attempt should be about a half-demon, half-human with an identity crisis or about survivors living in a biodome after an apocalyptical event. In the end, she chose to write short stories to hone her skills. After a few years, some of those stories evolved into a theme, and her first novel was born.

Jessie McClure lives with her elderly dog and family in the Pacific Northwest. Her home's location makes it easy to walk amongst the trees and lose herself in her stories.

Visit Jessie-McClure.com for news on upcoming book releases. As a bonus for signing up to receive announcements, Jessie will share one of her unpublished short stories. She promises not to send spam or act obnoxious in any way.

Jessie can also be reached at Jessie@Jessie-McClure.com with any questions or comments you'd like to pass on.

Made in the USA
Las Vegas, NV
21 November 2020